FORGET AGAIN

CIELO DEVLIN

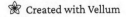 Created with Vellum

PROLOGUE

Something he had been searching for had come back.

Something he had been longing for.

The scene set before him tugged on a memory deep inside his mind.

A grin spread across Zane's face.

This was what he wanted, wasn't it?

In the memory, he saw a smile stretch wider and wider, and maybe...

Maybe Zane wanted to leave his past behind him.

Because if HE could do something like THAT...

What kind of person was he?

CHAPTER

ONE

Hospital machines buzzed in his mind. After the fourth beep, he forced his eyes to open. A television screen was on the wall, reflecting the face of a terrified teenager. His fingers trailed the cotton bed sheets covering him. Did he have a name? He tried to find the answer but his mind was covered in a thick fog of disarray. For whatever reason, tears pricked the corners of his eyes. A horrifying pain shot through his limbs, and he stiffened. He raised a pale hand with familiar, chewed fingernails. The middle finger on his right hand had a device clipped onto it. He looked away from the bright lights on the ceiling, a jolt of fear running through him when he saw the tubes going inside his nose. The thought of them being inside of his stomach made him want to vomit. A weird breathing machine was attached to his face, but oddly enough the machine made it harder for him to breathe.

A scream pierced through the hospital walls. It took him a while to figure out it came from him. A nurse with long blonde hair tied into a bun burst into the room. Her eyebrows struggled to knit together, and he suspected she had gotten some sort of botox.

"Get this off of me," he murmured, desperation leaking into his voice.

"Calm down." She held up her hands as if calming an angry bull, her lips fighting a frown.

"What's going on?" His words grew quicker. "I don't— Who are you? It hurts. Everything—" He paused. "Everything's so bright." The light from outside the window reflected off the white walls, and straight into his eyes. It didn't help with his headache at all.

"It's okay, Zane." The nurse smiled.

Was that his name? Was he... Zane? A wave of disgust washed over him. Zane... He wasn't sure why but he hated that name.

She walked towards Zane's cot confidently, before sitting on the edge of the hospital bed. "You can call me Mrs. Valentino." He struggled to read the writing on top of the nurse's light blue scrubs. Her full name was Claire Valentino.

Zane flinched when she grabbed his hand. "Stop," he snapped. It was difficult not to trust the nurse with the friendly smile, but Zane didn't know her. And he definitely didn't know if he could trust her. She released his hand, keeping a safe distance away from him.

"Mrs. Valentino," he said carefully. "What happened to me?" His eyes narrowed.

"The doctors are still trying to figure that out, sweetheart, but I can help you get those nasty machines off of you." She reached toward him, something dark hiding beneath her reassuring expression.

"Don't touch me!" Zane's voice hitched, and the tears that had been pricking his eyes fell. The nurse's baby blue eyes widened.

He looked away. "Sorry."

"It's quite alright. It must be quite a shock to wake up here, not knowing who you are, or what you're doing here. I understand, Zane. More than you think I would." She tapped the side of her head with her index finger.

"How so?" Zane demanded.

Mrs. Valentino winked. "Sorry, sweetheart. I like to keep my secrets." Zane crossed his arms, staring down the strange nurse.

"How about I get to keep my secret if... I give you..." Mrs. Valentino grabbed a piece of candy from her pants pocket. It was hardly a fair trade in his opinion, but he was too exhausted to care. Zane took it, before giving Mrs. Valentino the smallest of fake smiles. While his tired mind was distracted by the shiny wrapping, she gently grabbed the weird device on his finger and took it off. "Just let me go get the doctors, okay, sweetheart?"

Zane relaxed slightly. "Okay."

Her shoes clicked against the tile floor. He took a deep breath and tried to focus. Breathing felt strange with the tubes, but it helped. Zane could almost see the things he knew he SHOULD know. He could almost make sense of it but the memories fell through his fingers like sand. Zane didn't even notice that a doctor had entered the room with a nurse by her side. The doctor was asking him all sorts of questions but he wasn't paying attention. He didn't even register that Mrs. Valentino wasn't there with her. He didn't even feel the tears slipping down his face.

"He's in shock," The doctor remarked.

"How long has he been awake?" The nurse dragged a hand down his face until half of his face turned red.

Zane pointed to the weird hospital breathing and feeding tubes. "Can I take these off? She said I could," he muttered.

"Of course." Zane watched as the doctor's dark hand reached for him, and his eyes drooped. As his last thoughts fled into the darkest corner of his mind, he held onto the fancy wrapped candy Mrs. Valentino gave him.

"Was someone in here before us?" the faint voice whispered.

Zane jolted awake a few hours later, his groggy mind finally cleared.

"He's awake!" A confident-looking doctor said, his hands in his medical coat.

Zane slowly sat up, his back to the pillow. He squinted when the sunlight cut into his eyes. "You seriously need to close the blinds on those windows." His hands flew to his face. The tubes and breathing machine were off of him.

"A ventilator," the female doctor explained. "It was necessary. My name is Dr. Smith." She smiled. "And this is also Dr. Smith, but you can call him Trent to avoid confusion." She pointed with a delicate finger to the doctor beside her. "He's a bit of a handful, but once you get to know him I think you two will get along." Trent rolled his eyes.

"Why am I here?" He glanced around the room. A few white chairs were set up by the window, the tile floor spotless. That was something Mrs. Valentino failed to answer. But the answer had to be on the clipboard Trent was holding with a vice-like grip. He was almost scared to hear what they had to say. Trent and Dr. Smith exchanged a glance.

"Um. Well..." Trent trailed off, his hand on the back of his neck.

Dr. Smith looked him in the eyes and said, "You were found on the streets unconscious. You've been asleep for four days." She looked at him sympathetically. "You were bleeding from several gashes, including your head so we had no choice but to bring you here." Her voice was soft, yet clear and concise.

"I don't have to... pay for this, do I?" Zane asked, dragging a shaky hand through his unruly brown hair. Dr. Smith blinked

6

slowly. Zane's eyes widened. "I didn't exactly call 911! And I don't have any money that I know of—"

"No. It's okay." Trent smiled, a look of reassurance on his face.

"But the ventilator, and my wounds! It must have been expensive to—"

"You don't have any debt to pay," Dr. Smith interrupted. "And we still have no idea who called the ambulance for you. But don't worry about anything, Zane."

"Can I go back to my family then?" Zane asked. Dr. Smith winced. "What?" Zane sighed. "You have to know who they are." There was something strange about not remembering his parents. Such a huge part of his life had been ripped away from him.

"We don't even know who you are," Trent muttered.

"But Mrs. Valentino said my name is Zane?" he challenged.

"Okay, Zane... We'll find out what we can," Dr. Smith wrung her hands together, avoiding Zane's gaze. "Trent, could you go fetch some pills?" She shot Trent a look full of meaning. "I can ask around... see if anyone knows the boy." Dr. Smith was mostly talking to herself now. And that was okay. Because it gave Zane time to think. Because when he mentioned Mrs. Valentino? There was no flicker of recognition in their eyes. Was Mrs. Valentino even real? She had to be. Because Zane had the evidence in his hands. A fancy candy that was wrapped with shiny, yellow paper.

TWO

J ust a few more days and his life would be his again, if a foster home counted as that. Zane glanced at the pills on his bedside table, his eyebrows furrowed. He didn't know what they were for, but then again he didn't know a lot about anything. All he knew was that the only person who knew his name was someone called Mrs. Valentino. Dr. Smith looked at him weirdly whenever he mentioned seeing Mrs. Valentino, always changing the conversation effortlessly. Their last conversation switched over to Zane needing a shower. He agreed with her. One look in the mirror confirmed that. He looked awful, and not in an ugly kind of way. Although his recently acquired scars didn't help. There were bags under his eyes, and he desperately needed a haircut. Zane kind of wanted to burn the weird blue dress he was wearing.

"Stupid dress." Zane tugged at the rough fabric. No matter what Trent said about it being necessary he would never be convinced it was anything other than an ugly dress. Zane glared at his ratted brown hair in the wall-length mirror. It hung over his eyes, and no matter how many times he raked his fingers through it, his hair still ended up being a greasy mess. "I hate you." He pointed a pale finger in desperate need of sun at the mirror.

"Zane, no matter how much you insult your hair it's not going to go away." Trent sauntered into the room, before setting a plate full of food on Zane's bedside table. "Technically the nurses are supposed to bring you food, but I wanted to see how you were doing."

"That's only because you refused to give me scissors," Zane remarked. "And I don't need a babysitter."

"Yes, well maybe you shouldn't have tried to use a knife to cut your hair," Trent snarked. *"With great power comes great responsibility."*

He knew the last sentence was a quote of some kind, but where it was from he couldn't remember, though it itched at the back of his mind. Zane opened his mouth to answer. Nothing came out. It wasn't his fault that they'd given him a steak knife with his lunch, or that it had been the only thing he could try to cut his hair with. Zane had cut open his finger with the dull knife, and he couldn't help but notice that the story had somehow spread throughout the hospital. Dr. Smith had been furious, banning him from even looking at sharp objects. His temper had gotten the best of him, and he ended up shouting at her.

"I don't know. It was just bothering me like crazy. You of all people should understand what I'm talking about." Zane's guilt slipped into his voice as he pointed at Trent's gelled hair.

"I'm afraid I don't. My hair is always perfect." Trent patted his hair. "But that's beside the point! You owe Dr. Smith an apology. I have other patients to get to, Zane. I'll bring your dinner over later."

Zane winced. "Yeah, okay. Thanks."

"Don't forget to take the pills Dr. Smith prescribed," Trent reminded on his way out. He hesitated. "Also, you mentioned someone named Mrs. Valentino... Who is she?"

"She's the nurse who visited me when I woke up. She was blonde?" Zane explained, his confusion deepening. His eyes drifted to the pillow where he had the piece of candy stashed.

Trent's lips pressed together in a thin line, his forehead creasing. "Never heard of her. I'll look into it." Trent shrugged, closing the door behind him.

Zane snatched the tiny, almost yellow pill from the white dish on his lunch tray. Zane had no idea what it was supposed to do, but... he swallowed it. The jello looked tempting but Zane was still really tired despite the fact he had slept for most of five days straight.

After a long, soapy shower, and a thorough brushing of his hair with a proper hairbrush he finally looked presentable. He still had to wear the stupid dress, but it was a start. Zane grabbed the TV remote from his bedside table and flicked on the TV. He had to relearn everything about the world, and this seemed like a good way to do it. Zane started with something that Trent seemed to quote a *lot*. Superheroes. Zane traversed the different channels until he came across Marvel movies. He had to admit the Marvel movies were... pretty gory. Lots of blood. Murder. Zane knew it was all special effects or whatever. But it was all so... familiar. As if he had experienced something similar in real life. And that was the part that scared him.

"Seriously? A Marvel movie is *all* it takes to make you look like a ghost?"

Zane shot up, his gaze instantly going towards the doorway. A girl was standing there, with her blonde eyebrows raised. Zane quickly turned off the TV.

"Uh no? I mean I—" Zane stammered. "Shut up." He muttered.

The girl smirked. "You're fun to make fun of. Although I did expect someone... a little different." It was Zane's turn to raise his eyebrows.

She leaned forward and inspected him, making Zane glad he had taken a shower. "Don't you think the whole complete amnesia thing is a little weird?"

Zane shrugged, silently urging his face not to burst into flames. A good first impression had officially gotten thrown out of the window, and he silently vowed to never watch a Marvel movie again.

"Look, I heard about how you mentioned someone named Mrs. Valentino. She visited me too when I woke up. And yeah, I have amnesia too. She was superrrr creepy. She asked me a bunch of questions and failed to answer the one question I asked."

Zane's heart rate spiked, and he quickly snatched the piece of candy she gave him from underneath his pillow. Zane twirled the candy. "So she is real..."

"In case you were wondering, I asked her *who the hell she was*. Sure it said Mrs. Valentino on her name tag, but honestly? Can you really trust the only person who knows your name?"

"Can I trust you?" Zane asked skeptically.

"I don't care if you trust me or not," she admitted. "I just want answers. I think you want answers too." She pointed at him with a finger that was noticeably not shaking. The girl might not have been scared, but Zane was. He was terrified of the possibility of never remembering his past life. He was terrified of always being one step behind because he had lost memories of at least 12 years. Not that he would tell *her* that.

"What's your name?" Zane asked.

"Gemma. Gemma Walton," she smirked, a hint of pride in her voice.

"I'm—"

"Zane. Yes, I know. I heard about the knife incident. I also looked at your medical file. B positive."

Slightly creepy that she knew his blood type.

"I'm O negative apparently." She grinned. "I already have a bit of a criminal record as well. Although I didn't cut my finger open with a dull knife."

Zane looked away for a moment, his gaze shooting back to her. "Wait... A criminal record?"

Gemma's lopsided grin widened. "I stole a neurologist's keycard. But to be fair, I DID end up returning it to him."

Of course. The only other person who knew about Mrs. Valentino was a delinquent. "So... what you're saying is..." The puzzle pieces in his brain slowly pieced themselves together. "You're trying to find Mrs. Valentino?"

"Took you long enough." She tossed her ratted blonde hair behind her shoulder. "And I'll let you help me. It'll be fun!" She giggled. "We could be a team." Gemma smiled at Zane. "This is the part where you're supposed to agree wholeheartedly."

"Er... Yeah. I guess we're a team." He raised his fist in the air half-heartedly.

"Good." She nodded. "See you later, Scaredy-cat." Gemma gave a two-finger salute before leaving.

He wasn't sure what he thought of the strange girl. She was somewhere between endearing and annoying. He didn't even know what he was supposed to think. He was glad she had found him, at least. Zane supposed he could just make it up. He could act like he knew what he was doing. He could act like he wasn't scared. He just hoped no one would see through his facade.

THREE

Z ane poked at the disgusting hospital food. He had to drench the potatoes in ketchup for the taste to be bearable. The sausages weren't much better. They were a mix between rubber and cement. The food was barely digestible, but it was free, and he was broke.

Trent stepped through the doorway, glancing at the drenched potatoes. "Delicious, isn't it?"

Zane scoffed. "If you enjoy eating tires, then yes."

Trent reached into his medical coat, bringing out a small container of jello. "I'm not really supposed to bring you this but —" he set it down on Zane's tray. "I can't leave you to suffer like this. Just don't let Dr. Smith catch you. She'd freak out if she saw you eating this."

Zane raised his eyebrows in surprise. "Thanks." He set the tray on the foot of the bed before turning to face Trent. "Does she have zero taste buds or what?"

"I don't know, but she lectured me for twenty minutes when she caught me eating a cookie." He smirked. "Her lecture hasn't exactly deterred me though. I bought cookies for my lunch break today, so if Dr. Smith asks, act oblivious."

Zane frowned when odd feelings of guilt slipped into his mind. He wasn't sure why he felt weird about lying to Dr. Smith, but the answer had to be somewhere in his past. Or it was completely unrelated. Personally, he thought it made him more of a Scaredy-cat than he was already. He shook his head to clear his mind from his less-than-pleasant thoughts.

"Trent... Why are you wearing scrubs with puppies and kittens?" Zane studied the different huskies, golden retrievers, calico kittens, and black kittens in different poses littered across Trent's white scrubs.

"Casual Friday." He tore a hand through his hair, succeeding in ruining the delicate gel work.

"Does that mean I get to wear something other than this dress?" Zane tugged on his hospital gown.

Trent laughed. "Afraid not."

"So that's the only reason you decided to show up to work covered in puppies and kittens?"

"Not the only reason, Sherlock. I get to read stories to some kiddos today and they love animals. And..." Trent paused for dramatic effect.

"And?" Zane pressed.

"I look fabulous," Trent said sarcastically, gesturing towards his scrubs.

Zane snickered, his thoughts beginning to drift away from their conversation. Would he and Gemma really be able to find Mrs. Valentino?

"Are you okay, Zane?" Tren asked.

Zane hesitated. He felt fine. Absolutely peachy. Except for the fact that Mrs. Valentino could be evil. Gemma could be evil too. She just HAPPENED to be the only other person who knew about Mrs. Valentino? Was he forgetting something? OH YEAH, he had amnesia, no family to go home to, and apparently, he was a sensitive little Scaredy-cat!

"Did you remember to take your pills?" Trent asked.

His pills... What did they even do? Okay so MAYBE Zane had forgotten. But the question still remained. What were the pills for?

"Trent, what are the pills supposed to do?"

"They're just to help jog your memory!"

That was a lie, according to the slight dilation of his pupils, and a fidget with his dog and cat scrubs. Were medical professionals even allowed to lie to their patients? Zane's trust in Trent wasn't exactly damaged. He was sure Trent had his reasons for lying. Zane couldn't bring himself to confront him, however.

"So what's wrong, Zane?" Trent sat down on the edge of the hospital bed, moving the food tray out of the way. Zane simply raised his eyebrows, pointed to his head, and gave a tight smile.

"Oh. Right. Well, I have a break in ten, and if you'd like we can play poker or something. It might cheer you up. Maybe even jog a few of those memories of yours."

"I can't ask you to—"

Trent patted Zane's knee. "It's fine, Zane. I have a feeling it'll be fun."

"Isn't it illegal for minors to play poker?" he asked, his voice monotone.

Trent snorted. "We're not going to use actual money, Zane." He headed down the hallway, and Zane watched his animal scrubs get farther and farther away.

"Hey, Scaredy-cat!" Gemma greeted, peeking around the door frame.

Zane jumped. He didn't expect to see her. She had probably been waiting for Trent to leave.

"You're just proving my point further," she teased. "Anyway,

I have a lead. Follow me." By the time he registered what she said she was already halfway out of the hospital room.

"A lead?" he echoed, slightly confused. Zane brushed his messy hair behind his ear, took a deep breath in, and followed the girl with a criminal record. They headed up a flight of stairs until they were on the fourth floor. When Gemma SAID she had a lead she seemed to have FAILED to mention the fact that following said lead would involve breaking into a private office. SHE might be a delinquent, but Zane was not. Zane paused in front of a wooden door, his eyes scanning the words on the front. *Ms. Lily.*

"We can't break into a private office!" Zane hissed out through his teeth.

Gemma snatched his wrist and yanked him into a hallway out of sight of a group of doctors passing by in deep discussion. "You want answers, don't you?" Gemma nudged him with her fist.

"Well yeah, but it's still breaking and enter—"

"Cool, let's go!" she interrupted, stepping closer to the door. Gemma used a small piece of metal, that looked like she bent it herself, to pick the lock. After a few moments the lock clicked open.

Zane didn't even have time to protest before Gemma dragged them both to the other side of the door. They found a tiny office with a computer in the center and papers scattered everywhere. Gemma didn't pause to take in her surroundings, instead she walked towards the computer and turned it on. Zane sent a paranoid look over at the door. It wouldn't hurt to lock it. So he did.

"We're going to need a password—" Zane started.

"I'm in!" Gemma shouted triumphantly.

"Of course you are," Zane muttered before walking behind the desk and peering over Gemma's shoulder. She clicked on a file labeled "Cameras," and selected footage from two days ago.

"Who are you, Mrs. Valentino?" Gemma wondered aloud.

Zane rolled his eyes. "Do I even want to know how you knew the password?"

Gemma pointed to the calendar on the wall. "Birthday," she answered vaguely.

She pressed a few more buttons and fast-forwarded through the footage.

"How long is this going to take?" he asked, remembering that he was supposed to play poker with Trent.

Gemma scowled at him. "Seriously, Zane? How about - 'Wow, good job Gemma! You're so cool, and did I mention you're wicked talented? I would never have been able to do this without you!'" she said sarcastically.

"Okay, it was *kind of* impressive," Zane admitted.

Zane jumped when someone knocked on the mahogany door of Ms. Lily's office. Even Gemma jumped. They were busted.

CHAPTER
FOUR

Z ane pressed his ear against the door, straining to hear the strangely muffled voice.

"Hello? I have those papers you wanted." It was Trent. Zane would know the relaxed voice from anywhere. Neither Zane nor Gemma said a word.

"Hey, Dr. Paulson! Could you help me hide these? I don't want Dr. Smith to have a heart attack." Trent's voice echoed from down the hallway, followed by snickers from his fellow hospital staff.

Zane could only assume that the mysterious thing he was requesting help with was some sort of treat, although he had no intention of asking. Eventually, his footsteps faded away completely. Zane couldn't help the laugh that escaped his lips. His laughter seized when he saw Gemma's surprised expression.

"What is it, Gemma?" Zane asked.

She turned to look at Zane, her eyes wide and her chin resting on her hand. "According to the security cameras, Mrs. Valentino doesn't exist. Wow. Just when I thought she couldn't get any creepier. Maybe she's some sort of ghost that's haunting us. Oh! Or maybe I'm crazy and imagining everything, including you! That's weird to think about." Gemma leaned back nonchalantly in the black swivel chair she was seated in, her hands behind her head.

He was pretty sure he wasn't a part of Gemma's imagination, but the very notion made him shudder. He shook off the nerve-racking thoughts and plastered a smirk onto his face.

"See, I was thinking. If we're going to be a team I think we should call ourselves team Zane-Gemma. Or maybe instead we could call ourselves Zane's team. I'm obviously the leader here." Zane adjusted his hospital gown while waiting for Gemma's reaction. She took the bait.

A disgusted look grew on Gemma's face, almost as if she had taken a bite out of a lemon. "Excuse me?"

Zane grinned when Gemma abruptly stood up.

"I was nice enough to start this special team and THIS is how you repay me? That's hurtful, Scaredy-cat." Her voice took on a teasing tone. "Besides, I have the brains in this whole operation. And arguably the looks as well." Gemma tore a hand through her hair, grinning with her eyebrows raised.

"Scooch over then, Brainiac." Gemma wasn't lying. Zane couldn't find any footage of Mrs. Valentino. Zane did find out that Trent swiped a lot of cookies under Dr. Smith's nose, although hilarious, not what they were looking for.

"Weird," Zane muttered. "Actually it's more than weird. I think Mrs. Valentino deliberately deleted all of the footage of herself."

"Oooo! This is on a whole new level of weird. Is she some sort of secret spy or something?" Gemma asked excitedly.

Zane skipped through the footage, although he wasn't expecting to find anything.

He clicked on a camera facing his hospital door and selected the 12:00 PM footage. He played the footage until 12:03 PM. Nothing.

"Wait!" Gemma scooted herself closer to the computer. "Look at this." She reversed the footage before playing it.

"What am I looking at?"

"It's really subtle," Gemma admitted before replaying the footage from 12:01 to 12:02. After a few seconds, a flicker ran across the screen like ivy and a blurry figure showed up for barely a second before disappearing.

"We should tell someone about this," Zane suggested.

"Are you crazy?" Gemma narrowed her eyes at him. "You're cute but there's not much going on in that brain of yours."

Zane widened his eyes. "I thought you said that you had the looks out of the two of us?"

Her face turned a light shade of pink. "It was just a joke. I'm not that conceited, Zane. Well anyway, the first person you tell is usually working with the bad guy. That or they tell the wrong person the wrong thing."

"Rightttt," Zane said skeptically.

"Oh fine, Scaredy-cat. Tell someone and prove me wrong." Gemma grinned at his newfound reluctance.

Zane narrowed his eyes. "That nickname is getting old."

She sighed. "Oh cheer up. I'm just teasing you!"

"Anyway, we have evidence. What are we going to do with it?" Zane asked.

Gemma leaned forward. "We're going to find more evidence, and then we're going to find Mrs. Valentino."

FIVE

"Ha! Four of a kind!" Trent slammed his cards down on the white table they were using to play cards.

"How?" Zane could only stare at the seemingly innocent cards in exaggerated horror.

Zane only had two of a kind, so he reluctantly pushed his 500 dollars toward the center of the table. Obviously, Zane didn't actually have any real money, but monopoly money was a good substitute.

Zane chewed on a snickerdoodle cookie bitterly. Patients glanced at Trent and Zane in an amused way. They probably thought he was the doctor's son. Trent crossed his arms across his chest, clearly smug about the win.

"Proud about taking all of my money? How will this boy, with *amnesia* no less, make it in the world?" Zane inquired.

Trent rolled his eyes. "I think you'll be okay. I'm pretty sure monopoly money isn't accepted in most places in the United States."

Zane jumped when a hand placed itself on his shoulder.

"Nice to see you two getting along," Dr. Smith commented. He relaxed when he heard the familiar voice.

"Poker? Are you sure he's old enough?" she asked, eyes widening.

Trent chuckled. The light from outside shone through two large windows in the surprisingly big cafeteria, causing Dr. Smith's bronze skin to gleam. Unfortunately, the lighting made Zane's skin appear even more ghost-like than normal.

"How are you feeling, Zane?" she asked.

"Pretty terrible considering I just lost 500 dollars playing poker," he said with a lack of enthusiasm.

Dr. Smith let out a laugh. "Well, I am so sorry, Zane. But that's what you get for betting with my husband."

Trent conspicuously set a manual on top of the cookies hiding inside of the monopoly box. She tucked a curly ringlet behind her ear before lunging forward as fast as a snake and snatching the box of cookies hiding underneath the instruction manual. Trent's eyes widened.

"Just remember..." Dr. Smith wiped cookie crumbs from the corner of Trent's mouth. "You can't hide anything from me, dear," she said sweetly.

His brain caught up to what Dr. Smith said a minute too late. She had called him her husband. "Wait, you guys are married?" Zane blurted.

"Yes, yes we are." Trent, Trent SMITH, smiled in a lovey-dovey way at Dr. Smith causing Zane to gag.

"I'm out!" Zane slid his chair back before moving hurriedly towards the elevator doors.

"Watch out!" someone from behind him exclaimed.

By the time he heard the words he had already bumped into a tall young adult holding a black briefcase. Zane fell to the floor and by the time he opened his eyes, the guy was gone. He wasn't far enough away, however, that Zane couldn't hear the words he said that were barely above a whisper.

"Code nightshade!" the man snapped, his voice low and menacing.

Zane immediately headed toward Gemma's room, by going up the elevator and turning down different hallways. Once he got there he slipped inside room 333.

"Gemma I—" He trailed off when he noticed Gemma was no longer wearing a hospital gown. She was wearing a baggy gray sweatshirt and ripped black jeans, along with black and white sneakers. She grabbed a pack of bubble gum from her sweatshirt's pocket, opened it, and plopped a piece in her mouth.

"I know, I look *amazing*, don't I?" Gemma asked as though she already knew the answer to the question.

Zane swept a hand through his unruly brown hair—a habit he had learned from having overgrown hair—jealousy stewing inside of him. Of course *he* still had to wear the stupid dress.

"Yeah, these were the clothes they found me with but they were *covered* in blood." Gemma smirked. "Kinda glad I don't remember what happened, but I'm preeeetty sure I won whatever fight I was in." She twirled a strand of her ratted blonde hair.

"Uh huh," he said doubtfully.

She rolled her blue eyes at his skepticism. "You're probably not here for the fashion show, are you, Zane?"

"Actually I think I found something—or rather someone—who can lead us to Mrs. Valentino."

She gasped and clapped her hands together excitedly. "Tell me all about it!" She sat down on the edge of her hospital bed and patted the spot beside her. Zane joined her. Gemma rested her chin on her hands and gestured for Zane to tell her about the lead.

"I was in the cafeteria heading towards the elevator doors in a hurry and I bumped into this guy with a leather briefcase. We both fell to the ground but he ended up running off. The weirdest part was he whispered, '*Code nightshade.*'"

"You do know there are A LOT of crazy people in this hospital, right? Are you sure he has anything to do with Mrs. Valentino?" He could see the skepticism brewing behind her eyes. Zane's hope slowly deflated. Gemma was probably right. But the guy... He looked so familiar. "He wasn't a patient though. It had to have meant *something*."

"Well, you know..." A grin grew on Gemma's face. "We could always break into—"

"No! No more breaking into private offices!" Zane exclaimed. "You seriously need to stop with this delinquent routine."

Gemma's grin faltered for a second. "If you seriously want to lose this OH so IMPORTANT lead, fine by me." Zane could almost hear an edge to her voice but he shook it off. After all, she was Gemma. What could possibly bother her?

CHAPTER
SIX

Z ane was an idiot. He practically fell over himself trying to get out of the hospital cot. His mind still couldn't process the entirety of his stupidity. A sudden realization had struck him, something that could possibly change everything. It made him realize just how important memory truly was. When Mrs. Valentino was reassuring him, she said it must have been strange waking up not knowing who you are or the place you were in either. But... how did Mrs. Valentino know that Zane didn't know who he was? Especially if she didn't work for the hospital. It made him wonder if his case of amnesia was an accident... or if his memory loss was planned. If it WAS planned, then what did that mean? That he was some sort of lab rat? And... why him and Gemma out of everyone else in the world? It sucked not knowing anything. Seriously sucked.

"One step at a time, Zane." He headed towards Gemma's room, but was intercepted by Dr. Smith. Her curly hair was tied back into a ponytail and her arms were covered with pen ink. Presumably, last-minute notes were scribbled down on whatever surface she could find.

"Hello, Zane." She studied the guilty look on his face and held a look in her dark brown eyes that said she wasn't impressed. "Care to explain why you're wandering the halls on the opposite side of the hospital nowhere near your room?"

"Yes I..." Zane winced. He could lie. And probably get away with it. But how could he lie to the person who most likely saved him from dying? Maybe he could just stall for a little while and take care of something he needed to anyway.

"Actually, Dr. Smith, I need to apologize." Zane rubbed the back of his neck nervously. He imagined how apologizing to Dr. Smith would go, but it was so much easier in his head than out loud. "I sort of flipped out at you when you caught me with that knife. And yeah, I was a little freaked out already about the whole amnesia thing." He tapped the side of his head. "But that doesn't change the fact that I still yelled at you. And I was so angry." He paused. "Not just at you!" Zane added hurriedly.

A smile played on Dr. Smith's lips. "It's all right, Zane."

The stall worked out for him because Dr. Smith left without asking him what he was doing. So, technically he didn't lie.

"Nice job avoiding her question, Scaredy-cat." A voice said in his ear. Zane cursed himself for jumping.

"What's got you looking so pale?"

Zane turned around and if he squinted hard enough he could see genuine concern in her blue eyes. "Do you remember Mrs. Valentino?"

"Yeah?"

Zane took a deep breath in. "She knew I had amnesia before I woke up."

"What do you mean by that?" Gemma asked.

"She commented on how weird it must be to wake up not knowing who you are. She KNEW. How could she possibly know? What if our amnesia wasn't an accident?"

"You don't know that," Gemma protested.

"If we aren't some sort of experiment, then what are we, Gemma?"

"I don't know," she muttered. "But hospitals have a bunch of fancy equipment so they could have seen something wrong with our brains, and Mrs. Valentino probably saw the paperwork." Gemma trailed off. For the first time, Gemma seemed... vulnerable. Her confidence had slipped. She was just as perplexed by the situation as he was.

"Anway, Scaredy-cat, we could always get proof of your mystery man! Lily's private office has plenty of footage! You don't have to come if you don't want to, but you can't stop me." She narrowed her eyes, daring Zane to try. He said nothing. Maybe he should have.

CHAPTER
SEVEN

Z ane could find no trace of Gemma anywhere. It had been hours and she never came back. She had quite literally disappeared. Around every corner Zane expected Gemma to be there. She never was, and he was seriously thinking of breaking into Lily's private office to find out where she had gone. Zane couldn't exactly ask Trent or Dr. Smith 'What happened to the girl who was in room 333?' Because that would lead to questions. Those questions would lead to lies. And those lies would lead to soul-crushing guilt. He was sure that his past self would have known what to do. Actually, he had a nagging feeling that his past self would have gone straight to Lily's office. A sigh escaped his lips when he rounded another corner on his way to the cafeteria. Still no Gemma. He paused in front of a bright green elevator, his gaze flickering to the stairway. It was *right* up those stairs. He could just take a tiny little peek to make sure that Gemma was okay. Were morals seriously more important than Gemma? Zane thought about this for a moment before coming to a conclusion. No, they weren't. Besides, if he wanted to be normal again he needed to start acting like his past self. Zane headed up the stairs, until he reached the floor the office was on.

Zane slowed down as he approached it, pausing when he saw the slightly open door. He hesitantly walked towards Lily's office and twisted the gold knob. The office was still messy. But he wasn't alone. For a moment his hopes rose, and he thought it might be Gemma. It wasn't Gemma OR Lily. It was the guy he bumped into in the cafeteria. Zane watched in silent surprise as he inserted a USB into the side of the computer before tapping his fingers on the wooden desk impatiently. What would Gemma do? She would probably confront the strange man in the long, black coat. Zane would probably choose to run. He could've chosen fight or even flight, but instead, he froze.

Zane accidentally leaned against the door and...

Creeeeak.

The man's fiery gaze turned on Zane.

"Uh... Hi. I see you had the same idea as me." Zane pointed at the computer monitor with a shaky finger. Zane subconsciously memorized the guy's face. He didn't even think about it and he could, if asked, tell you that the young adult had short-cropped black hair, high cheekbones, and brown eyes with golden flecks in them. A storm of anger threatened to break through the calm facade the stranger was displaying.

"Do I know you?" Zane asked nervously, causing the guy's anger to falter and his eyebrows to raise.

Almost instantly, the young man snatched the USB from the side of the computer. In a matter of seconds, he jumped through the open window behind him. Zane rushed towards the window as shock enveloped him. The guy used whatever he could to climb down the wall, his movements quick. Zane saw him reach the ground and step around a wall, out of sight. It didn't stop him, however, from flying down the hospital stairs and out into the lobby. Zane stepped toward the exit but he was stopped by a receptionist who made eye contact with him.

"Hey, honey, head on back to your room please. I can help you find your way back if you need." She had a friendly, round face framed by red hair and she was leaning over the side of the receptionist desk to talk to him.

Zane nodded, frozen in his tracks. There wasn't much he could do and whatever footage proof there had been of the guy was probably also gone. He was out of leads. Except for the strange symbol that had been on the USB. A flower. Not just *any* flower... A *lotus* flower.

After going back to his room, he waited for either Trent or Dr. Smith to arrive, walking back and forth as he waited.

Once Trent stepped through the doorway Zane stopped pacing. "Trent! Can I borrow your computer?"

Trent's eyes widened. "Sure, Zane. I'll be back in a few for it."

Once Trent brought his computer back, Zane sat in a chair in the corner. Zane opened the computer before pressing the power button. He had doubts, but he still put the lotus flower on Google's search bar. He glared at the computer screen, as if that would make it load faster. Once it did, he clicked on a website that looked especially promising. The results made his stomach churn. Apparently, the symbolism of the lotus flower was all about "rebirth" and "second chances." Could the whole amnesia thing be considered having a second chance? That had to mean the mysterious guy was a part of this experiment, for a lack of a better word. Or maybe he just really liked flowers. All Zane knew was he was done panicking about everything. Not that he had a choice in the matter. He blamed the amnesia for messing with what he thought used to be a level-headed brain. He made a list in his head of the predicament he was in, all of the facts, encounters, and possibilities he could think of, and tucked it safely in the back of his brain. His thoughts weren't safe on paper, but then again they weren't really safe in his brain either. Especially considering he had recently forgotten everything about... well, everything. Zane yawned. He should probably return Trent's computer—which he *borrowed* because he was *not* a thief—and sleep on it.

"Maybe just a few more minutes of research," Zane muttered.

"Hey, can I have my computer back, Zane?" Trent peeked his head in the doorway of Zane's room. Zane had flipped through so many websites about the lotus symbol that his eyesight had turned blurry.

"Yeah sure." He hopped up from the blue chair in the corner, closed the computer and handed it to Trent.

"Find what you were looking for?" Trent asked.

"I did. Thanks, Trent."

"Sure." He looked suspicious but didn't question the vague answer.

Zane needed to find Mrs. Valentino. He needed to find the mysterious boy with the lotus symbol on the USB. And most importantly he needed to find Gemma. But first? He needed to get rid of the stupid hospital dress.

"Hey, Trent? About the dress I'm wearing..."

CHAPTER

EIGHT

Z ane studied himself in the bathroom mirror. He definitely had a sense of style. Or at least used to. He tugged on the fancy black vest, and his eyes studied the white dress pants tucked into dress shoes. His hair still looked awful, but overall he didn't look bad. He fidgeted with his long sleeves, his fingers poking at the gashes on his face. They were healing, but he would have scars for the rest of his life. There were still small bloodstains on his clothes that had been too difficult to remove, which made Zane wonder if it was his. Maybe some of it was Mrs. Valentino's blood. Or the mysterious guy's blood. He tucked the piece of candy Mrs. Valentino had given him into his pocket. Trent and Dr. Smith were waiting for him in the cafeteria, which was directly across from the bathroom.

Zane pushed open the bathroom door, walking towards the cafeteria table where Trent and Dr. Smith were sitting. An air of confidence followed him.

"Looking sharp, Zane," Trent commented.

Dr. Smith simply raised her eyebrows. Of course, he picked that moment to trip. He didn't fall but he still felt slightly embar-

32

rassed. Images of laughing faces entered his mind as he stood there, eyes focused on the dirty floor of the cafeteria. The images of the laughing faces expanded and suddenly it wasn't his own mind creating them. It almost felt real. He stayed there for a moment. Processing. Face flushed. A tangible memory flashed past his eyes. It was of someone he cared about laughing, and he had felt embarrassed just like he was now. Then it was gone. He shrugged it off and slipped into a spot opposite Trent and Dr. Smith.

"So, it's your last day in the hospital..." Dr. Smith started. Zane's heart sank. They were going to send him into foster care, or to a group home, or wherever sad, lonely orphans were sent.

"We don't think you would like to be sent somewhere all alone never knowing if..." Dr. Smith wrung her hands together.

"We were thinking you could come home with us," Trent admitted. "At least until we find out who your parents are," he added hurriedly.

Tears pricked the corners of Zane's eyes. "Yeah. That sounds nice."

Zane stared at Dr. Smith and Trent. They gave him reassuring smiles in return. What did they think of him? When they saw him did they pity him? Or maybe they actually cared about him. What were Dr. Smith and Trent Smith's reasons for taking him in? He supposed he would find out eventually. But he hadn't even realized that doctors could adopt their patients. Zane still couldn't forget how Trent had lied about the pill. It felt as if his stomach was being punched, and at the same time, he was receiving a Nobel prize.

Zane shuffled his feet underneath the table. "I'm going to head back to my room." They didnt stop him.

He turned the knob to his room and slipped inside. His jaw dropped. He would have been less surprised to see a clown juggling.

"Looking sharp, Scaredy-cat. The blood really makes your eyes pop."

He took a startled step forward. "What?" His voice was quiet and barely above a whisper.

"Miss me?" Gemma teased.

"Yeah," he admitted, his eyes wide.

"Anything happen while I've been gone?"

The stress from earlier caught up to him and made his head throb. "A lot has happened since you've been gone." He massaged his temples.

"Headache?" Gemma's forehead creased in concern.

He nodded. "Why did you leave for so long? I couldn't find you anywhere."

"I didn't. I was caught, and they kicked me out of the hospital. Not to mention they sent me to this stupid group home." Anger slipped into her voice and lightning flashed behind her eyes.

"I'm sorry." He reached out to put a hand on her shoulder but stopped and let his hand drop to his side.

"Don't be, Scaredy-cat." A familiar smirk resurfaced. "So what happened exactly?"

"You'll need to sit down for this," he suggested. Zane sat down at the foot of his bed and Gemma sat down next to him. "Where do I begin?"

Twenty minutes passed before Gemma was completely caught up. "Let me get this straight. A man with a symbol of a lotus flower downloaded footage from Lily's computer and most importantly." Gemma paused. "You broke into a private office by yourself... WITHOUT ME!?"

Zane winced. "Yeah?"

"That hurts, Zane."

"That was a one-time thing! Well, technically a second-time

thing! But the point is I wouldn't have had to break into the office if you hadn't been caught."

He still couldn't believe it. For all he knew, she could've been kidnapped by the flower-obsessed guy. She still looked the same with her unruly blonde hair and baggy clothing but there was something she wasn't telling him. For now? Zane was just glad she was back.

"What are we gonna do?" he muttered.

"What do you mean?" Gemma asked.

"How are we going to stick together? I'm going to be living with Dr. Smith and Trent but I doubt it's near the group home you're staying at. Where is it anyway?"

Gemma shifted her feet, seemingly deep in thought. "Relax! You couldn't get rid of me if you wanted to. You would *die* without me, Scaredy-cat. You've already become such a disaster in the time I've been gone." She smirked, but Zane could see Gemma's own doubts hiding behind her teasing expression. Zane couldn't bring himself to laugh. "My group home is by this really old church. You don't need to know the exact address, but if you ever need to find me look for the church with the red roof. I already peeked into the Smiths' files anyway. I know their address so uh..." She stood up and walked over to the window. It was covered in rain droplets that looked eerily like spider eyes. "I'll find you, Zane."

"When will you be back?"

Her smirk disappeared. "I won't be gone long, Zane. But the other orphans will be wondering where I've gone and, trust me, they love to gossip." The word orphans had slipped off her tongue almost too easily.

Gemma pushed the window open and her face was pelted with rain, but she didn't seem to mind. "Try not to miss me too much, Zane."

CHAPTER
NINE

*Z*ane had to leave everything he knew behind, and he wasn't sure if he would be able to do it. Or who would be lurking around the corner when he left.

"Ready to go, Zane?" Trent asked.

"I packed everything I own," Zane answered cheerily. He glanced at his fancy vest and made sure the candy Mrs. Valentino had given him was still in his pocket. It was somewhat comforting, especially since it was one of the few things that proved he wasn't crazy.

"Trent..." Zane adjusted the collar of his shirt.

"Yeah?"

"Are you sure about this?" Zane asked.

"About what?"

"Me living with you," he said quietly.

"I'm sure."

Zane followed Trent down the hallway and to the front doors of the hospital. The only place he knew. The only place he had ever been. He took a deep breath and stepped through the doors.

Awkward silence accompanied Zane on the car ride. He

wasn't going home exactly. It was more of a temporary house that he would be staying at. Zane wasn't sure if that made things better or worse.

"So." Dr. Smith coughed awkwardly. "Any hobbies?"

"Um. Not that I can recall."

"Ah. I see." Trent added, tapping his fingers against the steering wheel.

"Food preferences?" Dr. Smith asked.

"I like jello." Trent's grip on the steering wheel tightened.

"Oh. I see." Dr. Smith's voice was strained. He had never seen her look so jumpy before. They were just as nervous as he was. "We'll need to get you new clothes."

"If it's too much trouble, I can just go into foster care. I would hate to be a bother." Zane wrapped his arms around himself and forced himself to watch the colorful trees fly by.

"No, Zane, we're happy to take you in. It's just we've never taken care of a kid before. We don't want to mess anything up," Dr. Smith admitted. "We wanted children but..." She looked down at her stomach, and the silence filled in the blanks in Zane's mind. Dr. Smith couldn't have children. With all the extra time Zane had in the hospital he had watched a few different doctor shows to try and figure out his amnesia. He hadn't. But Zane figured out a lot of different things about other conditions and health issues.

"Sorry," Zane mumbled, the tension in the car reaching an almost suffocating level. A concern suddenly crashed into him. What if Gemma couldn't find him and she had forgotten the address? They might never see each other again, and he would have no one who believed him. As his worries swirled faster and faster, the trees started to get blurrier. A memory struck him like lightning and he stifled a gasp. His vision turned blurry, and suddenly he could see again. But he wasn't in the baby blue prius. And he might have been able to see but it felt like he was hearing someone else's thoughts.

Zane rolled his eyes at his classmates. They were struggling to identify the meaning of a book for English class. If they thought THAT was hard, they should really try sneaking into a school without means of identification and not being caught. It had been surprisingly easy to hack into the school's computer and put himself in as a transfer student.

What a bunch of idiots. Zane thought to himself. He fixed a strand of his hair that had fallen out of place, head resting as his chin as he watched the teacher explain the book. Zane wasn't really listening, but he didn't need to.

"Zane!" his friend Max whisper-hissed.

He twisted around in his seat and raised an eyebrow at his raven-haired friend.

"They found us." Max's blue eyes were wide with alarm.

Zane dropped the pencil he was holding and it landed on the threadbare carpet.

"What was that for, Zane?" Trent asked in an amused way. "You see a ghost or something?"

Zane blinked the memory away. "I remembered something," he admitted. His brain felt like it had been stuffed full of cotton.

"That's great, Zane!" Trent's grin widened, as he flicked on the car's blinkers.

Was it? And who WAS he? Some sort of foreign spy? He shoved it into a part of his mind labeled "Deal with later." He just couldn't right now.

"Our apartment is half an hour away. We can put on some music if you'd like." Dr. Smith drummed her fingers on the thin armrest.

Zane shook his head. After a few more minutes of awkward silence, he let his eyelids droop.

"We're here!"

Zane forced his eyes to open. His neck had a painful crick from staying in the same position for so long. Trent drove the car into a parking space and turned off the engine. Zane pushed the passenger seat door open and stepped out. His foot touched down on concrete, and his hazel eyes surveyed a tall apartment building. Dr. Smith and Trent joined him in his sightseeing.

"We're on floor 13," Dr. Smith commented. "Not as bad as it sounds, I promise. There's an elevator we can use. Unless it's out of order, which has only happened once."

"Considering you haven't let me eat any sweets in our apartment I'd say otherwise—"

She proceeded to punch Trent's arm. "Sweetheart, care to rephrase that?" Dr. Smith batted her eyes.

"Ouch!" He rubbed the part on his arm she had abused, an extremely exaggerated reaction. "At least I have a witness for this domestic abuse." He smirked at Zane. Dr. Smith rolled her eyes.

Zane looked away from the weird flirting. He still couldn't wrap his head around the fact that the two of them were married. The two of them were such an odd pair.

Trent's gaze focused on the ground. "Ready to see the apartment?" he asked.

Zane simply nodded. Words couldn't express the complicated emotions doing backflips in his stomach. Nor could they express the strange tangle of conflicted emotions constricting his throat when Trent pushed the plain apartment door open.

"Uh... I'd say put your stuff wherever you want but considering you don't own any—" Dr. Smith proceeded to punch Trent's arm for the second time. The apartment room looked as though Dr. Smith had decorated it, but every once in a while Trent's unique personality peeked through the frilly throw pillows and velvet curtains. Zane could see Trent in the valentine stuffed bear with a heart stomach on top of the fridge, the hat thrown carelessly on the small dining room table, and the coffee stain on the white carpet. But it wasn't the lavender candles or the Paris paintings that caught his attention. It was the poster hanging from the wall in the living room. Trent's face in the middle of it was the thing that surprised him the most.

"What's that about?" Zane asked.

Dr. Smith put her coat on the rack by the door. "Trent refuses to take it down. He starred in a local church play and can't stop bragging about it."

"It's an accomplishment no matter how small!" Trent protested. "Plus they got my good side." The poster was of him wearing a type of robe with a cane in his hand. Whoever made it did a great job with photoshopping the background. He was just surprised Trent had time with his job. "Anyway, are you hungry, Zane?" Trent asked brightly, already rushing over to the kitchen. Zane looked at Dr. Smith for an explanation. She joined Trent in the kitchen without so much as an eye roll.

CHAPTER
TEN

Thoughts seemed to dig into his mind like daggers, draining him of rationality. Zane studied the popcorn ceiling intently, his eyes slowly adjusting to the darkness. His fingers twirled the edges of the wrapper on the candy Mrs. Valentino gave him. It was his first night in the Smith's apartment and despite the surprisingly comfortable couch, he couldn't fall asleep. Fear and anger mixed together in his brain, succeeding in making Zane even more confused than before.

Max.

He used to be friends with someone named Max. And someone had found the two of them. Was it Mrs. Valentino? Was Max somewhere out there with no clue as to who he was? Zane flipped onto his stomach and put his pillow over his ears. Unfortunately, the blue pillow wasn't able to drown out his thoughts. Zane thought of the fear on Max's face. What if... What if Zane was the bad guy? And the only way to stop him was to wipe out his memories? Speaking of the devil... A memory, like a spark, faint at first, surfaced in his mind. He didn't know if it was caused by him thinking about something, like Max, or if it was random.

Being chased down meant you had to improvise so as to not be caught. And unfortunately the only empty crate they found barely fit the two of them in it.

"Your elbow is on my face!" Zane complained.

"Shhh! They'll hear us!" Max warned. "Stay still!"

"If it means getting out of Max cuddle-time I don't mind!" Zane snapped, but stopped moving anyway, not daring to breathe.

"Last crate!" The captain of 'The Annabeth' called out.

"What if they find us again?" Max whispered.

"They won't." Both of them stopped breathing when their crate was lifted into the air.

When Zane woke up, he was expecting to be inside of the cramped crate, but instead he was on a couch. It took him a moment to realize it had just been a memory.

"Good morning!" Trent said from the kitchen. "I'm making pancakes." Zane rubbed the sleep from his eyes, panic causing his breathing to grow unsteady.

"If you don't like pancakes we have cereal," he added hurriedly.

"Pancakes sound good," Zane mumbled, glancing down at his shaky hands.

"Whipped cream and strawberries? Or do you prefer maple syrup?"

"Can I try both?" Zane asked, his voice wavering. He just hoped that Trent didn't notice. He hopped off of the cream-colored couch and the blood rushed to his head. Zane ignored the sudden nausea.

He glanced at the bathroom door, knowing he couldn't do anything until he calmed down. "Can I actually get a shower first?"

"Sure."

He was able to borrow a pair of shorts and an oversized shirt, and after the shower, Zane hopped onto a barstool next to Dr. Smith. She was hunched over a cup of coffee and her eyes were drooping. Trent turned off the stove and shoveled eggs into a small glass bowl. He set two plates of pancakes in front of Dr. Smith and Zane.

"Thanks, honey," Dr. Smith mumbled.

She walked over to the fridge, grabbed a bowl of different fruits like strawberries and blueberries, and dumped a ton of them on her pancakes. Zane snatched the maple syrup and drizzled it on the top of his stack.

"So, Zane, you said you remembered something?" Trent asked in between bites of his makeshift breakfast burrito. He had stuffed eggs, sausage, and syrup in the middle of a pancake. Zane had to admit it did look delicious.

"Yup." Zane stabbed his pancakes and tore a piece off.

"Was it a good memory?" he continued.

Was it? Considering he was being chased down by an unknown group of people, probably not. Zane shoved the piece of pancake in his mouth so that he didn't have to answer. The sweet pancake turned bitter in his mouth with Trent's next question.

"So, who's Max?"

"How do you know about Max?" Zane tapped his fingers on the counter nervously.

"You were talking in your sleep last night," Trent admitted sheepishly. "I had gotten up to get a glass of water and I heard you. I wasn't sure whether to wake you or not. You seemed pretty distressed."

He suppressed a sigh. "He's a friend. Or at least he used to be before the whole amnesia thing." Zane tapped the side of his head.

Dr. Smith gulped down the rest of her coffee. "If you want to talk about it we're here for you, Zane."

"Thanks."

He didn't.

He didn't want to talk about it at all.

For a while they ate in silence.

"Zane, I was thinking later today we could go buy you some new clothes. Specifically, clothes that aren't bloodstained?" Dr. Smith raised an eyebrow at Zane.

"Sure." Zane shrugged before taking another bite of syrupy goodness.

The awkward silence returned.

"So—" The three of them said at the same time. Moments passed, and when no one said anything he kept eating. Eventually he cleared his plate and set it in the sink. He thought about saying something else but it seemed pointless.

"Hey wait!" Dr. Smith raised one hand in the air, which was stretched out toward him. Her face was frozen in the same hesitant expression. "Okay. We're going to have to break the ice eventually. And I don't want to force it but when I say ice I mean the sink the Titanic worthy iceberg between all of us. The uneasy silence is killing me, and I have no doubt it's killing you two as well. Soooo..." She wrung her hands together, turning toward Trent with a hopeful look in her eyes.

"Er. Sweetie?" Trent's face turned pale. "Are you sure?"

Zanes' confusion deepened.

"How about you go first, Trent?" Dr. Smith nudged him in the side.

"For what?" The nervous tone of Trent's voice convinced Zane that he knew what Dr. Smith had planned. She continued staring at him with that hopeful expression.

"The things I do for you," Trent sighed. "Okay. We want you

to feel comfortable while staying with us Zane. So we're going to tell you some things about us. And you don't have to tell us anything in return either. I know you're been really scared Zane."

He shifted uncomfortably at the accurate observation.

"But you're not alone in that. I'd tell you how much I fear losing my precious wife but she would probably kill me." Trent shot an 'I told you so!' look at Zane when Dr. Smith simply smiled and flexed her fingers as if preparing to punch him should he try any more funny business.

He rubbed his chin thoughtfully. "I should probably tell you something about when I was younger." Zane leaned forward, his curiosity growing. "It might be extremely surprising to you." He said in a joking tone. "But in highschool I was often bullied. That's kind of why I'm a doctor now. I did it out of spite, Zane." His expression grew serious. "The reason we even met is because I wanted to prove someone wrong. It really bothered me that people said stuff about me." He studied his fingers intently. "And I want you to know if you ever need help with anything, even if it seems minor compared to that... We're here for you. We might not be your parents but we're the only guardians you have, and we want to be good ones."

Dr. Smith nodded. "We all go through struggles, Zane. But having someone there to support you makes it easier. We want to be those people. I was lucky enough to have my parents there for me but I was extremely rebellious in my childhood. I did wrong things but I ended up surrounding myself with good people," she said quietly. "We just hope we can be those good influences for you."

Two pairs of eyes turned towards Zane. He forced himself not to throw open the apartment door and go hide at the bottom of the ocean forever. They said he didn't have to tell them anything. But he kind of felt obligated to.

"I…"

Who he used to be dug up a lot of complicated emotions. Zane couldn't exactly mention he used to be some sort of spy with a fake identity. Yeah, no. He wasn't going to mention that for a long time. Or… Well… Ever.

"I…"

Max, Mrs. Valentino, the flower boy… Zane just wasn't ready to tackle the whole, shady individuals are stalking me thing.

"If you're not ready to open up to us, I understand. It's like we said earlier. You are not obligated to tell us anything. We've only known you for five days, Zane. It wouldn't be fair, expecting you to put your heart out on the table," Trent admitted. "We just wanted you to get to know us a little better, and let you know that we're there for you."

"No! I just… It's complicated."

Dr. Smith adjusted her purple blouse, her intense but well-meaning gaze staring right through him. "You have plenty of time, Zane. Take as much as you need."

Zane took a shaky breath in. Maybe there was something he could share that wasn't a big deal. "It kinda scares me how normal violence is for other people," he muttered. "I mean, watching people murder and bleed out on tv shows is just considered normal. It's terrifying because people find that entertaining. And yeah, it makes me kind of a Scaredy-cat…" Zane narrowed his eyes at the reminder of Gemma. "The whole waking up covered in blood thing kind of ruined that for me."

Zane didn't miss the shock that flashed behind their eyes. The silence returned but it was anything but awkward. It was a nice kind of silence.

Dr. Smith set her hands on her lap before straightening her posture. "Zane, I can honestly say that you are a breath of fresh air. Not many people have strong morals these days."

Zane looked down wrinkling his nose when he saw the blood stain on his sleeve. "You said that I could get new clothes right?"

"Yes, of course. When would you like to go shopping for new clothes, Zane?" Dr. Smith asked with a smile. "There's no rush either."

Zane couldn't stay cooped up in the apartment forever, even if he wanted to. "How about tomorrow?"

CHAPTER
ELEVEN

P op music blared from the mall speakers, making him
grimace. Crowds of people were everywhere, and there
was no telling who was hiding among them. Murderers, kidnappers, or even his own personal *stalkers*.

"Zane, what kind of clothes were you wanting?" Dr. Smith
turned to him, her hands holding on to her small, black purse.

He glanced down at his blood stained outfit. "Literally
anything else besides this." Zane let his hand rest over the
wrapped candy safely tucked away in his pocket.

She looked at him strangely, shaking her head as if to get
something troubling out of her head. Zane assumed it was
concern. Dr. Smith said nothing, but she didn't have to. They
walked past a group of teenage girls with brightly colored hair,
who gave him the side-eye when they passed. They took one
look at his unkempt hair and sneered. Zane winced, grabbing his
hair and using it to further cover his face.

An hour passed before Zane picked out the amount of clothes
Dr. Smith deemed reasonable. He turned to the cashier, who
chewed gum loudly.

"That'll be two hundred," she said, eyes studying them with disinterest.

"Two hundred dollars?" Zane whispered.

"It's fine, Zane." Dr. Smith reassured.

The teenage cashier looked at them in annoyance, her tan finger twirling a strand of her equally fake platinum hair. Zane narrowed his eyes at the cash register.

"Are you sure?" he asked. A memory so sharp and clear pressed against his temples, forcing him to pay attention to it.

"Are you sure?" Max asked nervously.

"It'll be fine." Zane reassured while rummaging through various boxes.

"Won't they find out?"

"They won't." Zane surveyed the carnival tent, which had red and white stripes. They were in the main tent, where everyone performed. The only other hint of human life was the leftover popcorn scattered on the floor.

Max shrugged. "They always find us."

"Fine. I lied. We can't hide forever, but just for a little while..." He picked up a small tophat from inside of a particularly heavy box and put it on his head. "You can be with your own kind." Zane stuck a round red styrofoam ball on Max's nose. "Clowns." He explained when he saw Max's confused expression. The confusion turned into annoyance, and Zane's lips curled into a smirk.

Zane blinked away the memory. The cashier already had all of his new clothes in bags and Dr. Smith was handing her the money.

"I'm sure, Zane. You need normal clothes."

"But—" Dr. Smith glared at him and Zane reluctantly closed his mouth.

"Smart boy," the cashier commented. He didn't know her very well, but he already decided he disliked her.

Something Zane had begun to learn about malls was that

they really were the perfect place for stalkers. The variety of people blended in, no matter what they looked like. Whether they had colored hair, curly, or straight. Everyone just turned into a blur, along with the rest of the crowd. And that meant that you couldn't tell one face from another. Zane thought he was crazy when he saw a familiar brown-haired guy. A guy who had jumped out of a window. He was looking at various sweatshirts, but every once in a while he would look up at a mirror. With Zane's reflection smackdab in the middle of it. Zane was feeling a little reckless at the moment. If he was going to be stalked he would have fun with it. A slightly darker thought entered his mind. If this guy was going to hurt him, then he would have already. Which meant that what he was going to do next wouldn't really matter that much. While the clerk and Dr. Smith were busy, Zane stuck his tongue out and held up his middle finger. The look on the boy's sharp face was worth it. Zane snatched the bag from the counter.

"All right! Let's go!" Zane hooked elbows with Dr. Smith and dragged her out of the store.

"In a hurry?" Dr. Smith asked dryly.

"Every minute of the day is important!" Zane answered with a quick look over his shoulder. The boy had abandoned the sweatshirts. Zane tried to speed up but Dr. Smith refused to move.

"Zane, slow down."

"It's just that maybe I can—" Zane looked around for the boy. He was nowhere to be seen.

"Are you feeling alright, Zane? Maybe you should sit down for a second." She guided him to a bench, before digging into her purse. Dr. Smith brought out her phone. "Stay here for a second, Zane." She headed away from the bench, but she was still close enough that she could see him.

Zane sunk deeper into the bench he was sitting on, trying his best not to listen in on the conversation Dr. Smith thought he couldn't hear.

"He's getting worse," she whispered.

A pause.

"I know."

Another pause.

"Are you sure?"

Dr. Smith frowned after hearing something the other person said. "Okay." She agreed. She gave a thumbs up to Zane, which included an obviously fake smile. Zane wanted to ask what she had said okay to, but he couldn't bring himself to. He couldn't even maintain eye contact. That's when a memory that felt so similar to what was happening struck him.

"How is he doing?" A tall man whose name Zane still didn't know asked.

"He's getting worse," An uptight voice admitted. A voice belonging to HER. The one who Zane thought he could trust. The one he had done everything for.

"How so?"

Zane peered through the keyhole, his heart pounding.

"He's so close to finding out, and he keeps fighting back."

"Interesting." The man turned slightly, enough to where Zane could see the blue lotus banner hanging from the wall.

"Remember the treatment we discussed? I think it's time we implemented it."

"Are you sure? I think you'll be able to gain his trust back again—"

"No. There's no way around it. He knows what the Evermoving is really trying to accomplish. If he brought that information back to—" Her eerie blue eyes snapped towards the keyhole. "It looks like we have an eavesdropper..."

Panic pounded against his chest, and he shuddered. There was no way out of this.

"Zane..." The voice started out quiet, but gradually grew louder.

"Zane!"

"ZANE!"

"What?" He snapped back to reality, focusing his gaze on a slightly frustrated Dr. Smith.

"Let's go."

Zane blinked away the rest of the memory, fragments of blue still lingering in the corner of his vision. "Yeah, sorry."

Memories were coming back to him quicker than ever, and each time they raised more questions. He used to be on the same team as the boy who jumped out of the window? And did he run away with his friend, Max? Were they both a part of the Ever-moving? His temples started throbbing, but he forced himself to keep walking towards the exit alongside Dr. Smith. He wished that his memories were a little more organized.

CHAPTER

TWELVE

Z ane threw his blanket to the side and quietly tiptoed to the apartment door. He couldn't sleep. It felt as though he was being torn into a dozen different directions at once. Zane *needed* to get out of the apartment. He reached blindly towards the coat rack until he found Trent's brown coat. He grabbed the gold key from the pocket and opened the apartment door with it. Zane hesitated, placing the candy Mrs. Valentino gave him underneath his pillow. The door creaked as he pushed it open. Once the door was shut behind him, he let out a breath he didn't know he had been holding. What would Trent and Dr. Smith think if they saw him sneaking out like this? Would they immediately send him to a group home? Or into foster care? Finally admit that he was too much trouble? The lights in the hallway were off and it was pitch black. Everyone in the apartment complex was likely asleep. Except for Zane. Even so, he pushed away his fears and kept walking.

The city was still loud, even at night. Honking cars, drunk pedestrians, suspicious men in black coats... He kept his head down, his eyes fixated on the uneven sidewalk.

"What are you doing, Zane?" he muttered to himself. He wasn't really sure if he was being honest. He broke into an office but he didn't have any problems wandering the streets at night? Then again it *was* his life. This choice didn't affect anyone besides himself. Except maybe Gemma, he realized too late. Zane inhaled deeply. He had found his way into a park, and with no one else around, it was almost peaceful. He was sitting on a bench, the crickets being the only thing keeping him company. Zane's palms grew sweaty. What if that stalker was still around? He stood up abruptly and started to walk home. Zane wasn't stupid enough to go out into a park while people were stalking him. Except he was, considering he had done exactly that. If he was smart enough for the crazy things he did with Max, then he should have been smart enough not to wander out alone.

"Well, well, well. What do we have here?" A voice purred from behind Zane's shoulder. He tensed when he felt a warm breath on his neck. The scariest part was he didn't recognize the voice. This wasn't the guy who messed with the hospital computer. And it definitely wasn't Mrs. Valentino.

"You're all alone. It took you long enough. You don't know how long I've had to wait. " The person behind him pressed a knife to his throat. "Do me a favor? Don't scream."

He forced himself not to move, even as a chloroform-soaked cloth was pressed against his nose. As soon as he fidgeted, the knife pressed harder into his throat, and he forced himself to stay still. Soon his vision blurred and he went limp.

"I can't believe it!" A voice that sounded female exclaimed excitedly. "This guy is almost impossible to capture! You don't think he let us, do you?"

Zane forced his eyelids open before letting out a shriek. It was no longer night, and Zane's brain felt strangely fuzzy.

"Are you sure we got the right one?" A tall teenage boy asked.

Zane surveyed the strange campsite they had brought him to,

and twisted around to get a better look at the ropes that bound him to a tree. His gaze finally settled on a boy and a girl who wore dark clothing. The girl had medium brown hair and the boy had cropped-back red hair.

"What's your name?" the girl asked. "Mine is Dani. And trust me when I say you won't be able to use it to find me." Zane tried pulling against his restraints but they didn't budge.

"Hello? She asked what your name was," the boy said in an exasperated voice. Zane kept pulling against the restraints.

"It's a simple question, really. Here. Let me show you." The boy pointed to himself. "Myyy... Nameee... Isss... Tomm..." He said in a condescending way.

"Why did you bring me here?" Zane stopped struggling against the restraints, glaring at them through the hair that had fallen over his eyes.

"Because. You're the little pet of some of our dear friends. And you should know plenty about them. Zane, I believe?"

"Is this about the Evermoving?" Zane blurted.

"Finally something!" Dani adjusted her round spectacles, one hand on her hip.

"I don't even know anything more than their group name! Which to be honest is kind of stupid!" Zane dug his fingers into the dirt ground so that they couldn't see he was shaking.

"Don't lie to us!" Tom snapped, his amber eyes pinning Zane in place.

"I don't know anything." he murmured.

"Are you refusing to tell us what you know?" Tom asked.

"I think you'll change your mind soon enough." Dani dralled, while reaching in a brown pouch attached to her belt. She pulled out a small vial filled with a clear liquid. She smiled. "One drop of this and you will feel excruciating pain. I have something that will relieve that pain after you tell us the truth. So open up."

"Wait! I'm serious! I don't remember anything about—" Tom

forced Zane's mouth open and Dani opened the vial. She let one drop fall onto his tongue. He blinked slowly.

"Was that supposed to do something?" Zane asked in an amused tone.

He suddenly folded over from what felt like a knife stabbing his insides. Zane gasped as the pain spread quicker than a disease. He squeezed his eyelids shut, his breathing ragged and uneven.

"I left a long time ago!" he wheezed out. "With Max!"

"What else?! What are the Evermoving's secrets?"

"I don't remember! Just stop!" Zane pleaded.

"Tell us what you know!" Tom demanded.

"I don't know anything!" he shouted.

"Liar!" Dani snarled.

"They made me forget!" Zane screamed, tears pricking the corners of his eyes. "I wish I knew but I don't know anything anymore! I don't know where Max is! I don't even know my last name! Let alone who my parents are!" The pain worsened, and Zane could barely breathe.

"All I know is I found out something about the Evermoving that they didn't want me to..." The pain was so bad that Zane couldn't even speak anymore. Someone placed a hand on his shoulder, but Zane couldn't see who it was. Tears had obscured his vision and the only thing he was aware of was the horrifying pain that had crippled him.

"The antidote!" Tom demanded.

Something was injected into his arm and the pain subsided. Zane's head fell forward and he squeezed his eyelids shut.

"Seriously? We kidnapped a member of the Evermoving who has amnesia?" Dani crossed her arms over her chest.

"He looks pathetic," Tom said.

Dani proceeded to elbow Tom. "That's rude! Remember he isn't on the Evermoving's side anymore."

"He's probably faking," Tom muttered.

"What if he isn't?" Dani asked.

"If he isn't, then we just tortured an innocent bystander. Wait..." Tom frowned. "Oh."

"Uh, YEAH." Dani snapped.

"Why are my ears ringing?" Zane asked nervously.

"We tortured an innocent bystander, didn't we?" Tom asked. Dani simply nodded.

"Why are my ears ringing?" Zane repeated.

"Shhh... Go to sleep, Zane." Dani commanded while pressing another chloroform-soaked cloth to his face. He didn't have the energy to fight her.

Zane awoke with a gasp, suddenly falling off of a couch. His head hit the leg of a coffee table. Zane sat up and snatched the sticky note attached to his chest.

Sorry for the misunderstanding! -XOXO Dani

He was in the Smith's apartment again. Zane couldn't help the hysterical laugh that escaped his lips.

A misunderstanding?

A misunderstanding!?

Zane debated calling the police. But who would believe him? He was kidnapped and somehow these kidnappers snuck him back into his apartment? Zane stood and ran towards the apartment door. He flung it open and looked left and right, making sure Dani and Tom had actually left. Zane reluctantly closed it, making sure to lock it just in case his kidnappers decided to come back.

"You slept through breakfast." Trent was leaning on the kitchen counter, eyebrows raised.

Zane practically jumped out of his skin. "You could say that." Zane shrugged and played off his shock with a smile.

"A girl stopped by earlier."

Zane immediately thought of Dani. But no, she wouldn't have let Trent see her. Unless he was in on the whole thing.

"It was Gemma from the hospital. Did you two meet there?"

Zane hesitated and shrugged, trying to avoid the question.

"Dang, it's been maybe a week since you've woken up and you already have a girlfriend?" Trent teased.

In his annoyance, he didn't hear the apartment door open. "We aren't dating!' Zane protested, realizing too late he should have denied knowing her.

Trent proceeded to ignore that statement. "She got really annoyed when I said you weren't awake yet," he admitted. "You might want to have a bouquet on hand. Maybe add in a box of chocolates?" Trent suggested, a mischievous glint in his eyes.

"We are NOT dating!" Zane attempted yet again.

"Would that really be so bad?" a voice asked, while trying to hold back laughter.

Zane winced. He knew it was Gemma. What was she even doing here? It was too risky. He couldn't bring himself to turn around. She walked forward and gave Zane a side hug. Zane avoided eye contact.

"Am I embarrassing you?" she asked with a smirk.

"Hello, Gemma." His smile was so tight it should have snapped in half. In reality, he was glad to see her. They had a lot to talk about. And now instead of two people, they had four to find.

"If you'll excuse us, we have to talk," Gemma admitted.

"Talk about what?" Trent asked with a smirk.

She winked in response. "Love bird stuff." Trent shooed them away while gagging.

"You're literally married," Zane challenged.

"Aw, you're so cute when you're angry," Gemma teased, her voice barely above a whisper. Zane knew she was trying to make him even more frustrated. But his mind was too focused on Dani and Tom.

"Alright. I'm just going to borrow him for a few. Let's go, Zane." Gemma dragged Zane out of the apartment, their elbows linked. The door closed and he turned towards her.

"So, you met the Smiths in the hospital? What exactly did you tell them when you saw them again?" he asked.

She smirked. "I told them I'm staying in this hotel, and we met just before you left the hospital. They both seem to like me. I think they're just happy that you're acting like a normal teenager."

After stepping inside the elevator at the end of the hallway, they headed to the first floor. The lobby wasn't exactly private, but when you're being stalked you aren't really safe anywhere. At least that's what Zane assumed. They sat down on a couch in the corner, and he kept a close eye on everyone who entered through the glass doors. "You would not believe what happened—" Zane said at the same time as Gemma.

"You first," Zane suggested, mostly because he wasn't sure how to tell her he was kidnapped.

"So, it turns out it IS possible to be kicked out of a group home," Gemma admitted. Zane's eyes widened. "Also I think I'm being stalked by this girl?"

"Wait! Back up. You got kicked out?" Zane asked, concern lacing his voice.

"Yeah... Technically I wasn't kicked out, but I'm being moved to a different place. Apparently, I was too difficult," Gemma trailed off. "I only started a small fire."

"Gemma!" Zane scolded. "What in the world did you do?"

She rolled her eyes. "It's fine, Zane."

He jumped up from the velvet sofa they were sitting on. "What is wrong with you?" The grin disappeared from Gemma's face.

"You could have just behaved! Or literally ANYTHING ELSE!" he exclaimed exasperatedly, gaining the attention of the apartment staff.

"I..." Gemma winced. "It wasn't that big of a deal. And they weren't exactly nice to me."

Zane's anger immediately dissipated. "Sorry." He sat back down next to her. "My emotions are just kind of through the roof right now."

Gemma's fingers dug into the purple fabric on the sofa. "We didn't deserve to have our memories erased," she murmured, blue eyes narrowed.

"No." Zane hesitated when he saw the tears building in her eyes. He put a hand on her shoulder and they sat in silence for a moment. "Would this be a bad time to tell you I got kidnapped?"

THIRTEEN

"WHAT?!" Gemma's voice echoed throughout the hotel room, and suddenly everyone's eyes were on the two of them. Soon enough they looked away from the outburst.

Zane clamped a hand over her mouth. "Do you want everyone to hear?!"

"What do you mean you got kidnapped!" She screeched quietly, voice muffled through his hand.

He took a deep breath in, gripping his jeans so his hands wouldn't shake. "Have you heard of the Evermoving?" She shook her head. "I recovered a memory about this group or organization, or whatever they are. Apparently I was a part of it. But I discovered something I wasn't supposed to. And so did a friend of mine. I guess whatever information I had, my kidnappers wanted. They were both younger, maybe young adults or teenagers. Their names were Dani and Tom."

Gemma hummed thoughtfully. "Why would they tell you their names?"

Zane shrugged. "Dani said it didn't matter if I knew."

"And where was this at?"

"This one park. It's like a couple minutes away from here."

Gemma suddenly snatched his wrist and began dragging him out of the hotel. "We're going back there."

He planted his feet and Gemma came to a stop as well. "We don't have anything to defend ourselves with," Zane pointed out.

"They won't make an appearance in broad daylight. So suck it up Scaredy-cat We're going to investigate this lead."

After some more convincing, he showed her where he was kidnapped. The small wooden bench looked so harmless during the day.

"Are you sure this was the spot?" Gemma lowered herself to the ground, studying surrounding dirt paths intently.

"Yup. They used chloroform. One of them had a knife." He paused, hand flying to his neck. Zane was pretty sure the knife had broken through his skin. He also lowered himself to the ground, dirt clinging to his shirt.

A young couple gave them weird looks as they passed. They began whispering about teenagers and drugs. Zane moved toward where he thought he was standing when either Dani or Tom grabbed him. Sure enough, a tiny speck of dried blood was on the ground.

"Gemma. Come here." He stood up, glaring down at the ground. The proof was right there.

She walked over to him, eyes widening when she saw it. "Weird. Zane, what did you tell them?"

Zane chewed his inner lip, fingernails digging into his palms. "I had nothing to tell them." A cool wind pressed against his face, blowing his messy hair upwards.

"Hey." Gemma poked him on the arm. "You still haven't told me everything that happened. What did they do to you?"

He finally looked at her. "Gemma, they..." Zane paused when a mother and her daughter came into view. The two of them waved, but he couldn't bring himself to smile back. Once they were out of sight he continued. "Tortured me for information I didn't have."

Gemma slowly brought him into a hug, saying nothing. Her arms were wrapped tightly around him, and he hugged her back. Zane could almost smell the chloroform in the air. He squeezed his eyes shut, taking a deep breath in before pulling away.

For a while they searched for anything Dani and Tom had left behind, but they found nothing.

"I should head back to the apartment," Zane said.

Gemma shook her head. "I'm coming with you." She nudged him with her elbow. "We can't risk you getting kidnapped again." The words were almost a joke, but there was a serious tone in her voice. When they got to the entrance, he said a quick goodbye to Gemma. Once he got inside the apartment, he took a seat on one of the barstools.

"You alright, Zane?" Dr. Smith said, causing Zane to jump.

His eyebrows furrowed together. Zane spun the barstool around to face her. "I guess."

Dr. Smith sighed. "Trent mentioned something about a girl stopping by?" Zane nodded, dragging a hand down his face wearily. Dr. Smith sat down next to him. "What happened?" Her eyes softened in concern.

"It's nothing. You wouldn't understand."

"Try me."

Zane was PRETTY sure that Dr. Smith had never been chased down by people, or kidnapped, or lost all of her memories because of the Evermoving.

"Stop pretending to be my mom," Zane snapped before he even realized what he'd said. But it was true wasn't it? Trent and Dr. Smith really were doing that. But in a few months, they were going to discard him like an old shirt.

Dr. Smith blinked rapidly, hand over her chest.

"Stop pretending like we're a family." He curled his fingers into a fist. "Because we aren't. You expect me to feel grateful for letting me live here. But it's just like Trent said. This. Is. Temporary."

"Zane—"

"Stop." Zane held up a hand. "The only reason." Zane's voice cracked and he paused for a moment. "The only reason I'm here is because you'd rather not deal with an actual commitment." He hadn't really meant what he said, but it felt good to say. It gave him power.

Zane could see the anger boiling in Dr. Smith's eyes. He ignored the rage and continued to glare at his glass of water as if it were the source of all of his problems. She left, but he could almost feel her anger in the other room.

CHAPTER

FOURTEEN

Zane studied the handwriting on the sticky note until his
eyes drooped and the words became blurry. He had so
many questions and zero answers. Just one answer was all he
needed. One reassurance that not everything was a mystery.
Something tangible. But he had nothing. No leads, no helpful
memories, and now? He was trapped in a place that wasn't even
his, and under constant surveillance by Dr. Smith and Trent.

"Who are you?" he snarled. He continued to glare at the
green sticky note until finally... Something clicked. There was
something off about the lettering. Was it possible for him to
know two languages without even realizing it? Because he was
pretty sure the writing wasn't in English. Zane reached for the
shopping bag beside his makeshift bed -which was actually just
a couch- and grabbed the black hoodie on the top of the stack.
This time. Zane thought. *I wont get kidnapped.* He slipped on the
hoodie and left the apartment silently, his steps as quiet as a
cat's.

Google translate was his solution. Unfortunately, google
translate proved to be another dead end. The writing didn't

match up with any of the languages on google translate, making Zane think that maybe it really had been written in English. He shut down the library's computer and started browsing the shelves.

"Looking for anything in particular?" a quiet teenage girl asked. Zane forced himself not to jump in surprise.

"Um yes. I'm looking for books on languages?" he said, though it sounded more like a question than anything else.

The girl tossed her hip length hair behind her shoulder. "So why are you in the fantasy section?

"I didn't realize I was," he replied honestly.

The girl smiled politely. "I'll help you. The books on language are this way." She started walking to the other end of the library, and Zane quickly followed her.

"What's your name?" she asked.

He hesitated. What if she was a part of the Evermoving? But she looked kind and honest. Against his better judgment he said, "Zane."

"I'm Robin. Is this for a school project?"

"School project?" he echoed then shrugged. "Um yeah. It's for school."

"In the middle of summer?" Robin raised an eyebrow while reaching for a book. Zane opened his mouth to respond. She held up her hand. "Things happen. You don't have to say a word."

Zane glanced at the book in her hands. "I'm sure Spanish is nice but I was hoping for a book about more obscure languages?" Zane was ninety nine percent sure whatever Dani wrote wasn't in Spanish.

"Hmm..." She murmured while trailing a finger over the spines of the books. "Aha!" She took a book with an orange cover and the title, "Dead Languages, What Languages Used to be, and Their Changes in Time."

"Thanks."

Robin grinned. "You're welcome."

He took the book from her and flipped through the first couple of pages. "This is perfect."

"Do you have a library card?"

Zane froze. "A what?"

Robin frowned. "No wonder you're in summer school."

He coughed in order to hide his laughter. "Do I need one?" Zane shut the book.

"Yes!" she exclaimed. "You do." Robin finished in a quiet voice, her face flushing.

"Okay... How do I get one?"

Robin covered her smile with a hand. "I'll help you."

Half an hour later with a book and a new library card in hand, Zane snuck back into the apartment. He crept into the kitchen for a snack but was promptly interrupted.

"Where were you?" He winced before turning towards the living room. Dr. Smith and Dr. well... Smith were sitting side by side on the couch, both of them looking unimpressed. What was the point in lying? Going to the library was a normal, innocent thing to do.

Zane held up the orange book with a smirk. "The library?"

"We live in the city, you know. You could have been kidnapped." Dr. Smith commented. Zane wanted to laugh. He could have been?

"I wasn't." He threw his hands up in the air. Answers were more important than *possibly* being kidnapped. Again.

"Zane, you can't be so reckless. You should have at least told us first," Trent said, a touch of exasperation coloring his normally even tone.

"I'll tell you next time," Zane promised. He set the book inside his hoodie's pocket before fleeing to the bathroom and locking himself inside. He sat down, grabbed the book and sticky note, and poured over the pages.

"Huh," he murmured.

The writing looked similar to a number of languages, he found out. But most of all the writing on the sticky note looked like a really old version of a mix between English and French. Probably. It would have been nice to remember what languages he did or didn't speak. Maybe it wasn't a different language at all, but a form of code that was stored somewhere in his memory.

The next day, Zane found himself being drawn back to the library. Maybe it was because of the large collection of books or the fancy chandeliers hanging from the ceiling. But if he was being honest, it was because he finally had someone in his life who was completely normal, and didn't know about his strange past.

"Wait you're saying—" Zane broke off, his own laughter interrupting what he was trying to say. "Your mom thought you were doing drugs because some Pixie Stix spilled on your desk?"

Robin snorted as she nodded rapidly. "She sat me down at the dinner table and she gave me an entire lecture about—" she paused, and a fit of giggles escaped her lips. "A lecture about the side effects of cocaine! And after she was finished, she asked me why I was taking drugs!"

Zane grinned. "What did you tell her?"

"I told her I wasn't! And that the powder was just from my Pixie Stix! Her entire face turned red!" Robin's laughter subsided enough to where she could finally speak again.

"What about you? Have your parents ever assumed anything crazy like that?"

Zane's smirk disappeared. Robin froze. "Do you have parents?"

"I'm living with this couple but... They aren't my parents or anything." He tapped his fingers on the library table nervously. "I need to tell you something." Although it was nice that Robin didn't know, he didn't want to keep the truth from her. "I have amn—"

Somebody coughed loudly behind him.

"I have amn—"

The coughing continued. Robin didn't look annoyed, but she did seem curious. "I think she wants to talk to you." She pointed over his shoulder.

Zane groaned. "I'll be right back." He stood up abruptly, turning towards the source of the coughing. Gemma was halfway hidden behind a bookshelf, gesturing for him to come closer. Her hair had surprisingly been brushed.

"Gemma what's going on—"

She pulled him behind the bookshelf. "I found Mrs. Valentino again."

Zane's eyes widened. "Really? Where?"

"I think she was following me or something. I went back to the park to see if Dani or Tom were there. They weren't, but I think she was wondering why we were there yesterday. There are people following us, Zane. And I don't know who, but someone is watching." Gemma cracked her knuckles. "Whatever reason our memory is gone, it has to be important. I think they're making sure we don't remember the wrong thing. I just don't know why they would go as far to erase our memories, when we can easily remember parts of it. And I also don't know why they didn't just kill us."

Goosebumps appeared on his arms. "We're also extremely popular it seems. I just don't know who is connected to whom."

"What did the guy in the office look like?" Gemma asked.

"He was slightly taller than me, with sharp facial features, black hair, and brown eyes." She sucked in a breath. "What?" Zane demanded.

"I think Mrs. Valentino and this guy are working together. Do you think he deleted the small piece of proof we found?"

Zane closed his eyes. "Yeah. Probably. But they're clearly not doing a very good job of being discreet. If Mrs. Valentino and this guy are from the Evermoving and ended up giving us complete amnesia, you'd think they would be able to go completely undetected."

"Yeah, well we're not exactly normal. Whoever we were before this, we were clearly capable of some things. Maybe we have like crazy observation skills."

"Probably. In a memory I recovered, Max and I snuck into this school. Somehow we put ourselves in as transfer students."

Gemma rubbed her temples. "Gosh, this is hard to wrap your mind around."

"Never mind that. Do you have a place to live now?"

Gemma sighed. "Yeah. The police found me and I was sent to some shady foster home."

"And hold on... Did you see anything else at the park? Maybe something that could lead us to Mrs. Valentino?" Zane knew this was the most important thing he could ask.

"She didn't know I saw her but she was with that one guy like I already told you. It looked like they were arguing."

"About?" Zane's curiosity grew.

"I don't know," Gemma whispered. "They were gone within seconds. I didn't even see where they went." Zane let out a breath he didn't know he had been holding.

"Where were they? We could go back, try and find them..." Zane's brain seemed to work twice as fast, dishing out plans faster than he could process them. "If we find her again, we could force her to tell us about our past! We could finally figure out why we woke up in the hospital at the same time, both with amnesia. Maybe even—"

"Scaredy-cat, I'm going to have to stop you there." She shifted her feet awkwardly. "I don't think Mrs. Valentino would let herself be found. We've been lucky these last few times."

"Do you think they're toying with us?" This had been a concern of his for a while but saying it out loud made it sound so much scarier.

Gemma blinked back tears. "Yeah. Maybe." She shook her head abruptly, replacing her concern with mischief. "Anything else you want to tell me? Like who is that girl at your table?"

Zane ignored the last question. "I've actually been studying something..." He pulled the sticky note out of his pocket and showed her. "First of all, I don't think this is in English. Second of all, I can read it."

"Hmmm..." She narrowed her eyes at the strange letters on the sticky note. Gemma suddenly let out a startling laugh. Zane's eyebrows raised.

"Sorry, it's just this girl has a sense of humor. I mean—XOXO? The entire thing is just... Wow." She paused for a moment when Zane shot her a fierce glare. "No you're totally right I'm sorry. It's probably not in English." Gemma squinted at the sticky note. "Or she just has terrible handwriting...? Do you think we could use it to track Dani down?"

Zane sighed. "The writing is just so weird. But maybe." He brightened. "Aren't there people out there that deal with this sort of stuff?"

Gemma rolled her eyes. "Give." She pointed to the sticky note and Zane reluctantly gave it to her. He regretted it when she walked past him, preparing to talk to Robin.

"Wait!" He whisper-yelled, but Robin had already seen Gemma.

"Hey girl!" Gemma greeted with a small wave of her fingers. He smiled tightly, his eyes wide in annoyance.

"Hi." Robin smiled at Gemma, though it seemed kind of forced. "How are you?"

"Can you read his handwriting? I've been telling him it's

terrible for years but he won't believe me." She rolled her eyes and presented it to Robin.

"Umm..." Robin hesitated. "For a while, I thought Zane had lied about being in summer school." She giggled. "I guess he didn't. Okay, let me see. 'Sorry for the misunderstanding XOXO Dani'? What misunderstanding?"

Zane's entire face turned red. "Okay! Thanks for that Gemma!" He snatched the sticky note from Gemma and said a hasty 'gotta go' to Robin. He quickly stormed out of the library doors, the sticky note safely tucked back inside his pocket. He hopped down the library steps, his gaze fixated on the ground. Leaves crunched underneath his feet.

*How embarrassing, h*e thought to himself, his face turning a deeper shade of red. Not only did Robin think his handwriting was awful, but his lead was gone.

"Zane! Wait up!" Gemma hollered.

He kept walking, trying desperately to get his embarrassment under control. He let the cold air combat his hot face until he could finally turn towards Gemma with confidence.

"Wow. Your face looks like it's on fire," she commented.

He knew she was just trying to get him to turn red again, but apparently, his face didn't get the memo because yet again, it looked like a beetroot. Gemma coughed to cover up her laughter. Zane groaned before flipping his hood over his head. He pulled on the drawstrings until his face was completely covered.

"Stop that," he demanded.

"Summer school?" she asked with what Zane suspected was a grin. It was hard to see through his hood.

"Shut up," he said through his teeth.

"Awwww! Scaredy-cat. You don't have to hide from me." She reached for his hood but he managed to duck out of the way.

Zane sighed. "Gemma, do you remember anybody from our past?"

"I assume you're bringing this up because of Max?" she asked.

Zane took off his hood and glanced around. The setting sun sent shadows, from the trees and cars, dancing across the ground. "Yeah," he admitted reluctantly. "We used to be friends." His hand curled into a fist. "I wish I knew where he was. He could answer a lot of our questions. If you know anyone like that, this whole search could be over sooner."

"Hm. So Max is for sure a good guy?"

"Probably." Zane shrugged.

"Okay," Gemma said, "I guess we'll find out eventually right?"

They continued to walk, silence accompanying them. Zane was the first to break it. "When do you think you'll visit again?"

"I don't know. Maybe we should make it a weekly thing. Although I know it'll kill you to not see me for that long." Gemma teased.

He settled his gaze on the ground, satisfied with her answer. Weekly updates should be enough to sort through any new information.

"Gemma!" A shrill voice shrieked over the buzzing sound of traffic.

Zane turned to where a tall young woman was racing down the sidewalks. She was wearing a yellow plaid dress, and her hair was done up in ringlets. He could only assume she was Gemma's guardian.

"That's my cue." Gemma smirked. "See you soon, Zane."

CHAPTER
FIFTEEN

Z ane poked at the breakfast food on his plate, distracidly arranging a frowny face, two eggs as the eyes and bacon as the frown. He had very quickly run out of things to do in the Smith's apartment.

"So what did you think of Tellerman, Dr. Reed's patient?" Trent's knife clicked against his plate.

Dr. Smith glanced at him. "Could you be more specific?"

"The one where the blood was just oozing out of him, and he refused to take painkillers," Trent said while taking a bite of pancake.

"The guy with the knife wound?" Dr. Smith questioned.

"That's the one!" Trent grinned.

This was the reason he hadn't eaten anything on his plate. They had been going back and forth all morning. He decided to go for it and nibble on a piece of toast.

"He was brave, and I admire him for daring to annoy Dr. Reed," she admitted. "I don't think I've ever heard anyone talk back to him. Wasn't the wound infected too?"

Trent leaned forward, his eyes glinting with mischief. "Yup.

Tellerman was kind of a pain, but you can't help but admire him." Zane tried his best not to gag, the piece of toast sinking to the bottom of his stomach. He didn't want to react. His past self wouldn't have. So why should he?

"He also had this nasty w—"

Unfortunately, he still wasn't Zane. At least not yet. "Is this some sort of punishment for sneaking out?!" Zane said exasperatedly.

Trent frowned. "Huh?" He glanced at Dr. Smith for a moment, before realization lit up his face. "Oh. Right. Sometimes I forget that hospital talk isn't exactly..." He chuckled. "A normal conversation topic?" Trent scratched the back of his neck nervously. "Sorry about that, Zane."

"It's fine." Zane let himself relax and took a giant bite out of his bacon.

"I think there was also pus," Trent commented, his lips curling into a smirk.

"Trent! Seriously?" Zane widened his eyes at Trent, who looked smug. He received a shrug in response.

"We'll try to keep the hospital talk to a minimum," Dr. Smith reassured.

"Thanks." Zane adjusted his blue hoodie, and his frustration began to die down.

"Speaking of the hospital—" Zane prepared to glare at Trent. "We need to get to work." He finished with an amused glance at Zane.

Once the Smiths left the apartment, he went back to the library. Robin was there to meet him. "Robin?" Zane leaned back against his library chair.

"What's up, Zane?" Robin peered over the book she was holding.

"We're friends, right?" he asked hesitantly.

"Of course." Her face scrunched up in confusion and worry. "Why?"

"No reason." He focused on the book that Robin had picked out for him. It was a book about witches and wizards, but he was having a hard time with it. Too much was on his mind.

"So what school do you go to?" she said, finally breaking the silence. Zane blinked slowly. His mind processed the question and he tried to figure out the name of a nearby school.

Zane couldn't, so he improvised. "I've kind of been skipping."

"School?" Robin asked cautiously.

"Yup," he confirmed.

"Why?" Robin's lips drooped into a frown.

"I don't know," Zane muttered.

"I have a feeling you do," she pressed.

"This year has been kind of hard for me," he answered vaguely, before reading the next line in his book.

"Are you really skipping school because of that?" Zane wanted to tell her everything. But he couldn't. The words were locked inside of a steel safe, and he wasn't sure if anything could open it.

"Robin, there are some things that I can't tell you," he warned.

She set her book down and leaned forward. "Can't or won't?" How could he be friends with Robin while hiding so much from her?

Zane flinched. "I have to go." He tucked his book underneath his arm, leaving Robin to wonder what in the world he was hiding. He ran down the library stairs two steps at a time, worry plaguing him. He couldn't be honest with Robin. If he told her the truth, Robin would think he was a weirdo, or absolutely insane.

Dr. Smith and Trent said he was found in the streets. Maybe he could find something there. He wasn't sure what, and Zane didn't even know where to go. Zane just didn't want to go back to the apartment yet. He stuck close to crowds, a justifiable paranoia of being kidnapped following him. By the time he walked his worries away, he found himself in a broken down part of town. It was almost like it had been forgotten. There were a group of young adults playing baseball in the streets, their knees scraped and bloody. What really caught his attention, however, was a small black building tucked into the shadows. He approached it, although not because he thought he would find a lead there. It was because there was a sort of calm familiarity surrounding it. But then again, if it felt familiar, maybe he would find someone who used to know him. He opened the glass doors and the smell of whisky pressed against his nose. On the far wall there were dozens of drinks lined up on the shelves, and a long counter stretched from one end of the room to the other. There was also a door on the back wall, likely storage or a bathroom. He turned his gaze toward a crowd surrounding a young man holding a tall glass of alcohol. They were shouting his name, though he wasn't sure the young man was hearing what they were saying.

"Tim! Tim! Tim!" They shouted.

Zane's heart barreled into his ribcage, and he prepared to flee the vulgar establishment. He glanced behind him and found that the baseball team was in front of the exit. Loud cheers erupted when Tim downed the rest of the alcohol. Cheap lights hung from the ceiling, shaking as the crowd started cheering louder. The baseball players approached the bar and Zane had to go further in to avoid them. Neon lights afflicted his eyes, and loud music blasted in his ears.

Tim slammed the glass down on the counter, making eye contact with Zane. His steps were unsteady as he moved. "Look who is it! My old pal Zane!" The man named Tim set a hand on Zane's shoulder and he quickly pulled away. Now that he could see Tim better he realized he had long red hair like a lion's mane and a square-shaped face. That, and he smelled like he had been swimming in a pool of alcohol.

"You know me?" Zane focused his gaze on the exit.

Smith chuckled. "Very funny, Zane. You used to be in here more than I was." Surely it was because he was hiding. Just like when he and Max attended school to avoid the Evermoving.

"What?" He was almost as unsteady as the drunkards around him.

"So what are you doing here anyway?" A grin lit up Tim's face.

"Zane?!" One of the older baseball players exclaimed in shock. He could barely see him, since he was behind his friends.

"You better believe it!" Tim's amber eyes were wide with delight.

"Good to see you!" The baseball player left his group to join them. "Where've you been?"

Zane had a burning desire to find out who he was. Nothing would change that. But he used to be an alcoholic?

Zane shuddered at the thought. "I have to go—"

"No way!" Tim interrupted. "You need a drink before you go!"

"I'm— I'm a minor! It's illegal for me to even be in here!" Zane protested.

"Really? Never stopped you before." The baseball player said.

"I need to get out of here," he muttered, unsure whether or not they had heard him.

They exchanged a worried glance that didn't go unnoticed. He wasn't feeling overwhelmed because of his unlikely friends. It wasn't because the alcohol and loud music was too much for him. It was because the environment felt so normal.

Tim slung an arm around his shoulder and guided him out of

the bar, the other guy trailing behind. Once they were a ways away from the bar Tim spoke. "Are you alright?"

"I'm not who you think I am," Zane warned, ignoring his question.

"Nonsense! You're Zane, our old pal." Tim lowered his voice, and his headache was grateful.

"Is this about your fight?" the baseball guy asked.

"My what?" Zane narrowed his eyes, trying to mentally command his brain to remember.

"That was a long time ago, Troy." Tim shook his head. "Never mind that. What's wrong with you?" He squinted, one finger pointed at Zane.

"I kind of have amnesia?" They both started howling with laughter. "You don't believe me." Zane muttered.

"Well actually you've never pulled pranks before. Not once. But you seriously don't remember us?" Troy's eyes widened.

"No."

"Hmm." Tim sighed. "Probably for the best."

"Why?" Zane asked.

"We didn't exactly leave off on good terms," Tim admitted, while the baseball guy nodded in agreement.

"What happened?" Zane frowned. Their eyes darkened.

"You said some things. Flipped out on us. You're not really Zane right now. Without his memories, you're more like um." Tim squinted at Zane. "A shell."

Sometimes he really did feel like just a shell. But why did he flip out on them? He wasn't even sure if Tim and Troy knew. "Why did I come here, anyway? Especially if I'm not old enough to drink?"

Tim shrugged. "The bartenders never said anything. And I don't think I've actually seen you drink anything. Scratch that, I saw you drink a mimosa once."

Zane's hands flew to his head, his fingers pressed against his temples. A headache pierced the layers of his mind until it started to become a memory.

His eyelids felt like they were glued together. Maybe he shouldn't have had that drink. He hated the fuzzy feeling it gave him.

Zane's eyes shot open in an instant, landing on the person sitting next to him. "So why are you here? What do you want?"

"Zane, look. You were with the Evermoving for years. I'm sure that you have important information." The person's face was blurry, and he couldn't see what he looked like.

"You already have Max on your side. And besides, if I say anything they'll know." Zane tensed at the thought.

"But we need you. You know something important. And besides, the Evermoving never leaves any loose ends behind. They'll find you again."

Zane took a deep breath in. He couldn't think about it. As soon as he even considered telling someone... They would do something to him. Max might have been able to switch sides after they left, but Zane? He had never really escaped.

The memory was instantly ripped from his mind, and he found himself back on the city sidewalk.

"Zane!" Tim snapped his fingers repeatedly in front of Zane's face. "Can you hear me?" Zane nodded.

"How many fingers am I holding up?" Troy had a lopsided grin on his face.

"Four?" Zane said, confused.

"Troy," Tim warned with a glare. Troy rolled his eyes, clearly frustrated at missing an opportunity to mess with Zane.

"Relax, Timmy. Let's get the party boy home. Zane, where are you staying?" Troy shifted his weight to one foot. The two alcoholics seemed to hold their breath.

"I'm staying at this apartment complex near Lai's Park," Zane told them.

"We'll bring you home!" Tim's demeanor instantly changed, almost as if a heavy weight had been lifted off his shoulders.

He wasn't sure how he felt about putting his life in the hands of a drunk driver. "That's okay I can find my way back–"

Tim clapped Zane on the back, causing him to stumble. "Nonsense! It's the least we can do for an old friend." Zane glared at Tim but he didn't seem to notice.

"We'll drive you! Just let me go grab my keys." Tim walked, or more accurately, stumbled back into the bar, leaving Zane with Troy.

"I would ask how you lost your memory but I can only assume that you don't remember." Troy smirked.

"You're rude, you know that right?" Zane snapped.

"Actually I'm drunk," he corrected, his smirk widening.

"Right." Zane turned towards the bar doors silently willing Tim to return. Not that he was much better.

Troy squinted. "Seriously, how long have you been a mindless zombie?"

Zane decided to ignore the zombie part. "Almost three weeks," he admitted reluctantly.

"So how does this whole amnesia thing work anyway? Do you remember anything?" Troy asked.

He hesitated. Should he really place his trust in a stranger? "Sometimes I remember things. I still remember how to read and write but I don't remember people or places. Sometimes things feel familiar I guess." Zane exhaled sharply. "So yeah. That's about it." He could see the pity in Troy's eyes and he hated it. It was worse than his usual arrogance and rudish mischief. Relief flooded him when Tim pushed open the bar doors, keys in his hand.

"Let's go!" Tim pressed a button on the keys and a loud noise blasted in Zane's left ear causing him to jump. He turned towards the surprisingly nice red convertible.

"I don't think I've ever seen you get scared." Tim walked to the other side of the car before hopping over the door. He landed on the driver's seat, before inserting the key. With one twist the car roared to life.

"I'm not exactly myself anymore."

"True." Troy threw his baseball cap on the dashboard before taking the passenger's seat. Zane sat in the back, being careful not to scratch the expensive looking convertible. Tim didn't bother with a seatbelt, so to protect his pride he didn't either, although he wanted to. Once they got out of the shady neighborhood, Zane relaxed. They were now in a part of the city where the houses were nicer, though the streets were still covered by litter. Troy turned on the radio, blasting loud rock music to Smith's dismay.

"Troy! Turn the music off or I will knock your lights out!" Tim yelled angrily. With more than a little reluctance, Troy turned off the radio. "Thank you," Tim said, more than a little grumpiness in his tone.

"So... When did the three of us meet?" Zane asked, not for an answer but to break the awkward silence.

"One year ago," Tim answered, vaguely and cautiously.

"You were such a mess back then too!" Troy added with a grin. "I found you hiding in the bathroom crying–"

"Okay! Never mind. Forget I asked," Zane interjected.

Tim sighed. "It wasn't that bad. You were barely sniffling."

"No, he was full on sobbing!" Troy corrected.

Tim hesitated. "Yeah," Tim finally agreed. "You were sobbing."

Zane sunk further into the leather seat. So much for protecting his pride. Apparently, it had already been murdered in cold blood a long time ago. But they had known him for two years. They had to know about his past. He started to ask, when Troy interrupted him.

"You know, I think that brunette lady was checking me out."

"Which one?" Tim asked distractedly.

"All of them of course, but there was this one woman..." Troy sighed. "She was as pretty as a rose."

"You say stuff like almost every time I see you," Tim said while pinching the bridge of his nose.

"This one was different," Troy retorted, folding his arms across his chest and rolling his eyes.

"Plenty of fish in the sea," Zane said, repeating the words from a city billboard. It was covered in flowers and cheesy slogans, apparently advertising a dating app.

"Ha!" Troy snorted, twisting around in his seat to look at Zane. Zane raised his eyebrows at the skeptical baseball player.

"You only get so many chances at true love, Zane." Troy made a heart with his hands. Zane suddenly regretted his walk through the city. Besides, what was the possibility of running into old friends by chance? And what if it wasn't a coincidence that Zane had found them. What if it had been planned? What if he was just a puppet, following his master without question?

"I guess," Zane responded distractedly, his eyes focused on the apartment complex in the distance. He silently prayed that Tim and Troy wouldn't ask for a tour. Tim drove into the apartment's parking lot, not bothering with turning off the engine. Zane carefully opened the car door, making sure to not slam it closed.

"Thanks for the ride."

Tim narrowed his eyes. "Zane?"

"Yeah?" He avoided Tim's gaze.

"Try not to wander the streets alone. Especially in your newfound condition, okay?"

Zane glanced back at the apartment. "Fine."

He entered the doors, avoiding eye contact with everyone inside. After taking the elevator, Zane reached the Smith's apartment and knocked on the flimsy door. He wasn't sure anybody heard him because classical music was blasting loudly in the Smith's apartment. He knocked louder and eventually the classical music was shut off. The door opened from the other side and a very worried Trent stood in front of him.

"Hey," Zane greeted.

"Hiya." Trent smiled, but his lips were pressed into a thin line, ruining his normal carefree image. "Who were those people in the car with you?"

Zane cringed, his eyes drifting to the apartment window.

"Zane." Trent's voice was dangerously low. "You can't take car rides with people you don't even know." He grabbed Zane's wrist and dragged him into the apartment. Zane's heart was heavy, his eyes wide with shock.

"I–" He started to say.

Trent planted his hands on Zane's shoulders. "When Dr. Smith gets home, the three of us are going to have a talk, okay? You can't keep sneaking off–"

"But I–"

"BUT NOTHING!" Trent snarled.

Zane wrapped his arms around himself, focusing on the Paris painting hanging on the apartment wall.

"Dr. Smith was called back into work today because of an emergency. But when she gets back, you're in big trouble." Trent's voice was cold and furious. He tore a hand through his hair viciously, stomping into the apartment complex's hallway.

"I'm going to go make sure those guys are gone. You better be here when I'm back," Trent warned with a glance over his shoulder.

Once Trent had disappeared, Zane held out his hands, noticing they were shaking. He had never seen this side of Trent before. Usually he was calm and carefree. Zane didn't want to see Trent angry ever again.

Two hours of dread later, and Dr. Smith was back. "You've been acting very irresponsible," Dr. Smith said, causing him to sink further into the couch. "We thought you'd been making trips to the library but apparently you've been going somewhere else. Somewhere with alcohol perhaps?"

Zane straightened in alarm.

"You reek of beer and cigarettes and I'm scared for you," Dr. Smith admitted.

He looked back and forth between Dr. Smith and Trent. They both had decided to stand, but they seemed to have opposite reactions. Trent looked furious and ready to strangle Zane, whereas Dr. Smith looked mostly concerned and exhausted. They both seemed equally disappointed, however.

"I'm going to take some time off to look after you, okay?" Trent said slowly, eyeing Zane like a delicate China doll. Somehow, he managed to sink even lower into the couch. "Just until we know you're okay," Trent added.

The three of them jumped when Dr. Smith's phone rang. She quickly grabbed it from the side table and answered the call immediately. "Now?" A tinge of annoyance was hidden in her tone. She hung up and turned towards Trent.

"I have to go. Hospital emergency," Dr. Smith explained, suddenly looking as if she hadn't slept in a long time.

She turned towards Trent. "It's the same one," she added.

"Okay." Trent pulled her into a quick hug. She smiled tightly at Zane, wiggled her fingers, and left.

"So, Zane, who were those men anyway?" Trent asked, crushing Zane's hope of getting out of the interrogation. Beads of sweat gathered on his forehead, and he knew he couldn't tell Trent the truth. Nobody could know about his past. *Nobody.* Not Trent, not Dr. Smith, and definitely not Robin.

CHAPTER
SIXTEEN

All of Trent's questions were met with silence. Zane didn't budge once, partly because he didn't want to put Trent in danger. Trent eventually gave up and he thought about escaping the suffocating apartment. Trent, unfortunately, was in the same room and he couldn't afford to be caught. Not again. That and he couldn't help feeling panicked at the idea of seeing Robin or his drunk friends again. And yet there was a dangerous curiosity compelling him to find out more... Begging him to ask questions. Urging him to find more pieces of his past. Demanding for him to complete the puzzle. He needed to know who he was. His fingers twitched as his mind raged a war of indecisiveness.

I can wait, he thought.

"Zane, I know you watched a few movies in the hospital. I was thinking that we could watch something."

Chop.

The sound of a knife cutting into a tomato.

"Fine with me," Zane muttered.

Chop. Chop.

"Probably nothing with the avengers," Trent added, the knife starting to cut faster. "But who knows, maybe your perspective has changed."

Chop. Chop. Chop. Chop.

Zane kept silent, knowing Trent wasn't looking for an answer. He waited for the next chop, but it never came.

Trent plopped down beside him. "What are you in the mood for? Dinner is already cooking." Zane shrugged, eyes focused on the ground.

"You're probably too old for Mary Poppins. Everyone loves Harry Potter though." Trent reached for the remote on the side table before turning on the tv. "What do you say?"

"Sure," Zane responded, his frustration growing. He sat through the movie no matter how much he wanted to scream, cry, or do something to get his frustration out. Trent and Dr. Smith had brought him into their home and he was being such a jerk... He didn't want them to be his parents, or his caretakers. He just wanted his *real* parents. Whoever or wherever they were. Zane tugged on a loose thread from his sweatshirt, wrapping it around his finger over and over again. He slowly unwrapped it, instead bringing his knees to his chest. Trent glanced over at him, and he quickly switched into a different sitting position. One that didn't make him look like an upset little kid. He focused on the movie, watching as Harry spoke to a snake. Trent looked at him again and he realized his leg had been thumping up and down against the floor. He set his hand on it, forcing himself not to fidget. Trent sighed, finally deciding to pause the movie.

"Is there something wrong, Zane?" he asked, his eyebrows raised, and his lips curled into a tight smile.

"No," Zane responded quickly. Maybe too quickly. "You can go ahead and play the movie," he added, while resentment boiled in his mind.

"Okay," Trent said hesitantly.

"Okay," he said in return.

Once Trent was focused on the tv, he snuck away to the kitchen.

"What are you doing?" Trent asked.

"Getting water–" A knife seemed to cut through his brain in the form of a memory.

"WHAT ARE YOU DOING!?" A voice screamed as rain slammed against his face. He barely registered who it belonged to, far too focused on the bodies lying beside the garbage can. A hand placed itself on his shoulder, but he shoved it away. It was too late. He had seen the evidence.

"They haven't forgotten what I know," Zane said, his voice drained of emotion. "And this was a warning. If I say anything they're going to kill me."

"Getting water," Zane finished firmly. His eyes were squeezed shut, trying to block out the images of disfigured bodies.

"Got it," Trent responded with a thumbs up.

He forced his eyes to open and dragged his feet to the kitchen cabinet with glasses. He hesitated, his heart racing from the recent memory. He reached his hand out, his entire arm shaking.

"Keep it together, idiot," Zane muttered fiercely. He paused for a few moments, taking slow, deep breaths.

Trent's hand reached above his head, opening the cabinet and taking a glass. He moved over to the fridge, letting the water fill the cup halfway. Trent opened his mouth, about to say something, but seemed to decide against it. Trent handed the glass to Zane, already heading back to the couch. He took an unsteady sip, before setting it back down. Had Trent heard him? He snuck back to the couch, sitting as far away from Trent as possible. But not far enough away that it would be noticeable. He didn't want to hurt Trent anymore than he already had.

He forced himself to sit through the movie, occasionally

glancing over at Trent. Zane focused on his breathing, refusing to let Trent know how anxious he was. He closed his eyes, once again being afflicted by the recent memory. Zane quickly opened his eyes before shoving his hands in his blue sweatshirt; that way Trent couldn't see them shaking. He was still feeling the fear from the memory, the intense panic eating him from the inside out.

I'm fine, Zane thought. *It's over.* So why was he still terrified?

Zane grabbed plates from a drawer and helped set the table, trying his best not to glare whenever Trent tried making small talk. He had already grasped at several straws, one of them being the weather. Zane had stopped shaking from fear, so all that was left was annoyance.

"Zane, have you remembered anything else recently?" Trent looked over at him while scooping the avocado into a large bowl.

Zane tensed, his fingers strangling the arms of his hoodie. "Not really." *Technically the truth*, he thought.

"Bits and pieces here and there," He admitted, his grip tightening. He released his vise-like grip on his hoodie so he could finish setting the table. Zane grabbed three forks from a drawer, before setting them on the plates.

"Is Dr. Smith going to eat with us tonight?" he asked, internally begging Trent not to continue asking about his memories. Between the dead bodies, Max, his confusing past filled with illegal activities... He couldn't tell anyone about them. He would end up in jail, rotting away for the rest of his life. Or worse, killed.

"I don't know," Trent faltered. "They really need her in the hospital right now. She's had this patient for a while and it's not looking good." He froze. "Not important." Trent smiled. "Let's eat." He held up a wooden spoon while gesturing to the table. Not looking good? Zane cringed, already feeling guilty for making Dr. Smith's day worse. Zane took a seat, though he felt too sick to his stomach to eat anything. Across from Zane, Trent stuffed his face with food.

"Are you going to eat something?" Trent said, though it sounded more like a baby babbling.

"Maybe." He focused his gaze on the table.

"Well, I—" Trent's phone rang. Trent sighed and pinched the bridge of his nose. He took the phone from his pocket and held it up to his ear. "Hey! I thought I told you I'm taking time off." Zane watched the conversation happen, but other than that said nothing. "Oh," he murmured, his eyebrows knitting together. "Are you sure?" Trent paused. "I have to take care of personal issues, I really can't come into work today."

"Personal issues?" Zane muttered under his breath, with more than a little bitterness.

"I can't," Trent said firmly. "Are you sure it's that serious?" He set the phone down reluctantly. "I have to go."

"Okay." He shrugged.

Trent got out of his seat, hesitating on his way to the apartment door. "Don't go anywhere, okay? I wouldn't leave if it wasn't serious."

He couldn't help but scowl. "I won't." The door closed, so Zane made himself useful by putting the food into the fridge. Once everything was put away, he laid down on the couch, the palms of his hands pressed against his temples.

Were these people still after him, waiting for the right moment to end his life?

Was that why he had been covered in blood?

Was it a failed attempt at killing him?

Did they even know he was still alive?

The door creaked open, and he briefly wondered if he was going to die. He let his hands fall away from his face, smiling when he saw Gemma.

"You look rough." She squinted at him and turned her head,

almost as if he would look better from a different angle. "Have you been getting enough sleep?"

"Have you?" he countered, noticing the deep circles underneath her eyes. Today she wore baggy sweatpants and a sweatshirt, her hair free and messy.

"It's kind of hard to live up to the expectations of my foster mom," Gemma admitted. "But you look like you've been dealing with the weight of the world." She took a few steps closer and studied him. "You're holding back from crying aren't you? Did someone break your heart or something?" she said, a half-hearted attempt at a joke.

Zane sat up and folded his arms across his chest. "I think I know why I ended up in the hospital," he whispered.

Gemma sat down beside him. "Is that why you look like death?"

"I saw something I wasn't supposed to, and I know something I'm not supposed to." His breathing grew quicker. "I never– what if they're still after me– I don't want to die." He brought his knees up to his chest, his eyes squeezed shut.

Gemma stiffened. "Yeah, I don't want you to die either. But uh... Don't you think they would have come after you by now?"

"They probably never had a chance. Between the kidnapping and the whole hospital thing I've been pretty busy," Zane said sarcastically.

Or maybe they already got a hold of me. Zane thought darkly.

"I guess." Gemma set her head on his shoulder. "What are we gonna do?" She stuffed her hands inside her sweatshirt's pockets, and he put an arm around her.

"Try to survive?" He paused, his eyes lighting up with an idea. "Actually I met some people who knew me in the past. I'm sort of grounded because of them though."

Gemma's eyes practically fell out of their sockets. "Why

didn't you start with that!?" She punched him in the arm. "I need to go talk to them! Where do they live?"

"I found them inside a bar. It's not far from here." Zane trailed off, a quiet thudding of footsteps replacing the sound of their conversation.

"Zane! I'm back! It was a misunderstanding. Could you open the door? I forgot my key. It's in my coat pocket."

Gemma winced, before bringing her finger up to her mouth in the universal, "Be quiet!" She rolled underneath the couch, moving the flap on it to cover her body. Zane knew he would be in far worse trouble if caught home alone with a girl, so he went with it.

"Yeah, sure!" he called back, rubbing the spot where Gemma had punched him.

"The brown one?" Trent added.

Zane stood, before hesitantly approaching the apartment door. He shot a glance back at the couch before reaching into the coat pocket. Zane inserted the key before swinging the door open.

"That was fast," he said, his voice full of surprise.

"Yeah, well apparently the situation has already been taken care of." He laughed light-heartedly. "I love the staff but sometimes they can be total nitwits." Trent placed a hand on Zane's shoulder, leading him further into the apartment before shutting the door. Trent's eyes widened in surprise. "You put away the food?"

Zane scratched the back of his neck. "Um... Yeah, is that okay?"

"Of course it's okay." Trent ruffled Zane's hair, a grin on his face.

"You ate something before you put everything away, right?" Trent asked.

Zane dug his fingernails into his palm. "No?"

"You need *something*, Zane." Trent hesitated. "How about a granola bar or some pancakes?"

He shrugged. "Either."

"A granola bar it is!" Trent reached into the kitchen cabinet. "Chocolate or peanut butter?"

"Chocolate." Zane looked back at where Gemma hid, praying she would find a way out, and soon. If Trent found her, who knows what would happen.

CHAPTER
SEVENTEEN

Z ane put a smile on his face, almost as if he wasn't trying to hide Gemma from Trent. "What was the emergency?" He munched on the chocolate granola bar, letting the chips melt in his mouth.

Trent hesitated. "There's just a lot going on, but you don't need to worry about it, Zane. I don't want to trouble you with anything." His gaze darkened, his eyes focused on the kitchen floor. "I just wished we lived closer to the hospital." Trent tapped the side of his face with a finger repeatedly, clearly deep in thought.

Based on what he had heard from the Smiths, the hospital was full of horror stories. Although they seemed relaxed about it all, it had to take a toll. Zane could sympathize, already having a first hand experience with dead bodies. He hated that he could.

Trent leaned against the counter, his face scrunched up in regret. "I'm so sorry, Zane. I shouldn't have said anything. You're already going through a lot and I didn't need to put this on you too."

Zane shrugged, before taking another bite out of the granola bar. "It's whatever," he mumbled.

"Zane, I was thinking that we could head to the local nursery. Maybe get flowers as a little pick me up for Dr. Smith?"

"Um..." Zane hesitated.

What if he got kidnapped again?

What if they found him?

He could still smell the sweetness of the chloroform.

What if he saw Mrs. Valentino?

What if *they* made another attempt on his life?

"Sure," he said, knowing this would be the only chance at Gemma escaping without notice. He set down the granola bar, but paused on his way off the bar stool when Trent coughed rather loudly. Zane sighed, but stuffed the granola bar into his pocket anyway.

"I'll eat it on the way," He mumbled.

Trent smiled approvingly.

Zane pushed open the doors of the nursery, a faint aroma of flowers and herbs greeting him.

"Hey, Trent!" A worker in a green apron came over and hugged Trent. "We just got your wife's favorite flowers in stock." It almost sounded like he had been planning to say that. Which was an entirely stupid thought.

Trent patted his friend on the back before letting go. "Awesome!" Trent grinned. "We'll take two, Danny."

"We?" Danny asked in surprise, finally noticing Zane. "What's your name?" he asked, showcasing a smile with a gap in the front.

"Zane." He tried not to narrow his eyes at the stranger, but there was just something strange about Danny. Almost as if he was wrapped in secrets. Behind his coffee-brown eyes seemed to lie something... He actually wasn't sure what it was. Zane was torn between wanting to know Danny and being wary.

"Zane. That's an interesting name." Danny wiped his hands on his dirt-covered trousers. "Did you..." he paused, as if he was trying to find the right words. "Adopt?"

Trent hesitated, his eyes drifting to Zane. "It's complicated."

He laughed, but it was without humor. "Complicated," Zane muttered, his voice full of scorn. He glanced at the bags of soil on a wooden shelf, deciding to change the subject.

"What kind of stuff do you sell?" he asked

Danny's eyes lit up. "I'll show you!" He started to walk so Zane followed him. "Let's start in the greenhouse first! There's the usual stuff obviously, roses, lavender, peonies!" Danny moved his dark hands around in the air animatedly. "That's for the newbies though, for my favorite customers I reserve only the best stuff. I'll make an exception for you though, newbie," Danny teased.

"Actually we just came here for the one thing." Trent interjected, though he seemed amused.

Danny rolled his eyes. "Boring! Zane, what do you think?"

Zane couldn't help but wince at his tone. He was sure Danny meant well, but he sounded like he was talking to a toddler. He laughed anyway. "Definitely boring." The two of them turned towards Trent.

"You're a doctor," Danny pointed out. "You can afford it. And I have to spend some time with my friend's son!" Danny glared at Trent until he relented.

Trent laughed nervously. "I'm still in residency. But fine. Only because I want to support my friend. Just don't go overboard?" he pleaded.

"As I was saying..." Danny grabbed a brochure from his pocket and handed it to Zane. It was covered in flowers and he instantly put it in his pocket.

"We have a few really cool plants! Actually I can teach you some tips and tricks of mine." Danny grinned.

"Sure?" Zane raised an eyebrow at Danny's eagerness. He could see why Trent and Danny were friends. Danny grabbed a few tools from the backroom, gesturing for Zane to follow him outside. Twenty minutes passed before they returned to the cash register.

"Wow!" Trent's eyes widened in shock. Zane and Danny laughed at his reaction, but he couldn't really blame Trent. Twenty plants was a little excessive.

"Danny was really convincing," Zane pointed his finger at him.

"You're the one that kept asking questions." Danny nudged Zane in the side, while shaking his head disapprovingly. The loose curls on his head shifted further onto his forehead.

"So you're okay with spending money on flowers but not clothes?" Tren wrinkled his nose.

Zane shuffled his feet. "Yeah? It's for Dr. Smith though, right? Doesn't she deserve the best?" He didn't actually care about the flowers. Zane found them pointless, but Danny had been really excited to answer any and all of his questions. That and it gave Zane a chance to study his behavior away from Trent. Danny was hiding something. Zane just wasn't sure what it was yet.

Danny smirked. "Doesn't she?"

"She does." Trent glanced at the plants on the cart. "I guess that's fine."

Danny grabbed the cart and maneuvered it closer to the cash register. Zane set the flowers he was carrying on the counter. Dr. Smith was definitely going to be surprised.

"Where am I going to put these?" Trent wondered out loud while holding up his hands and squinting at the various plants.

Danny calculated the price of the flowers on a calculator, whistling at the result. "You might want to buy these with credit."

"I'll be able to afford it." Trent started to pull his wallet out of his pocket.

"If you say so." Danny shrugged. "It's seventy dollars," he whispered dramatically.

Trent snorted. "Oh no. What a tragedy."

"Darn." Danny sighed. "If only you had a friend that worked here and could give you a discount."

"Too bad I don't have one." Trent countered with a grin.

Zane cough-laughed.

"I'll take half of them." Trent offered.

"Three quarters." Danny countered.

Trent slid his wallet to Danny. "Fine."

"He's not usually this grumpy," Danny explained, tapping his fingers on the counter in thought. "Trent is usually a joy to be around. Just don't make him angry, okay kid?" Danny laughed good-heartedly but why had it sounded like a warning? Zane wanted to press for details, but how could he?

Trent opened the apartment door with his elbow, his face obscured by flowers. Zane prayed that Gemma had found her way out. The two of them set the flowers down on the kitchen counter, but he couldn't help but glance over at Trent every now and then. Danny's words echoed in his mind. Trent was a good person. He had taken him in and provided him with a roof above his head. Zane had no reason to question Trent's motives. His constant paranoia wasn't helping his case either. So why did he always have to reassure himself? What was Trent hiding, if anything? And did he want to find out?

"Dang it!" Trent chuckled.

"What?" Zane asked, startled.

Trent rubbed the back of his neck nervously. "I forgot the flower pots. She'll probably want to pick them out herself though."

He relaxed. "Yeah." Zane hesitated as an idea crept up on

him. He knew it was risky, but it could prove whether or not he could trust Trent.

"Trent." He took a deep breath in. "Have you ever heard of the Evermoving?" Zane tore a hand through his hair nervously.

Trent squinted at him. "Is that a TV show?"

"I read the term in a book. Forget I said anything." Zane shrugged, but internally jumped for joy. Surely a member of a strange organization would have been at least a little surprised to hear the name of said organization.

"What book?" Trent asked, while studying him intently.

"Not really important," Zane said.

"What book?" Trent pressed. "I might be able to help you figure out what it is." Why was he so interested? And did he have a reason to question it? Was Trent simply being curious?

"It's a book about some sort of lotus flower? I don't remember what it's called," Zane explained.

"Sounds interesting." Trent's eyes widened for a fraction of a second. "I might have to read it."

"Yeah." Zane leaned against the kitchen counter, his thoughts racing. The apartment door opened, and he turned towards it. Dr. Smith was in the doorway.

"Hey sweetie! We got you some flowers." Trent held up a yellow flower plant. He was pretty sure she noticed considering the entire counter was covered with them.

"Oh!" Dr. Smith set her keys down on the small table text to the door. "Thank you." She chuckled. "You really didn't have to. One would have been fine."

"I don't really think I had a choice. Danny was very insistent," Trent said.

"I have no doubt he was." Dr. Smith fought away a smile. "Did you two go together?" She took off her white coat and set it on the coat rack.

CIELO DEVLIN

"We did," Trent said, tapping his fingers on the counter and looking up at the ceiling distractedly.

"Danny seems to love his job," Zane added, his eyes sweeping the room suspiciously. Everything was perfect. Nothing out of place. But where were the pictures? There were no pictures of the Smith's family or friends, which bothered Zane. Maybe it was just his paranoia again. The pictures were probably all on their cell phones. He could always check. But what was the password to their phones? Gemma would have already figured that out.

"Yeah. What did you two talk about anyway?" Trent grabbed one of the plants and moved it closer to the apartment window.

"Just plants," Zane said vaguely. "Actually he told me you used to be a really mischievous kid." It was one lie, and it could help Gemma and him find answers. So was it really that bad?

Trent paused after setting down the plant. "I wasn't that awful I don't think." He turned around, his face scrunched up in confusion.

"Danny said you would say that," Zane added, frost cutting into his words, his gaze shifting to Dr. Smith who was also giving nothing away.

"Weird that he would say that considering we haven't known him for very long," Trent said cautiously. "Are you feeling alright, Zane?"

What was he even doing? All he had was a hunch to go off of, and an unhealthy dose of paranoia. But the nagging feeling he had wouldn't go away. A slightly stupid part of him told Zane to be more bold with his approach. An even stupider part of him listened to it.

"Did you ever find out who Mrs.Valentino was?" he blurted.

"Maybe you should get some rest, Zane. You seem tired," Dr. Smith suggested, while moving closer to him.

"I don't need rest," he protested. "I'm just curious."

"Zane, tomorrow we were hoping we could take you to visit

someone," Trent said. "Your mental state is a little fragile right now and we're getting worried.

"I'm fine." He blinked and images of pelting rain, the scent of dead bodies, a terrified Max, a blue banner, and the tent of an carnaval hit him all at once.

"We know you've been having a hard time.We just think…" Dr. Smith wrung her hands together. "It wouldn't hurt to visit Dr. Sandra."

"Are you taking me to see some sort of physiologist?" Zane asked, his eyes widening.

"If Dr. Sandra decides you don't need to visit her again then it'll just be a one time thing." Trent sighed. "We're not taking you into a slaughter house. It's just a mental checkup."

Zane shrugged, before leaning against the counter, his arms crossed against his chest. "Fine. I'm fine though."

"When we found you, you were covered in blood—" Trent started to exclaim but was cut off when Dr. Smith glared at him.

"I don't exactly have any memories of my attacker. So…" Zane threw up his hands, his smile tight. "No trauma!"

Dr. Smith looked at the ground intently, seemingly deep in thought. "That's for Dr. Sandra to decide."

Dr. Sandra wasn't going to decide anything. She wasn't going to find out about anything pertaining to his past either. A memory exploded in his brain, not even giving him enough time to prepare for it.

Zane was shoved through a door, falling on his face before he could do anything about it. The door was locked in a matter of seconds. He quickly got to his feet, before addressing the only other person in the room.

"Who are you?" He demanded.

"You can trust us. We want to help you," a curly haired man said, leaning back against his black swivel chair.

"I can't trust anyone," Zane snapped, his eyes scanning the office

before returning to the gaze of the mysterious man. "Especially not you or your organization. I was told my entire life not to trust anyone associated with it." He looked back at the locked door, already planning ways to escape. He should have tried harder to avoid capture.

"The same people that were training you since you were a little boy?" the man countered. "You're not a spy or some secret agent. You're just a teenager." He tapped his fingers on the desk, his eyebrows scrunched together. "I want to set you free from the prison you're in."

"What you want is information." Zane glared at him.

"Everyone wants something," he admitted. "It's an easy exchange. The identities of your accomplices in exchange for something that you want."

"And what if you can't give me what I want?" Zane challenged.

"Then we won't be as nice. There are lots of people who have you on a wanted list. I could easily turn you in." A hidden threat lurked in the man's eyes.

"Why do they want me so bad?" Zane couldn't help but roll his eyes. He knew what he'd done, and exactly what information he had that people would want. He just had to hear it.

"That's the thing... I don't know. I was hoping you could tell me."

Zane let out a bitter laugh. Had they brought him here because of a few rumors and whispers? The man in the bar had been more convincing than the rich, power hungry person in front of him.

"You raised a red flag on our system. You're clearly important, so who do you work for?"

"Who do you think I work for?" Zane asked.

The man looked hesitant.

"Do you even know anything?"

"I know that you left your organization recently. And for what reason, Zane? I'd rather die than let someone like you slip through my fingers. You're quite the mystery."

Zane looked the man in the eyes, a scowl on his face. "A lot of people leave it. And just so you know, nobody... And I mean nobody who has left has ever spilled their secrets." Zane's reasoning did nothing to deter him.

"There was something else I heard. You're special. In what way I'm not sure. Please tell me, Zane."

He took a step back, debating making a run for the window behind the wooden desk. Jumping and maybe surviving seemed like a better option than being interrogated. Maybe even tortured if they couldn't get him to slip up.

"Why are you special, Zane? Did you steal something important, perhaps hear something you weren't supposed to? Or are you a victim of a new piece of technology?"

Zane took another step back, but he bumped into a wall. There was nowhere to run. At least not anymore. And worst of all, he didn't have Max by his side.

"The appointment will be early in the morning. We'll wake you up around 6:00, so you should go to bed early," Trent explained, his words bringing Zane back to reality.

Zane nodded, relief flooding him. He was safe. No interrogations. No torturing. His hand drifted to one of the scars underneath his hoodie. "I'll get a shower tonight then," he said, only half focused on what he was saying.

CHAPTER
EIGHTEEN

T he baby blue Prius shook as they pulled into the parking lot. Zane had picked a gray sweatshirt and jeans, entirely plain and forgettable. He wanted Dr. Sandra to think he was a nobody. Somebody who was in the background. But he wasn't a nobody. At least there were people out there who didn't think so.

"I'll walk you in, and I'll be back in an hour." Trent turned off the car, before sending a text. Zane couldn't see who it was through the headrest. He opened the car door, glaring at the entrance of the building. Motivation posters were on the outside, all of which only fueled his rage. It was in between two taller buildings, a stout mushroom beside trees. Lining the outside of the small building was concrete, and there were a few flower pots beside the doors. Trent opened his own car door, and they headed inside. The doorbell chimed when the door closed. The lobby was painted a bright yellow, and chairs sat next to the entrance. A receptionist's desk was on one side, and an aquarium on the other.

"Hello, do you have an appointment?" The red haired receptionist asked.

"For Zane?" Trent walked closer to the desk, and Zane followed him reluctantly.

"Last name?" The receptionist asked, while tapping the computer keys. Zane glanced at her name tag, which said Lana.

"It should be under Smith," Trent said.

"Okay." She looked up at them, her eyes a startling green. "She's almost done. I'll let you know when to head in."

Zane shoved his hands in his pant's pockets and headed towards the chairs.

Trent put a hand on his shoulder, stopping him. "Be good, and answer her questions."

"I will," Zane lied.

Trent released him before tearing a hand through his blond hair. "I'll see you after the appointment." He smiled reassuringly before leaving. It should have calmed his nerves. But how could it, when Trent could be an enemy.

Lana tapped on the keyboard several times, her eyes drifting lazily to the black modern clock hanging on the wall. Zane followed her gaze, and for several moments he watched the hands move. He tore his eyes away from it and settled for looking out the window. Zane lifted his feet and let them rest on the chair beside him, hands behind his head. She coughed loudly, her eyes narrowed at Zane. He considered ignoring her, but in this scenario she was also a victim. Zane let his feet fall to the ground, tapping them impatiently on the tile floor. He stopped for a moment, before turning towards Lana.

"How are you?" he asked, causing the receptionist to grimace.

"Fine. You?" She made eye contact briefly, before typing what Zane assumed to be random letters on the computer.

"I'm great. How long have you been working here?" Zane asked.

If looks could kill, Lana the receptionist would have been an assassin. "A while," she said vaguely.

"Aren't receptionists supposed to be friendly?" The words slipped out of his mouth, and he didn't mean to make them that sharp.

She rolled her eyes. "I guess." His feet being on top of a chair shouldn't have caused the amount of anger in Lana's eyes. Zane wondered if she had some sort of grudge against him. Or if she was just tired of living the life of a receptionist. Either way it couldn't hurt to ask.

"Have we met before?" Zane studied her reaction intently.

"No," she said, a little too quickly, green eyes immediately looking down.

"We have!" Zane exclaimed, jumping out of his chair. Lana fidgeted with her leather jacket, her movements getting frantic. A voice in his head told him to run. The stupid part of him didn't listen. A door opened down one of the hallways. A salt and pepper head peeked out.

"I'm ready for you, Zane." Dr. Sandra's voice was like sea glass, polished and smooth. Glasses with wide, round, frames sat low on her nose, her eyes slightly squinted. Zane hesitantly walked towards her, wondering in the back of his mind when her previous patient left. Dr. Sandra smiled, her crows feet especially visible. One side of his mouth curved upwards, but she must have felt the dread coming off him in waves. Once he was inside she closed the door, taking a seat and gesturing for him to sit down as well.

"Zane, tell me a little about yourself." Dr. Sandra leaned back into her chair. Zane, who sat across from her, refused to relax, even as the scent of Sandalwood drifted through the air. The room was poorly lit, and almost everything in it seemed to be made from wood.

"I would but..." Zane snapped his fingers, a grimace on his

face. "I don't really know that much." He smiled, and Dr. Sandra unnervingly returned it.

"Is there anything you do remember?" She crossed her legs, spinning the pencil in her hand.

"Just bits and pieces." He wrapped his arms around himself, avoiding eye contact.

"Do you ever see glimpses of any faces? Or are they mostly places?" She scribbled something down in her spiral notebook, but Zane was sure he didn't give anything important away.

"A bit of both." He tapped his fingers on his knee, his eyes drifting towards the small window. It was at the top of the wall, square, and about the size of 3 bricks. Plants prevented any light from coming in. There was no chance of escape through there, however the door was still promising.

"Have you been having any negative thoughts recently?" Dr. Sandra asked, still alarmingly cheerful.

"Not really."

"But you have had negative thoughts?" she pressed.

Zane pressed his lips together into a thin line. "Doesn't everyone?"

"Could you be more specific? What have those thoughts been about?"

"Just about maybe not being accepted by the Smiths and never truly belonging with them." Zane answered vaguely. That was partly true. His thoughts drifted to Gemma. He wondered if she had confronted Tim and Troy.

"Do you think that in the past you didn't always feel accepted?" she asked.

"How would I know?" Zane challenged.

"You said you remembered bits and pieces didn't you? Surely there must be something you can tell me."

His thoughts drifted to the first memory he recovered. Mostly feelings of embarrassment, shame, and the sound of laughter. "I remember visiting a circus." Zane made eye contact with Dr. Sandra, silently challenging her to call him a liar.

"What did you see?" she asked.

"What does this have to do with anything?" Confusion as well as suspiciousness covered his mind like fog.

"Please answer the question, Zane." Instead of doing anything related to her request, he studied the flower prints on her green chair. "What did you see?" Dr. Sandra repeated.

"A clown." His lips curled into a tiny smile, the memory of Max wearing a red, styrofoam nose still fresh in his mind.

Dr. Sandra leaned forward, eyes pinning him in place. "Who were you with?"

"A friend I think."

Her smile faltered. "I'm trying to help you, Zane. Please cooperate."

He resisted the urge to squirm. "That's the thing. I don't really remember that much." That was true. "If I remembered anything important I would have told you by now." That wasn't.

"The only thing you need to know is that I woke up covered in blood," Zane explained.

"No." Dr. Sandra smiled again, and it sort of freaked him out. "I have more questions for you."

Zane held his breath.

"The Smiths said that you made a friend. Is that true, Zane?" She lifted one leg over the other. "How is that going by the way?"

"I did. And it's going fine." That was the last question Zane answered. For the rest of the session, Zane was deliberately uncooperative. He didn't care if it made Trent or Dr. Smith angry at him. If they had a problem with it, they could just stop paying for the sessions. And besides, there was something off about the whole thing.

Dr. Sandra began to ask him another question, but he interrupted her. "Nope! This session is over." He pointed at the clock on her wall, before moving toward the door. "It was fun. It really was."

Her facial features turned sour. "Okay. I'll see you tomorrow, Zane." Before he left she added something else. "And next time, don't lie to me."

Zane rushed outside, opening the back door to Trent's vehicle. Zane slammed the door to the prius shut. He smiled at Trent, but it was completely fake.

"So? How did it go?" He started the car while waiting for Zane's response. Zane couldn't prove it, but he could almost feel Trent watching him in the rearview mirror.

"Great." Zane was tired of second doubting the Smiths. He was going to find Gemma, and they were going to investigate. Everything. The Smiths, Dr. Sandra, everyone Zane suspected.

CHAPTER

NINETEEN

Gemma said she was going to go investigate Tim and Troy. So she had to be at the bar. Unfortunately he was still being baby-sat by Trent. Zane's leg thudded against the floor continuously, and he silently prayed for a chance to sneak away. Trent was on the other end of the couch, staring off into space. Dr. Smith was still at work, and even Trent was starting to get restless from doing nothing. Zane considered running out of the apartment. With the right timing, he would be able to outrun Trent easily. But then the police would get involved. And if Trent was one of the bad guys, he would inform Dr. Sandra, and whoever else was stalking him. So all in all, there weren't a lot of good options. But... If Trent WAS one of the bad guys... Wouldn't it be better to escape?

"So how long is this babysitting thing going to last? It's not like I got hurt or anything–"

Trent glared at Zane, nostrils flaring. "When you prove that I can trust you. I have no idea whether or not you'll sneak out again."

Zane threw his hands up, slumping against the back of the

couch. "Seriously?! I get one ride home and suddenly you think I'm some sort of rebel."

Trent shook his head. "I'm just worried, Zane." Trent's eyes darkened.

"Okay." Zane stood, holding out his hands where Trent could see them. "That's reasonable." He held up a finger. "But! Can I at least go to the library and get some books?"

Trent stood up as well, heading toward the front door. "I'll go with you." Zane's face crumpled as soon as Trent's back was turned.

Trent put on his brown coat, taking out the key from the coat pocket. "How far away is it?"

Zane fixed his dismayed expression once Trent turned around. "We can walk. It's only a few minutes away. Trust me, we don't need a car."

Trent nodded. "Okay."

The two of them headed toward the elevator, and Zane pressed the lobby button. His eyes flickered toward Trent as he weighed the consequences of ditching him as soon as they got to the library. Once the elevator door opened, they maneuvered around the people in the lobby, reaching the exit. The cool air from outside blew into their faces as soon as they stepped outside.

Trent shivered, setting his hands inside his pockets. "Are you going to be okay in that?"

Zane glanced down at his plain gray shirt and sweatpants. "Yeah. I'll be fine." He wasn't even cold.

"Alright. Show the way, Zane."

After an agonizing six minutes of silence, they reached the library. Zane realized too late he would run into Robin inside. His hand hovered over the doors.

"What are you waiting for?" Trent pushed open the door to the left of Zane. He followed Trent inside, despite his growing dread. Somehow he was going to have to figure out how to escape without Trent's notice AND avoid Robin at the same time.

"So what are you here for?" Trent asked.

"I'm just gonna hang around and read." Zane shrugged, silently hoping Trent would trust him to stay in the library.

Trent checked his phone. "I don't know if I can wait around with you for that long." Zane's hopes rose. "You might just have to grab a book to go." His hopes instantly deflated.

"Alright. Just let me look around." He started scouring the bookshelves, his fingers trailing the spines. Trent stayed by the entrance, and he slowly made his way farther and farther away from Trent. There weren't any other exits he knew of. Except maybe... His eyes caught the bathroom door. Maybe there was a window he could sneak out of. There were no bookshelves to hide behind. It was a straight line to the bathroom. Zane's heart picked up the pace, and he could hear it beating. He barely made it halfway before someone intercepted him.

"Zane?" He silently cursed. It was Robin. Her hair was in a bun, and there were barely visible circles under her eyes.

Zane laughed nervously. "Hey, Robin." He tried to step around her but she wouldn't let him.

"You never gave me an explanation." Anger flashed behind her eyes. "I deserve one."

He shifted his feet, shooting glances at the bathroom door. "I know! You do! But I..." Zane hesitated, when he saw her determined expression. She wasn't going to move until she heard the truth. "Look. I lied about being in summer school. And skipping. I woke up in the hospital with amnesia a while ago and I think my amnesia wasn't an accident." He kept his voice as quiet as possible. "I'm being stalked and I know it's not believable but... I didn't want to tell you because I thought it might endanger you. I sound insane but–"

Robin cut him off. "Is it the guy at the door you're trying to get away from? That's still not an explanation by the way." She glared at him. "But as soon as you get away from these stalkers you're coming back here and telling me everything. I'll help you, and you better not be lying. OR a complete psycho."

"Thank you," Zane whispered, brushing past her. They exchanged a brief smile, before he yanked open the bathroom door, locking it behind him. It was a relief to know Robin had his back. He just hoped he wouldn't regret telling her. What if she got hurt because of him? Zane shook off the thought and focused on escaping the cramped bathroom. He switched on the light, illuminating a singular toilet by the wall, a sink, mirror, and... A window. Zane fiddled with the latch until it opened with a click. He lifted the window, before climbing outside. Zane closed it and began to sprint. He could faintly hear someone banging against the bathroom door. The panic gave him more adrenaline, and his legs began to pump faster. He didn't stop until the library was far behind him, the entrance barely visible. The panic that had his heart in a noose began to loosen. Zane's sprint slowed down to a walk. That had been easy enough. Now all he had to do was find Gemma.

CHAPTER
TWENTY

Zane felt sick to his stomach. The smell of the bar wasn't any better the second time. Besides the occasional whiff of perfume, everything reeked of cigarettes and alcohol. He held his breath and went further inside. What if she had been stopped from going inside? Zane's stupidity continued to impress him. Clearly, in the past, he had been a regular. That was probably why he hadn't been stopped the first time, despite definitely being younger than the legal age. But what about Gemma? Although... She probably had found a way inside anyway.

He pushed past crowds of people, every one of them acting like overgrown toddlers. Zane wasn't going to come back here again. He looked over his shoulder, spotting Trent by the entrance. His heart plummeted. He shoved past more people, frantically searching for a familiar face. Zane froze when he saw a door off to the side. Seeing as it was his only option, he opened it. Zane closed it, surprised when he saw the alleyway leading out to the street. It was his lucky day. He rushed out of the alleyway, skidding to the right.

"Zane?"

He turned around, preparing to run if it was Trent. It was Troy.

"I thought it was you. What are you doing here?" Troy adjusted the sleeves of his leather jacket.

"I'm looking for this blonde girl. Her name's Gemma and it's really important that I find her." Zane sighed. "Have you seen her?"

Troy smirked at something behind him. "You could say that."

Something poked him on the elbow and he whipped around.

"What are you doing here, Scaredy-cat? Miss me or something?" She grinned, the corners of her eyes crinkling.

Zane didn't return the smile. "Gemma, I think the Smiths are a part of the Evermoving. They sent me to this psychologist's office and the receptionist there knew me. Her name was Lana, and Dr. Sandra was asking really weird questions. Gemma, we have to investigate while we still have a chance," he said in a hushed whisper, so that Troy couldn't hear.

Gemma's face fell. "Oh boy." Her eyes shifted to Troy. "Hey, do you think Tim would be willing to drop us off somewhere?" Troy gave a thumbs up, heading back inside the bar.

"Are you sure we can trust them?" Zane asked.

Gemma rolled her eyes. "Please. Those two are harmless. Where was this place anyway?"

"You don't have to come, you know. I could investigate the place by myself. I don't want them to think we're working together."

"Don't be an idiot." Gemma scowled at him. "We're going there together."

Tim and Troy appeared moments later. They were given a ride with no questions asked. Zane opened the passenger door to the red convertible, stepping onto the concrete outside the building. One of the motivational posters seemed to be mocking him, the bright yellow letters spelling out 'You can do it!'. Gemma stepped out beside him.

"Alright, good luck you two." Tim and Troy, confused as they were, didn't press for answers.

Zane waved at Tim, waiting until he began driving away before approaching the building's glass door.

"I don't suppose you brought something we can use to break into this place?" Zane grabbed the metal lock on the outside. The place had closed hours ago, although he wouldn't be surprised if it closed as soon as he left. He was pretty sure Dr. Sandra had no other patients.

Gemma nodded. "Step aside, Scaredy cat."

Zane watched as she fiddled with the lock using a bobby pin and a quarter. Considering she had those items with her, he wondered how many other places she had broken into. Zane also wondered what happened to the other tool she had. The lock clicked open.

His eyebrows raised in surprise. "Impressive."

Gemma grinned. "I know right?" Her delight instantly disappeared. "Come on. Let's find some dirt on this Dr. Sandra."

"Wait!" Zane grabbed her arm before she went inside. "Do you think there are any cameras?"

Gemma shrugged. "Only one way to find out." They stepped inside, and the bright yellow assaulted his eyes once again. The familiar doorbell chimed behind them.

Gemma instantly moved toward the computer, pressing the spacebar to turn it on. "Dang. Password protected."

"And you don't have a calendar to help you out this time," Zane teased.

She smirked. "True." Gemma maneuvered around the desk, eyes flickering to Dr. Sandra's office door. "Do you want to do the honors?" As soon as Zane opened the door to the office, the two of them were suffocated in a cloud of sandalwood. They began to root through the books on her shelf, and even flipped through several documents. But all of the books were blank, and the documents in the file cabinet had nothing to do with the Ever-moving or amnesia.

"Weird. At least we know that Dr. Sandra isn't who she says she is. Who buys blank books?" Gemma tossed one behind her, and it landed with a thump on the floor.

"Gemma!" Zane scolded. "We can't let her know we were here."

She scoffed, but picked it up anyway. "Why did we think that we could outsmart these people again?"

"Oh wait!" Zane tapped her repeatedly on her shoulder, and she turned toward him. "She wrote some things down in a spiral notebook when she was asking me questions."

"Got it!" Gemma started to rummage through more of Dr. Sandra's things, and Zane began to open more of her desk drawers. Just as his fingers grazed the top of the notebook, a faint chiming could be heard through the office door. They both froze, quickly shoving everything back into place.

"What do we do?!" Gemma hissed out.

Zane took a deep breath in. Him being here was expected more than Gemma's presence. He had a feeling that whoever opened the door already knew someone was inside. "Get under the desk."

Gemma's face crumpled, and his heart swelled. "What?"

"Only one of us has to get caught. It makes more sense for it to be me. Get. Under. The. Desk." Zane whisper-yelled. The door to the office began to open, and Gemma carefully crawled underneath the desk. Once Zane was sure that Gemma was completely concealed, he turned toward the now open doorway. It was Dr. Sandra.

"How long have you known about Max?" She studied him intently.

The color drained from his face. "What are you talking about?"

"You heard me." She tilted her head, and he couldn't help but compare the movement to a cobra. So innocent looking, but dangerous.

He began to head toward the door, hands held in the air. "I didn't mean to cause any trouble. I'll just be on my way."

Dr. Sandra instantly brought out a gun from underneath her long coat, pointing it at him. "Don't even think about it. Zane immediately froze.

Dr. Sandra tucked a strand of her hair back. Her eyes were still narrowed, but the unnerving smile was still present. "Answer the question, please."

He should have ran when he had the chance. Or at least kept his mouth shut. Was she one of the people that had been hunting him down? Was he going to die?

CHAPTER
TWENTY-ONE

This time there was no way out.

"Go on, dear." Dr. Sandra's face was no longer that of a friendly therapist facade. Every line on her face screamed evil and threatening. She pointed at a chair with her gun. "Sit."

He listened, the threat of death keeping him compliant. "What do you want?" Zane snapped, his heart beating faster every second.

"How long have you known about Max?" Dr. Sandra held the gun with confidence, her smile the opposite of her threatening tone.

Zane stared down the barrel of the gun, as she sat across from him. "I don't know who that is," he said, his voice even and steady.

"I didn't believe you were Zane at first." She drawled. "Honestly I thought you died. But as soon as you mentioned the circus..." Dr. Sandra trailed off, repositioning the gun to be aimed towards his head. "I knew it was you."

"That's a totally random coincidence. A lot of people go there in their lives." Zane narrowed his eyes.

BANG! The gun shot and he tensed, waiting for the bullet to pierce his flesh. His back was against the chair and his eyes were squeezed shut. No pain. He let his eyes open, and they drifted to the hole in his chair. The bullet was wedged in between the fabric.

"I recovered my first memory with Max a little while ago," Zane muttered.

"Describe it to me."

"We were in a classroom. Someone found us. We ran." Zane hesitated. "Are the Smiths on your side?" He blurted.

Dr. Sandra widened her eyes in surprise. "No."

Relief flooded him, at the same time dread did. Now he felt bad for running away from Trent. But both of the Smiths had been acting suspicious. Maybe Dr. Sandra was lying.

"What other memories have you recovered?" Surprise still lingered in Dr. Sandra's eyes.

"Max and I were inside of a crate boarding a ship called... The Annabeth?"

"That's how you escaped." Realization lit up her eyes.

"Any other memories?" she asked, drawing the gun closer to him.

Zane shrunk in on himself. "I remember eavesdropping on a conversation. Something about what the Evermoving was really trying to accomplish? Someone talked to me at a bar once, and confronted me about Evermoving stuff." He avoided mentioning the two drunk men, Tim and Troy. "There was another time that I found bodies near a dumpster and I remember thinking that somebody was going to kill me. I also remember being trapped inside of an office and somebody asking me questions." He took a deep breath in. "That's all."

"Are you sure?" Dr. Sandra looked like she enjoyed watching him squirm when her finger came to rest on the trigger.

"I'm sure." Zane's feet twitched, his will the only thing keeping him in the chair.

"I guess we'll have to wait until the rest of your memories come back..."

"Are you letting me go?" He blurted.

"No." Her smile resembled the devil's. His heart came to rest in his stomach. "I can't have you telling anybody else about your memories," she admitted.

"I won't!" He shrieked. "I swear! Don't—"

The door opened and Lana, the supposed receptionist, blew on something. A blowdart, he realized too late. The dart hit his neck and he quickly stood up. Zane's footsteps were uneven, pain making it hard to stand. A hidden door on the wall opened, and two heavily armed guards stepped out. Behind them were stairs leading downwards to a tunnel. They grabbed his arms and dragged him through the entrance. He couldn't see their faces through the masks. Zane struggled for a few more minutes, but eventually he lost consciousness. The last thing he remembered was being put inside of a white van.

Zane jolted awake, blinking rapidly and trying to see through the darkness. He was inside of a vehicle; that he knew. A white van, he remembered. He crawled across the floor, his hand connecting with a wall. He used it to stand up, trying not to fall over when the van hit a bump. He touched his neck where the dart had been, an ache being the only evidence. Using the wall as a guide he walked towards the wall separating him and the driver. Zane pressed his ear against it, listening for voices. All he heard was faint mumbling. Zane, using the wall again, headed towards the side opposite of where he was now. He felt for the handle, and tried opening the doors. It was locked from the outside. Zane took a step back and slammed his shoulder into it. The van hit another bump and he fell backwards. Zane quickly got up again, before slamming into the doors again. After that failed, he felt around the door for anything he could use to open it. His hand came to rest on the heavily tinted windows. Zane punched the window as hard as he could, biting back a scream. He withdrew his hand and shook it back and forth. The van came to a stop and he panicked, attempting to slam into the doors once again. They suddenly swung open, and he hit the air.

"GAH!" Zane fell forwards, his face connecting with concrete.

"Get up," a gruff voice demanded. He sounded male. The guard's arm latched onto his and lifted him up. There was still a mask concealing his features, so he wouldn't be able to identify him. The other guard stepped out of the vehicle.

"I thought we weren't supposed to harm him?" the other guard asked, amusement in his tone. His voice was like sand, rough and coarse.

"He did it to himself," the guard holding him explained, followed by cruel laughter.

Zane used his free hand to feel his face, his fingers touching something sticky and warm. Blood. He was inside of an underground parking garage, most of it empty. The ceiling was tall, and every once in a while the lights flickered. Zane was pushed forward and he stumbled into an odd speed walk. The guard kept one hand on his arm to keep him from running. Zane debated trying to take the gun from his holster, but he didn't have the guts to take a life. Or the strength to wrestle it from the guard's hands.

"Where's the bag?" the guard behind him asked.

"In the van."

Zane blew his hair out of his face, his face scrunching up in annoyance. He didn't hear the guard come back from the van and jumped when the fabric was shoved over his head.

"What floor were we supposed to bring him to?" the gruff-sounding man asked, his grip on Zane's arm tightening when he twitched.

"Level 1."

He was dragged forward by the guard, almost tripping over the entrance to what he assumed was an elevator. The guard adjusted his grip on Zane's arm when he leaned forward to press the elevator button.

Click. Click. Click.

"Pressing the button over and over again isn't going to make it go faster," the other man said, annoyed.

"Whatever."

Click. Click.

The elevator finally started to move, causing his stomach to jump.

"Where are you taking me?" Zane asked, attempting to lift the bag up slightly.

The guard holding onto him swatted his hand away before smacking him lightly on the head. "Shut it. Our job isn't answering questions," he muttered.

"Why didn't you put the bag over my head before you put me in the van?" Zane tensed when the elevator came to a sudden stop.

"Do I have to repeat myself? Our job isn't answering questions," the guard said exasperatedly.

"Our job isn't answering questions," Zane mocked under his breath.

The elevator made a sound like doors opening and they started walking again.

"Don't move." The hand holding him disappeared. A series of clicks and locks was all he heard. The bag was removed from his head. What he saw made him feel like a firework had exploded in his chest, sending burning embers all over his lungs and stomach. He was pushed into a small holding cell that smelled vaguely of vinegar. Zane quickly turned around in time to see them close the glass door. The masked guard with the gruff voice waved and they disappeared. Zane realized it was a type of one-way glass, something that was sure to drive him insane. He glanced around the cell which had a small, white bucket in the corner, no windows, and no bed. The walls and floor were smooth white stone but alarmingly bare. Except for the lotus flower engraved on the floor...

Tears pricked the corners of his eyes and he collapsed on the floor, back against the wall. Zane brought his knees to his chest, his palms pressed against his eyes. He wasn't getting out of this one. The people holding him here weren't teenagers with some lack of morals. They weren't going to let him go, either. He just wished he knew what memory could be so important as to kidnap him. And why had he accused the Smiths? He should have trusted them.

"I'm sorry," he whispered, his voice cracking. "If I ever get out of here, I'm never doubting you again," Zane promised.

Eventually, he fell asleep, but he wasn't sure if it was night or not. There was a small circle on the ceiling that produced weak light, but there weren't any windows or clocks. Zane lifted himself to his feet, his body aching from the uncomfortable floor. He made his way over to the glass door, his eyebrows scrunched together.

Zane's fingers curled into fists and he hit the door. Over. And over. And over again. Quiet thudding was the only thing that happened. So he hit the door harder and harder until his fists started to bleed. The blood made him even more angry so he hit the door again. Something in his hand popped, a jolt of fear keeping him from continuing his assault on the impenetrable glass. Once his fury started to fade, he felt around the glass door for some sort of latch or mechanism. There was a space between the wall and the door on the right so he tried to pull the glass towards him. When that didn't work he leaned forward to get a better look in the place the glass slid into. It was narrow and dark. Surely the door would be able to crush his arm. Just as he was about to reach into the small crevice, the glass, for a lack of a better word, opened. It was the guards who brought him here. Their heights were the same. Zane took a few steps back, his heart sinking.

"Since you apparently can't get enough of me, can you at least tell me your names?" Zane asked, studying them more closely. Their masks were made from a black fabric, part of which was covered by their hoods. Other than that they were dressed normally with average jeans and work boots. The only difference between the two was that the gruff sounding guard happened to be shorter. Still taller than him though.

"You can refer to me as Bluejay," The man with the gruff voice offered.

Zane tried to hold back a bitter laugh. "What kind of name is that?"

"Glad you still have your sense of humor," Bluejay said, clearly annoyed. "And it's a code name."

"What about you?" Zane turned towards the other guy.

"Don't call me anything. And you have to come with us," he explained, pulling his hood further over his face.

"Got it, Anything," Zane muttered.

"I heard that." Anything stormed into the cell and grabbed his arm. He was yanked into the hallway and he had to jog to avoid being dragged. He was definitely going to get bruises on his arms.

"Where are we going?" Zane asked, gaze focused on the ground.

Bluejay sidestepped to the right of Zane and Anything, hands behind his back. "You're going to visit Dr. Sandra and tell her everything you know," he said, extra emphasis on the word you're. "She thinks you might have left a few things out."

Anything tightened his grip on Zane's arm. "And if you refuse to have a nice chat..."

His imagination ran wild with images of torture. "I get it," Zane interjected, his face pale. While he had the chance, he glanced down both of the hallways. There were more holding cells to the left of his, and two hallways branching off of the end of the hallway. To the right was the elevator. It was a solid gray and required key card access.

"Ay!" Bluejay smacked him lightly over the head. Again. Zane was surprised that he hadn't hit him harder. It felt more like he was a misbehaving child than anything else. If it had been the other guard he would have ended up sprawled on the floor.

"Don't get any ideas. Let's go," Bluejay added.

"Aren't you forgetting something?" Anything asked. Even though Zane couldn't see his eyes, he was sure they were rolling. Bluejay reached into a seemingly invisible pocket on his sweatshirt and brought out the black bag.

Zane narrowed his eyes. "It's not like I'll be able to tell people about this place—"

"Shush." He shoved the bag over Zane's head. His vision turned pitch black.

"He got blood all over my gloves," Anything complained, before starting to walk.

Bluejay sighed. "Don't be a baby. We should probably get him bandages."

Click.

The sound of the elevator button being pressed. This time he felt for the elevator edge with his foot and managed to step over it. Anything let go of his arm, and he rubbed the spot that had been held in a vice-like grip.

Click.

The elevator started to go up, and his dread increased with every moment. Then it stopped. His breathing grew ragged. He started to shake. What if Dr. Sandra found Gemma and she ended up here too?

"Whoa! He's shaking like crazy." Anything held up his arm, presumably to Bluejay.

"What do you want me to do?!" Bluejay exclaimed, before taking a deep breath in. "It'll be fine. Dr. Sandra will deal with it."

"If he dies, she'll kill us," Anything said, his voice low.

"I think he's just scared," Bluejay's voice held shock in it. "The legendary Zane... So many stories about his bravery but he's just a Scaredy-cat."

The word turned his nervousness into boiling lava. Zane ripped the bag off his head, desperation driving him. He yanked the gun from Anything's belt, finger on the trigger. Anything managed to grab Zane, so he quickly pointed it at Bluejay while he still could.

"I'll shoot him!" he warned. Anything hesitated halfway through reaching for the gun.

"Do it." Bluejay took a step towards him, leaning forward so that the barrel was pointed at his head. Barely visible blue eyes were narrowed at him. He couldn't take another life. It felt so wrong. But in sparing Bluejay he was letting his own life be taken from him.

"Let me go and I won't," Zane promised.

"He's not gonna do it," Anything scoffed. "He's too weak."

Zane pointed the gun downwards and shot Bluejay's foot. His suppressed scream sounded like a teapot. The guard holding him momentarily released Zane, and when the elevator door opened he bolted. He didn't have time to look where he was going and ran down whatever hallway he saw first. He heard footsteps stomping behind him, so he risked a glance behind his shoulder. Bluejay was leaning against the elevator and Anything was seconds away from tackling him.

CHAPTER

TWENTY-TWO

I f he could see through the mask, surely he would see rage and murderous intent. Anything lunged forward and snatched his wrist so he couldn't move the gun. Before he could do anything else Zane drew his arm back and punched him in his stupid throat. He ignored the blazing fire that shot up his arms. Anything kept one hand on Zane's wrist, his other hand flying up to his injured throat. He started coughing, and he used the distraction to yank his hand away from Anything. Zane began to run down the plain hallways and tried his luck with one of the rooms.

His hand shot out toward the closest door in his reach. He quickly opened it and sprinted in before quietly closing the thick, wood door. It was a storage room, he realized. Zane didn't have much time. There would be members of the Evermoving searching everywhere soon. Zane flicked on the light switch, illuminating the messy space. Boxes took up most of the room, and the rest was covered by cobwebs. He tightened his grip on the gun, which felt warm in his hand. Zane couldn't stay here, but he had no idea where he could go. He knelt down beside the closest box and ripped it open. It was filled with blueprints. Finally, he had a bit of luck on his side.

Zane rummaged through it, and laid the blueprints beside him. There were seven stories, most of which were underground. There were two exits, one in the parking garage, and the second on the third floor. Apparently, there was also an interrogation room, which was on the floor he was on now. There were also stairs, but it was hard to tell where it was on the blueprints. He pressed his ear to the door, and when he heard no footsteps, slowly opened it. It didn't matter which way he decided to go, because he needed a key card for both exits. Bluejay was still at the elevator, and soon the word of his attempted escape would spread. He still had to try to escape. Both for himself as well as Gemma. Zane headed to the right, silently praying that he would get out of this place. He found a few more doors, and eventually he found the stairway. He walked through the doorframe and debated going down or up the stairs. Foot steps from the floor above him were the deciding factor. Zane jogged down the stairs, almost dropping his gun several times because of his sweaty hands. He wiped his left hand on his jeans before switching the gun to the other hand. He wiped his right hand on his jeans before switching the gun to the other hand again. Then he kept going. He rested his arm on the stair's metal railway as he descended, his finger never leaving the trigger of the gun. Until there were no more stairs.

Momentarily, panic consumed him as he stepped towards the double doors at the bottom. Zane pushed them open, looking behind him to make sure he hadn't been followed. That's where things got confusing. Every single hallway was the same white color, and the cells were evenly spaced. There were no land-marks, except the elevator he knew so well. Unfortunately it was nowhere in sight. Zane heard a cell door click into place, and he quietly headed towards the noise. Heavy work boot stomping led him to believe it was one of the guards. Who hopefully had a keycard. After a couple of turns, he turned to the right and saw part of the hooded figure. Luckily for Zane, his back was turned. After a few moments of stalling, he crept forward, preparing to fight him.

Zane rushed forward, pointed the gun at the guard and shouted. "Hands up!" The guard jumped, his hand instantly hovering over his gun holster. "Don't even think about it!" The guard grumbled, hand reluctantly moving away from the weapon. "Turn around!" Zane demanded.

The guard did as he was told, hatred brewing in his barely visible brown eyes. "What do you want?" His voice sounded like a knife being sharpened.

"Toss your gun to me." He did, and Zane quickly kicked it behind him. "Open one of the empty cells."

Once the cell door opened, Zane gestured for the guard to go inside.

When he was inside the tiny prison, Zane walked a little closer to the open cell. "Kick the keycard to me." Once it was kicked toward him, Zane scooped it up, tapping it against the side panel as fast as humanly possible. The glass doors shut before the guard could escape. Relief flooded him. He grabbed the other gun from the floor and headed down the different hallways until he found the elevator. There was one place he knew he could go. The underground parking garage had taken him here, and it would also get him out. It had to. He pressed the button and waited for the doors to open.

His foot tapped nervously on the metal floor of the elevator. It was taking forever to get to the parking garage, and he kept picturing the ways he would get captured again. Maybe he would get a good dose of karma and be shot in the foot. Or he could get run over by accident, and Anything would find him sprawled out on the pavement. Finally they opened, and he peeked out of the elevator. Zane dove behind the nearest crate, avoiding the gaze of unmasked people unloading a white van. He tried to figure out where they were going by their footsteps, panicking when he realized they were headed towards the elevator doors.

He scooted around the crate when they got closer, hiding from view. He didn't dare look behind him until the elevator doors closed. The parking garage, now that he had an actual chance to look around, had very few cars inside. A fancy red convertible was one of them. But what really drew his eye was the barn-shaped gray door. That was his way out. There was a console on the side where he could insert the keycard, and he would figure it out from there. He sprinted towards the white van, peering over the driver's window to check if it was still running. It wasn't. He would have to go on foot.

"Hey! Who are you?!"

The color drained from his face. He turned around. It was the group of people unloading the van. He quickly inserted the key card and the doors slowly opened. He sprinted down the dark tunnel like his life depended on it, because it probably did. His footsteps caused dust to rise from the ground, and it got caught in his throat. Tears spring to his eyes and he coughed.

"There's some guy in the parking garage!" a female voice said, her voice distant. "I think he had a gun!"

Every step he took echoed in the tunnel. It was far too late to turn back. After what felt like thirty minutes he found the end of the tunnel. Sweat dripped off of him, the gun almost slipping out of his hands several times. He reached blindly for the key card insert, and eventually he found it. It made a beeping noise before opening, the sunlight hitting his face. His heart sank when he saw them. Guards had been lying in wait for him. They tackled him to the floor, using his surprise to their advantage. Hands took his guns away. Zane struggled at first, until he saw the gun pointed at him.

"Did you really think that you were going to escape?" Anything asked, almost sounding disappointed.

"Yes," Zane lied, his breathing labored. He let his head rest against the concrete beneath him but before he got his breath back he was hauled to his feet. A black bag was shoved over his head once again and he was dragged back into the tunnel. Eventually he went up a familiar elevator and they took him down various hallways.

The bag was taken off of his head, and he was shoved into a dark room. Somebody forced him into a small metal chair and handcuffed him to the table. His heart rate skyrocketed. Dr. Sandra stood in the corner of the room, her messy bun gone and her hair framing her evil face. The door was shut and locked into place.

She smiled at his no doubt bloody and covered in bruises face. "Let's try this again. Tell me everything." Dr. Sandra took a step forward. "In detail."

"And if I don't?" he asked.

"I've been reasonable so far, Zane. If you don't I'll have to break you." She adjusted her collared dress. Zane didn't want to know what she meant by that.

"What exactly do you want to know?"

"Everytime you recover a memory I want to be the first person you tell," Dr. Sandra explained. "I also want to know everything that you do regarding Gemma and Max."

"Remind me again who Gemma is?" Zane shifted awkwardly in the uncomfortable metal chair.

"I know you've been talking to her. Don't play the idiot,

dear." Except she didn't know Gemma had been inside of her fake office.

"Did you find that out by watching the video footage you stole?"

Dr. Sandra blinked slowly. "What have you two been discussing?" She sat down in the chair across from Zane, the scent of sandalwood drifting towards him. Zane hesitated.

Dr. Sandra clasped her hands together. "One day I hope that you will be able to trust me enough to not think about lying to me."

"Kind of ruined any sense of trust when you kidnapped me and held me hostage," he muttered under his breath.

"A necessary precaution. You're far more dangerous than you realize, Zane. You almost broke out of a secure facility just five minutes ago! And you don't even have all of your memories back yet!" Dr. Sandra pursed her lips. "What have you two been discussing?" she repeated.

Zane tugged on the handcuffs, glaring when they didn't budge. The metal scraped against his swelled-up hands, causing pain to flare up in his fingertips. "Really nothing. It's not like we remember enough to have a full blown discussion," he said bitterly.

"Tell me again but with detail, dear." Dr. Sandra smiled at him.

"The first time we met, we talked about Mrs. Valentino." Zane gritted his teeth together, angry at himself for giving so much away. "Who is she anyway?"

"What *about* Mrs. Valentino?" Dr. Sandra questioned, ignoring his question.

Zane resisted rolling his eyes. "She visited us both in the hospital. We were talking about who she could be, because nobody else knew who she was."

"Where is Gemma now?"

"No," he whispered.

"Excuse me?" Dr. Sandra's eyes narrowed.

"No," Zane said, a little bit louder. "I can't tell you that."

"Why not?" Dr. Sandra asked.

"Because I don't even know where she is," he admitted.

She leaned forward. "Would you have told me if you did?" Zane stayed silent. "What has Gemma told you?"

"Be more specific." Zane fidgeted with the cuff around his wrist.

"What has Gemma told you about Mrs. Valentino?" Dr. Sandra said.

He glanced at the one way glass to his left. "Is Bluejay okay? I shot him in the foot earlier."

Dr. Sandra tapped her fingers on the interrogation table. "We're getting off topic. What has Gemma told you about Mrs. Valentino?"

Zane smirked. "I'm not a tattletail."

"Do you value your life? Because I'm starting to think that you don't." Dr. Sandra adjusted her spectacles with a calm demeanor.

"I do value my life. Gemma would kill me if she found out I threw her under the bus." Zane leaned back against the uncomfortable chair.

"Maybe you'll be more cooperative tomorrow. Hunger does take a toll on the mind." Dr. Sandra stood up and started to head towards the one way glass. She knocked on it twice. "I'll see you in the morning, Zane." The door was unlocked and she left.

Anything stormed into the room, handcuff key in hand. "You should have told her what she wanted to know."

"Why's that?" Zane glanced at the gun he had stolen. He didn't realize that it had a small dent on the side. It was useful information, which he could use to identify Anything.

"You'll find out if you keep this up," Anything snapped.

"Why do you care?" Zane asked.

"I care because I've dedicated my entire life to this place, and the information you have is important to everybody here. Now stop asking questions," Anything said sharply.

Zane was too scared to ask if he would be tortured. Anything yanked him out of the seat and shoved him towards the door. It was getting harder and harder to not fall over. Four men stood outside, towering menacingly over him.

"Is this really necessary?" He tried to see some of their facial features, but they were very careful with the masks and hoods.

"Did you almost escape ten minutes ago?" Smith pulled the bag over Zane's head yet again.

"Did you almost escape ten minutes ago?" Zane mocked angrily, quiet enough so that he wasn't heard.

The masked men seemed to walk rhythmically, each footstep falling at the perfect time. They reached the elevator, and Zane managed to step inside without tripping.

I failed an escape attempt, was threatened, and even gave away information in an interrogation, but at least I don't trip on the elevator anymore. Zane thought sarcastically.

The elevator came to a stop and soon enough he was back in the same cell.

The same.

STUPID.

CELL.

He already hated the four, white walls and the confined space. It almost felt like he was in some sort of mental asylum. If mental asylums had buckets to pee in, no food or water, and individuals that hid their identity. Maybe their plan was to make him go insane, because it was starting to work. Zane doubled over, a sharp-as-thorns memory crippling him. He fell to his knees, images flashing past his eyes. Soon it exploded into something he could focus on.

"If we ever get into trouble we need a code word," Max suggested, *a notebook in his lap and a pencil balancing on his fingers. The two of them sat underneath a tree, red and orange leaves blowing around them.*

"That's stupid. We're not dumb enough for that." Zane snickered. "We have people on our side now, remember? They wouldn't let anything happen to us."

Max's expression fell. "For how long? They know who we used to work for. Their entire existence is dedicated to uncovering the Evermoving"

Zane glared at the grass. "Right. The people who trained us to be their personal slaves," he said bitterly.

"What are you guys talking about?" Gemma's voice came from above them, her body sprawled over a tree branch.

"How long have you been up there?" Max asked nervously.

Gemma was a member of the organization, who was apparently good at eavesdropping. Unlike most of them, she chose to go by her real name and was very transparent with her past.

"Long enough to hear your conversation," Gemma murmured, a smirk on her face. "They taught you nothing."

"We don't have anything to hide from you, Gemma." Zane tore a piece of grass from the ground. "We were told we're safe here."

"Based off of your last conversation you don't believe that, do you?" Gemma sat up on the branch, stretching her limbs out. "You still have secrets too."

"I don't think—" Max started to say.

"Not you. Him." She pointed at Zane, before grinning. "I'll get you to tell me someday."

Zane glowered. "Whatever." Gemma hopped down beside them, her words muffled.

It felt like the memory was torn from his mind like fabric,

leaving his brain frayed. Zane blinked rapidly, slowly standing up and reaching for the nearest wall to lean against. He used to be on their side. And so did Gemma, from the very beginning. What was he *really* running from? Whoever was protecting him from the Evermoving or... The ones who held him hostage now?

CHAPTER
TWENTY-THREE

A gun was pointed at him. And Gemma was the one holding it. Zane started to take a few steps back but then... She shot him. She started to aim the gun at him again, but he woke up. Zane's eyes flickered open in time to see the glass door slide open. He quickly stumbled to his feet, rubbing the sleep from his eyes.

The abnormally tall man threw a black bag at him and he barely caught it. "Put it on."

Zane did as he was told and the guy guided him towards the elevator. He memorized the turns they took to get to the interrogation room, repeating them over and over again in his mind. The door to the interrogation room was shut, and he was yet again handcuffed to the table. Dr. Sandra took the bag off of his head, her hair in an extremely exaggerated messy bun.

"Are you feeling cooperative?" She smiled, fake kindness oozing from it.

"I'll answer your questions, if you answer mine." Zane narrowed his eyes at Dr. Sandra.

Her smile disappeared. "This isn't a negotiation. But..." She glanced at something imaginary in the corner of the room. "I'm intrigued. However you should know, if you don't answer my questions truthfully, I'm done being reasonable."

"It's a deal." Zane took a deep breath in. "What is the purpose of the Evermoving?"

Dr. Sandra looked at him in surprise. "To protect the world."

"From what?" Zane demanded.

"It's my turn to ask a question, dear." Dr. Sandra sat down on the chair. "What was the most recent memory you recovered?"

Zane winced. "I... was with my friends. We were with the organization that's against the Evermoving"

Dr. Sandra looked as if her soul had left her body. "What exactly happened?"

"I was sitting next to Max, under this tree and we were talking about how we left the Evermoving," Zane said carefully. "We were wondering if we could trust the people saying they would protect us. Gemma overheard everything and said something about me having secrets. The thing I want to know is–" Zane tugged on the handcuff. "Why did you kidnap me if I was on *your* side? Don't you already know everything that I do?"

Dr. Sandra chewed her lip as she decided what to say next. "We kidnapped you because we don't know everything. Even when you worked for the Evermoving, you were extremely secretive."

"Has Gemma recovered any memories?"

"Well..." Zane looked down at his feet guiltily. "A few but she didn't tell me what they were about. She just seemed nervous about it." He looked directly at Dr. Sandra and asked, "What do you want with Gemma and me? I know you want information from me, but what else is there?"

She adjusted the sleeves on her lavender-colored blouse. "The ones in charge wanted to help you reach your potential. You could have done great things. But the whole running away and getting amnesia put a damper on those plans." Dr. Sandra's eyebrows knitted together, her spectacles sliding down on her nose.

Zane lunged forward, the chain the only thing keeping him from strangling Dr. Sandra. She didn't move an inch. "Weren't you the ones who wiped our memories?!" He glared at Dr. Sandra, half of his body on top of the interrogation table, fingers stretched toward Dr. Sandra.

She stood up, an innocent smile growing on her face. "I think we're done here."

"No! We're not done!" Zane kicked back his chair, slamming his hands down on the metal. "I have more questions!"

Dr. Sandra walked around him to the exit. "And so do I. Only..." She tapped her chin. "You don't get to ask any. At least not anymore. You haven't changed, Zane. You're still as aggressive as ever." She opened the door and addressed the nearest guard. "Give Zane something to calm him down. He also answered a few of my questions so give him some food when he wakes up."

She disappeared from view, and his face fell. Two men stormed in, one of them masked, and the other wearing a lab coat.

"Hold him still," the lab coat individual said. He didn't fight when the needle was injected into his arm. Zane's vision grew blurry, and he barely registered that the black bag was put over his head. One of the guards had to practically drag him back to the cell. By the time he felt the elevator move, he was out cold.

Zane tried to stand, but it felt like he was trapped in molasses. He felt hopeless, pathetic, and *hungry*. So *hungry*. He settled for lying on his back, one arm over his face. Zane stayed that way until the stars in the corner of his vision started to fade. The glass door eventually opened, and one of the masked members stood there with an apple in his hand. Zane hesitantly approached him, and the guard extended the arm holding the apple. Zane narrowed his eyes suspiciously, before snatching the apple away from him. He bit into it ravenously, eyes drifting to the leg the guy had most of his weight on. Zane swallowed, making eye contact with the familiar blue-eyed guard.

"Bluejay? Is that you?" he asked, although he wasn't sure why he felt a tinge of guilt. He was one of the people who had assisted in kidnapping Zane.

"Lucky guess." Bluejay's voice was level, revealing no emotion.

"Sorry about the foot. I had to at least *try* to escape though." Zane laughed nervously. "I didn't." He shrugged, pointing at the cell that had become his new home. "Technically you did tell me to," Zane muttered under his breath.

"I'm not here to stay. I just came to deliver the apple." Bluejay sighed. "And honestly, the guy you call Anything is more angry about it than me. Don't do it again." He narrowed his eyes at Zane.

"Try to escape or... Shoot you in the foot?" Zane took another bite out of the apple.

"Both," he snapped, pressing his keycard against a small monitor beside the cell. The glass door proceeded to close.

Zane really needed to stop edging on the guards. They had complete control over what happened to him. Dr. Sandra probably wouldn't mind if one of them slugged him on the jaw. He finished the apple quickly, leaving almost none of the flesh on the core. He sat down in one corner of the room, throwing the core of the apple to the other side out of boredom. It didn't make a sound. That was another thing that made this cell the worst. It was completely silent, except for his breathing. He regretted not asking what the Evermoving was protecting the world from. It could be anything, from other countries, foreign spies, the group he used to be a part of... Zane wished of living in a small house, in the middle of nowhere, away from everything. It was a stupid dream.

He wondered if he could even trust Gemma anymore. If she was his enemy from the start, how long would it be before she betrayed him? Was she worth the risk? Maybe.

The door slid open once again, and Bluejay peeked in. "That was fast."

He jolted upwards, scrambling to his feet. "That's what happens when you starve someone!" Zane snapped.

"Aww poor thing. Do you need another apple?" he mocked, clasping his gloved hands together.

Zane folded his arms across his chest. "What do you want?"

"I'm just here for the core. Which you so kindly threw." Bluejay pointed at what was left of the apple.

"This whole feeding thing seems inefficient. What if I made a run for it? Again." Zane glanced at Bluejay's foot.

"I wouldn't let you get far."

Zane scoffed. "What about last time?"

"That—" Bluejay kept an eye on him while retrieving the apple with his bad foot. "Was a test."

"You let yourself get shot for a test?" Zane's eyes widened in alarm.

Bluejay shrugged. "I would do anything for the Evermoving, although that wasn't part of the plan."

"What exactly were you testing?"

"We wanted to know where you would go. Dr. Sandra said you'd try to run at some point." Bluejay picked up the core by the stem, stepping outside of the cell.

"You're just trying to justify being terrible at your job," Zane muttered.

"Whatever you want to believe." Bluejay brought his keycard next to the side of the cell, but hesitated. "A bit of advice? Tell Dr.

Sandra what you know. It'll be easier that way." His black hood seemed to drop even further down his face.

Zane took a step towards the exit. "What do you mean by–" The door shut in his face. He slammed his fist into the glass out of frustration. He winced, his knuckles sore from his previous outbursts.

"We still need a code word," Max said, as they watched Gemma walk back inside the headquarters.

"How about Bluejay?" Zane said, half joking.

Max set down his notepad, a grin growing on his face.

Zane narrowed his eyes. "I don't like the look on your face."

"Bluejay?" Max asked, holding back laughter.

"Okay so maybe we might eventually need a code word! Get over it..." Zane's chin rested on his hand.

"It's just kind of strange you would choose Bluejay. I expected something more ominous or subtle," Max admitted.

Zane shook his head. "I'm indulging your weird obsession with code words. It's not really a big deal." He rolled his eyes.

"What should the meaning for Bluejay be?" Max asked.

"How about, "it's me?" he said, a scowl on his face.

Max put his hands behind his head. "That works."

The memory passed through his head without warning or an after effect. The color drained from his face. He'd found Max.

CHAPTER
TWENTY-FOUR

D r. Sandra couldn't find out what he knew. This was one memory that would be his secret only. He just couldn't believe he had shot his friend in the foot. He wasn't sure what he should say.

Hello?

It's good to see you again?

Whose side are we on?

How have you been?

When are we escaping?

Zane paced back and forth, his mind like a roller coaster. The dead silence was the only thing keeping him company. Eventually, the lights dimmed even further, something he had never noticed before. Zane stretched out his hands, which hurt like crazy from punching inanimate objects. He hoped that Max's foot would recover, and that he would forgive him. After all, he'd had no idea it was Max.

His eyelids started to droop, but he didn't want to sleep yet. There were too many things to think about. Too much to process. He squeezed his eyes shut, frustrated tears running down his face. He just wanted someone he could trust. Someone who could tell him about his past. Such as who had planned to kill him? And who was responsible for those corpses? His limbs grew heavy, and yet he didn't allow himself to sleep. Even when his eyes began to hurt he stayed standing. His thoughts started to blur together and eventually, he passed out.

The door suddenly opened, and he lifted his head to get a better view. This time it was someone he wasn't familiar with. However, they were still masked, and scary large.

"Get over here." His voice was low, with annoyance leaking into it.

Zane hesitated.

"Now," the man snapped. "You have a visitor."

He stood up. "A visitor? Who?" Zane glanced behind the guard, but saw nothing of importance.

The man took a step towards him, shoving the black bag over his head before grabbing his wrist. He was yanked out of the cell and dragged towards the elevator. Their footsteps were joined by a few others, including the odd steps of Max. The guy let go of his wrist and he walked without a guide. Max, by the sound of the footsteps, pressed the elevator button. A hand was placed on his back and he was shoved inside. The pressure was enough to make him fall. Zane wasn't able to catch himself in time, and his head banged against the metal. He suppressed a cry of pain. His face had endured enough damage when he first got here. He was sure it was covered in bruises by now.

"We're not supposed to hurt him," one of the guards said, but he wasn't sure who.

"Did anybody actually say that?" The guard who pushed him asked, smugness in his voice.

"No, but it was strongly implied. You don't want Dr. Sandra to be angry, do you?" Max asked, his voice low.

"He's fine, aren't you?" The abusive guard grabbed the back of his sweat shirt and set him on his feet.

Zane brushed himself off and couldn't help but whisper, "Pushover."

"What did you just say, you little brat?" The elevator button was pressed and the doors closed before the angry guard could say anything else.

"Nothing," he quickly muttered.

A few of the other guards snickered, including who he thought was Anything.

They took the same turns to get to the interrogation room and soon he was placed inside. Zane used his free hand to take off the black bag, setting it on the table. He found that his hair completely covered his eyes now. Zane slicked it to the side, only to find the room empty. He glanced towards the one way glass, and back to the exit. The door finally opened and...

"Mrs. Valentino?" His jaw dropped in shock.

The blonde woman walked into the room, pausing to laugh. "No. Not Mrs. Valentino. That was my fake identity. Good guess though."

Zane's heart hammered against his chest. "What happened to Dr. Sandra?"

"Oh she doesn't work here anymore." Mrs. Valentino, or whoever she really was, grinned. Zane didn't want to know what that meant. "It's kind of funny how long you held on to that piece of candy. Good thing you never opened it and found the tracker."

His eyes widened. "What?"

Instead of the scrubs he was used to, she wore a short red dress with a plunging neckline. It was paired with a glittering diamond necklace, her hair up in an intricate bun.

"You belong with us now, and we'll protect you. I just regret how they treated a member of our organization." She set a hand on her hip, her eyes narrowed. "It won't happen again."

"You... didn't know what they were doing to me?"

Mrs. Valentino stepped towards him, her face softened with concern. "No." She gently touched the scrapes on his face. She drew back and clasped her hands together. "Luckily I'm here now, and Dr. Sandra will never bother you again. Instead of prying information out of you, we'll help you work through those confusing memories."

"Who's we?" Zane asked cautiously, his mind still focusing on the tracker part of the conversation.

"My husband and his team of scientists of course!" His eyebrows practically flew off his face. The sides of her eyes crinkled in amusement. "Just because I'm the leader of this organization doesn't mean I can't have a husband too."

Interesting. She was the one in charge? "How exactly are they going to help me work through these memories?" He still had several thorns of doubt embedded in his brain, and they weren't coming out anytime soon.

"My husband said, 'We will use emotions, smells, and phrases directly correlating to the previous memories of the young boy'." She deepened her voice for the last part.

"When are we going to start?" he asked, suspicion lacing his voice.

"When you finally get a good night's rest in a real bed." Her features softened once again as she looked at him. "I'm so sorry, Zane, for everything that's happened to you since coming here." She leaned forward with a key and unlocked the handcuff.

The worst part was, a tiny part of him believed her. Zane desperately wanted to. But what if they really *weren't* that bad? Dr. Sandra was just one member of the organization. Mrs. Valentino started to walk out of the room.

"Wait!" Zane shouted.

She turned to look back at him. "Yes?"

"What's in it for you?" He flexed the hand that had been trapped in the handcuff.

"Nothing." The word sounded weightless.

"Dr. Sandra said that I had important information stored in my memories." Zane narrowed his eyes. "Aren't you after the same thing?"

Mrs.Valentino's expression turned serious. "If you choose to share the information with me. It's your choice."

Zane couldn't help the tiny smile that curled his lips.

She turned back around, one hand on her hip as she walked. "Could one of you guide him to his new room?"

Not a holding cell. A room. Max walked to the front of the interrogation room, and Zane hesitated. He couldn't say anything. Not in front of the other masked individuals.

"You–"

"Need to put the bag over my head?" Zane finished, already taking it from his hands.

"No." Max reached for it back.

Zane took a step towards him and placed the bag in his hand. "So, what exactly do I need to do?"

He started walking. "Just follow me." Max waved him forward.

"So how nice exactly is this *room* I'm getting?" Zane asked, watching the turns they took in the corner of his eyes.

"I don't know. I've never seen it." Now that he knew Bluejay was Max, he could tell just how fake the low voice was.

Zane glanced behind him, only to notice Max was the only guard around. He didn't risk saying anything, because he was certain there were cameras.

Zane tore a hand through his hair. "Is Mrs. Valentino really any different from...*Her?*"

Max shrugged. "They're both good at their job. At least, Dr.

Sandra *was* good at her job."

Somehow Zane knew nobody would hear from her for a long time. "What is the leader of this organization trying to accomplish exactly?"

He froze. "I don't think I'm supposed to tell you that." He shook off whatever he was thinking and kept going.

"Why not?" Zane asked.

"Don't worry about it. Just keep following me. We're almost to the elevator."

Zane's eyebrows scrunched together, but he didn't say anything. "So Bluejay, what do you do when you're not here working for the Evermoving?"

"That's classified," Max said vaguely.

Zane had to stop himself from laughing. "Where are we going?"

"What do you mean?" Max took another turn, keeping his eyes on the elevator they were approaching.

"What floor?" Zane deadpanned.

"I'm getting instructions as we go." He tapped the earpiece lodged in his eardrum.

"Got it." Zane walked faster to keep up with him.

"Who's talking to you?"

"You really love asking questions don't you?" Max asked exasperatedly.

He kept quiet, his gaze focused on the ground. Soon they reached the elevator, and Max used his keycard before pressing the button. It opened and several individuals walked out of it and down the hallway they came from. Zane and, he still couldn't believe it, Max, went inside and headed to an above ground floor. *Floor 3*. It opened, revealing a giant ballroom style area with two stairways on opposite ends of the fancy entryway. A gurgling fountain was in the middle, accompanied by classical music. On the right side of the room was a giant window, and on the other side towering jungle plants. Max was already eight feet ahead of him when he finished staring. He ran to catch up.

"This is a lot nicer than the second floor." Zane paused to get a closer look at the fountain.

"I guess so," Max muttered.

They started going up one of the stairways. Zane almost felt bad for getting the white carpet dirty.

"Do you live here too?" His fingers trailed the wooden banister.

"Most of us do. The guards have rooms that are less fancy though." Max kept one hand on his gun, clearly remembering what happened the last time. It made sense, considering the exit was directly behind them. The glass doors were heavily tinted which meant that no one would be able to see him.

"Do the people outside of here know you keep prisoners in the basement?" Zane smiled tightly.

"Stop that," Max warned.

When they got to the top of the stairway, they turned to the right. Their shoes made tapping noises against the solid wood. Intricate but useless pillars leading up to the ceiling made up the center of the upstairs. It was almost like a gazebo, and doorways were around the circle-like shape outside of the pillars. The center of the room looked forbidden, like something out of a fantasy. Gold vines hung from the ceiling, making tinkling noises whenever they moved. They went around the circle, passing doors until they got to the fourth one. Max opened the ornate door, gesturing for him to go inside. The sight blew his breath away. Warm steam pressed against his face, and he headed further in. The bathing room looked like an indoor spa, with countless bottles of shampoo and conditioner by the edges of the steaming pond-like bath. The ceiling was high, and solid stone steps led to yet another door. Zane was guessing it was the bedroom. He turned around to say something to Max, but the door was shut in his face. Zane tried opening it, but it was locked from the outside.

Figures. Zane thought bitterly.

He walked around the bath to the stairs, his eyes scanning the room for cameras. He didn't see any, but that didn't mean there weren't hidden devices, listening to everything he said. Zane was going to have to search for them, but that could wait until after he took a bath. He headed up the stairs, and opened the door to his room. Everything was white, from the bed sheets to the wardrobe in the corner. The only thing that wasn't was the brown carpet. He opened the wardrobe, scanning through the different outfits. Everything was either a suit or jacket. He took out the less fancy option, a white collared shirt along with black pants.

Out of the corner of his eye, he saw another person in the room. He panicked upon seeing his face, covered in angry bruises and dried blood. He took a step towards the crazed boy, ready to fist fight the homeless-looking stranger. "Who are you?" He swiped his hair away from his eyes to get a better look. Zane was flooded with embarrassment when he saw the floor length mirror.

After taking a bath, he turned off the faucet before slipping on the new clothes. Zane let his hair dry to the side. It still looked awful but it was better than in his eyes. He cleaned the dried blood off of his face, and a wave of calm seemed to come over him. Zane headed back to his bedroom and stood in front of the one-way window. A chain link fence didn't make for a great view.

Better than the same four walls. Zane thought bitterly.

He got in bed, and let his thoughts fade. The hot water and steam had calmed his nerves, but he still knew he had to be cautious. He didn't really know *her* real intentions. Nobody did anything for free.

CHAPTER
TWENTY-FIVE

Z ane's craving to remember his past outweighed his common sense. He had a plan. A stupid plan maybe, but at least he had one. The exit was a hundred feet away, and the only thing that stood in his path was a *door*. If things went south with the memory retrieval stuff, then he would make a run for it. He probably should have already tried to escape, but he couldn't. Not now. Not when he was so close to finding answers to all of his questions.

Zane searched every crevice for anything that had been bugged, but he didn't find anything. He searched behind the mirror, underneath the wardrobe, but there was nothing. He was currently searching under his bed when someone knocked on the door. He jumped and his head hit the frame of the queen-sized bed. The knocking grew more insistent. Zane stood up, rubbing the spot on his head that hit the frame.

He headed downstairs, avoiding the leftover bubbles and with his eyebrows furrowed together said, "Hello?" The door opened to reveal Max, still disguised as Bluejay.

"What do you want?" Zane's forehead furrowed.

"They're ready to start helping you recover your memories," Max explained, glancing at his new look. "I can see that you're ready."

Zane was fifty percent sure there weren't any cameras or listening devices so he decided to risk it. "Bluejay." Zane widened his eyes, hoping that Max would get it.

"Yes?" he said, confusion in his tone.

"No..." Zane said cautiously. "Bluejay."

It's me, Zane internally screamed. *And I know who you are.*

"I don't understand." Max shifted his feet.

"I know who you are," he whisper-hissed. "What are you doing here?"

Max took a step back, glancing behind him. His gaze returned to Zane. Max held a finger up to his lips, his voice almost silent. "Don't say anything else. I'm on your side." Max's voice returned to normal for the split second he spoke.

"Is that side also the Evermoving's?" Zane asked, but Max stayed quiet.

"Follow me," he said in his fake, gruff voice. "Now," Max added, but Zane couldn't tell if it was fake or real anger. He pressed a finger to his earpiece. "We're heading to the lab now."

They stopped in front of two tall doors. They were bare, and had no ornate decorations like everything else on the above-ground-floor. Max knocked five times, and they waited ten minutes until the doors swung open to reveal a huge laboratory. There were dozens of desks cluttered with pieces of machinery and fridges full of vials. Not to mention the doors had opened automatically.

Max started to walk in but hesitated. He stayed like that for a moment, most likely listening to someone. "I can't come with you. Good luck." He walked out of the lab and when Zane didn't move, pushed him inside. The doors closed immediately.

"Hello, Zane," a woman whose face was covered by her notebook greeted. "They're getting ready for you on the other side of the lab. I'd like to go over how you receive your memories if that's alright. Go ahead and take a seat."

"Where?" He held back a smirk, glancing at the seats covered in paperwork or machinery.

She looked over the top of her notebook, revealing turtle-green eyes. "There should be two empty chairs somewhere." Zane found the circular chairs in the corner and took a seat. He was soon joined by her, her curly hair bouncing as she moved.

She flipped through her notebook before looking at him. "My name is Dr. Cass. Do you get any warning before you remember something?" She took the pen from the notebook's spiral.

"Sometimes. Most of the time my brain feels like it's splitting open before and after." His face scrunched up at the thought.

Dr. Cass's eyes lit up. "Interesting." She leaned backward, fiddling with a piece of her hair. "How often do you get these pieces of memory?"

Zane shrugged. "Maybe once every couple of days."

"What triggers them?" Dr. Cass didn't smile, but her eyes held encouragement in them.

"When something happens that's close to what already happened in the past." He crossed his arms over his chest. "So far my memories have been important pieces of my life, usually times of high stress." He winced at the memory of the dead bodies.

"Fascinating. I'm going to tell the lead scientist everything you just told me, okay?" She stood up. "Don't touch anything," Dr. Cass pointed at him with her eyebrows slightly raised before opening a door at the far end of the laboratory. Zane surveyed the room, spotting a total of three cameras in the lab. One was pointed at the exit, and the others gave a perfect view of all of the organized desks. Zane counted every minute Dr. Cass was gone, and it added up to twenty minutes. He straightened up when the door opened again, and they headed inside the other room together. It was painted with a vibrant yellow, the same as Dr. Sandra's fake lobby. The thing that stood out the most was the white machine in the middle of the room. The machine was similar to a lounge chair, but it had all sorts of lights and heart rate equipment as well as stuff he didn't even know the use for. A desk was in the corner, and behind it were two scientists.

One of them approached him, his hand extended. "Hello," he said dryly. "I'm the lead scientist, but I guess you can call me Dr. Valentino."

Zane blinked slowly, before shaking his hand. He couldn't tell if that had been a joke or not.

"We're going to start with simple memory retention. A series of images are going to pop up on the screen." The other scientist pressed a button and the projector on the ceiling turned on. "And hopefully," he tapped Zane's head, "it'll shake a few memories loose."

Zane took a step back from Dr. Valentino. "Got it." He resisted scowling at the lead scientist.

"Lie down and relax," Dr. Cass recommended.

He barely had time to sit before they started attaching things to his arms and chest. Zane tensed, trying his best not to punch one of them in the face. They put some sort of helmet on his head, which was extremely uncomfortable.

"Focus on the images. Don't think too hard about it. The memories should come to you naturally." Dr. Valentino and Dr. Cass went behind the desk. It started to project images, but they went by so fast he couldn't focus on them. Sounds were coming out of the speaker in the corner, but they were warped together in what could be described as creepy horror movie sounds. He tried his best not to fidget or look away from the pictures, but he couldn't help glancing away every now and then. Zane blinked rapidly, tears gathering in his eyes. Voices that weren't his own started talking in his head.

Strap him down and the girl too!

Where's Zane? Max's voice.

I love blueberry ice cream! Gemma's voice.

It's all gonna be okay, darling. Remember, we love you. Zane didn't recognize this voice.

Don't trust the Evermoving!

The code word for help should be finch. Max again.

Hey losers! Gemma this time, but her voice was full of affection.

Where am I? His own voice.

It all began to be too much, so he squeezed his eyes shut, his hands reaching for the helmet.

I never should have trusted you! Weirdly enough the voice sounded like Max.

Suddenly all the noise disappeared, leaving him in a heap on the floor. His breaths were uneven and his fingernails dug into his skin. The pain distracted him, until he could finally open his eyes. He regretted it when he noticed the room was spinning.

"Does that usually happen?" Dr. Valentino asked.

"He said it hurts sometimes," Dr. Cass offered.

"It doesn't normally feel this painful..." Zane muttered, gasping as if he had been punched in the gut. Somebody sat him up and a glass of water was pushed into his hands. Zane drank it slowly until his massive headache started to fade.

"I'll work on a new design," Dr. Valentino said, clearly frustrated. Through blurry eyes he watched Dr. Valentino storm out of the room.

Dr. Cass helped him to his feet alongside the other scientist in the room. "I'll help bring him to his room. Trevor, you can take care of the machine with our boss." Dr. Cass slung Zane's arm over her shoulders. He tried his best to walk alongside her, still lightheaded from the strange things they'd done to him. Eventually, they got to his room and she helped him to the bed.

"Have you had any food today?" she asked, concern lacing her tone.

"I don't think so."

"That's probably why you almost passed out," Dr. Cass murmured.

Zane sat down on the bed. "Who's in charge of that anyway?"

"I don't know. I promise that you'll get regular food. *Someone* clearly hasn't been doing their job properly." Dr. Cass sighed. "I'll bring you something from the break room for now. I think they're serving spaghetti." She smiled lightly. "Sit tight."

Zane watched her leave before swinging his legs onto the bed and resting his head on the pillow. What had the voices said again? He remembered something about ice cream. And a secret code word. His headache returned and he couldn't help but feel relieved when Dr. Cass returned with food. She set the tray of food next to him.

He looked at her out of the corner of his eye, hesitating for a moment. "Thank you."

Dr. Cass shrugged. "I'm just doing my job."

"Not everyone here is as nice as you." Zane's thoughts drifted to the abusive guards, and the threats he had received from Dr. Sandra.

She stiffened. "I'm sorry you feel that way."

"Me too." He avoided eye contact.

"I heard what Dr. Sandra did. How are you still able to keep going?"

Zane eyebrows raised in surprise. He turned to look at her, taking a deep breath in. "I don't know." The words felt heavy, and he was instantly reminded of the bags under his eyes. He exhaled, resting his head on his hand. "I guess I just have an urge to find out about my past. And..." Zane curled his fingers into a fist. "There are people I care about." Gemma, the Smiths, Max, and Robin. "They're keeping me going at this point."

"We should be able to fix the machine soon. I hope you get your memories back." Dr. Cass held a kind look in her eyes. Genuine kindness was something he hadn't seen in a while. She pointed at the tray. "You should eat. I need to get back to work."

Zane smirked. "Yeah. Okay." The spaghetti was surprisingly well made, and after he ate, he hopped off his bed to finish his search for any bugs. He didn't find any underneath the bed so he took the mattress off of the frame. He used the zipper on the side to open it and shoved his arm inside. He took the stuffing out and his fingers brushed against something that definitely wasn't cotton. He grabbed it, revealing a black circle. He quickly crushed it between his fingers. It made a static-like noise.

"I was wondering how long it would take for you to find that." Zane jumped to his feet, what was left of the bug dropping to the ground. He relaxed when he recognized Max from his uneven gait. He still had the disguise on, but at this point Zane had learned to recognize Max.

"Hey." The greeting felt redundant. Max closed the door.

"You really don't remember anything do you?" Max's voice, which was back to normal, seemed to drip with anger. Whether it was towards him he didn't know.

"Not really." Zane really wished he could read Max's facial expressions.

"We need to get you out of here as soon as possible," Max admitted.

"When?" He glanced to the side, guilty of not wanting to leave.

"Tomorrow night. And especially before they discover who I am." He laughed, scratching the back of his neck in a way that screamed he was completely terrified.

"Where exactly are we going to go after we escape?" Zane asked,

"The less you know the better." Max took a step forward. "And don't tell anyone anything you remember."

Zane winced. "Oops?"

"Oops what?"

He tore a hand through his overgrown hair, exhaling slowly. "Oops as in it's too late. I kind of exchanged information with Dr. Sandra."

Max grew still, fingers curling into fists. "What did you tell her?"

"I told her I remembered joining the rebels or whatever you want to call them," Zane cracked his knuckles, "and about Gemma recovering a few memories." He was suddenly hit with a wave of suspicion. "Take off your hood."

"Why?" Max asked, confused.

"I want to make sure it's really you." Zane took a step back.

Max stepped forward. "Seriously?" He nodded. Max hesitantly brought his hood back, revealing raven hair. Soon after, he took his mask off. This was Max. He had the same light brown skin, blue eyes, and voice. The knots in his stomach loosened, his nervousness dying down. Zane opened his mouth to say something else but Max interrupted him.

"No more questions until we escape." His eyebrows knitted together, a thoughtful expression on his face. "I'll fill you in on everything later." Max put the mask back on, before covering his hair with the hood. He paused halfway out of the door. "Don't. Tell. Anyone. Anything," Max warned.

"I won't." Max stood still for a solid minute. Zane held up his hands. "I promise."

He seemed satisfied with Zane's answer and left.

CHAPTER

TWENTY-SIX

Z ane didn't want to escape. He was so close to retrieving his memories, and it seemed like a waste to leave now. He bathed before dressing in a black and white suit. It was easier to tell time with the one-sided window in his bedroom, but he still felt like a prisoner. He was more of a willing prisoner now but still a prisoner all the same. Zane pressed his ear to the door, waiting for the sound of footsteps. He hoped they had managed to fix the machine. Zane was confused when he heard soft steps, so unlike the clomping of most of the guards. He took a step back, and a key was inserted into the door. It opened slowly, revealing Dr. Cass.

Her turtle-green eyes widened in surprise. "You're awake."

"Did he manage to fix the machine?" Zane asked, stupid feelings of hope creeping into the corners of his eyes.

She smiled. "Maybe." Dr. Cass started walking, and he quickly followed. "The doctor has a few different methods he wants to try out. He thought maybe we overloaded your senses, giving your brain too much to process. So we'll start out slow, but first we're going to get you something to eat."

Zane refused to let his stomach growl at the thought of food. "How long have you been working here?" he asked, partly for what could be important information, and partly for filling the silence.

She moved strands of hair out of her face before answering. "A year, maybe. It took ten years to even get in the door, including thirteen years at harvard."

"You don't look—"

"That old? I was an accelerated student."

"I don't remember school," Zane muttered, suddenly feeling extremely stupid.

"You will soon," Dr. Cass reminded him.

She opened the door three spaces from his, and they headed down a hallway. Once they got to the cafeteria, Dr. Cass stayed by the doorway. He tried not to seem too eager, grabbing a tray calmly and avoiding eye contact with the doctors. The guards were noticeably not in the room. Occasionally, however, one would grab something and leave. He grabbed about a dozen sandwiches, filling up the rest of the tray with chips and chocolate cake. He sat down at one of the only empty tables and inhaled the food. He got several dirty looks, but he ignored them, mostly because he was too hungry to care.

After eating, they headed back into the room with the machine.

"Hello, Zane," Dr. Valentino said, eyes focused on the computer. "Go ahead and take a seat."

The other doctors attached the necessary equipment when he sat down, and the project began projecting images one by one.

The first picture was of an underground tunnel, followed by a blaring voice from the speaker. "Run!"

There was a twenty second pause before the next image flickered across the whiteboard. This time it was a picture of Gemma,

Zane, and Max sitting underneath the same tree in his previous memory. More images flicked in front of him, and he soon realized it wasn't from the projector.

"Hey!" Gemma sat down between the two of them.

Max dodged her attempt at ruffling his hair.

"Hi Gemma." they said in unison.

She sighed. "You guys really like sitting on grass, and I don't know why."

Zane smirked. "Are you calling us boring?"

Gemma scoffed. "I wouldn't be dating you if I thought you were boring."

"Awww!" Zane made a heart with his hands, causing Gemma to throw grass in his face.

"Ew," Max muttered.

"Hey, we should take a picture!" Gemma suggested, holding out a cellphone. Zane leaned into the picture, and Gemma quickly took it before Max could scoot out of frame.

Gemma grinned. "That turned out great."

"Max is even in this one." He dusted the grass off of his shirt, smirking at his friend.

Max grinned. "My eyes were closed."

"Let's retake it!" Gemma suggested enthusiastically.

Max swiped the phone from her hands. "No more pictures," he pleaded, "You already have like fifty on that thing."

Zane bit back a scream. This memory felt more forced than the times before. More insistent. He tried to say something but they moved onto the next photo before he could. This one was of a small room, a cot in the corner, and a small nightstand. It had simple decorations, but it almost made him relax. That was before the memory began to be more insistent, banging on the doors of his mind. He focused on one thing in the room, until images started to flicker in his mind.

"Are you sure?" Gemma asked, reaching out to grab his hand.

Zane tore his hand from her grasp. She flinched, the hope in her eyes vanishing. "I'm sure," he snapped. "This was never going to work out."

She let out a scream of frustration. "I don't even know why I dated you!" Gemma tugged on her hair, tears welling in her eyes. "You've never told me you care about me! Or comforted me, or listened to any of my problems! You're just a selfish jerk!" She kicked the leg of his cot as hard as she could.

"Why'd you stick around for so long then!" he snapped, rising from where he sat on his bed, towering over her.

"I thought you would change," she whispered. "You were so charming when we first started dating. You always knew the perfect thing to say, the perfect thing to do..."

The memory faded slowly, before settling in his brain. Zane's heart wrenched. How could he ever have done those things? He swore he would apologize as soon as he saw her. *If* he ever saw her again. His head began to feel hot, and he managed to mumble something, but by then the next picture came on the screen. This time it showed a dark, abandoned warehouse.

"Your first job of course!" a staticky voice said from the speaker.

"What do you mean?" Zane resisted grinning. He couldn't show his emotions in front of her. She would just use them to her advantage.

"Your first job of course! You said you wanted to get back into the fray, right?" Mrs. Valentino asked, her eyes sparkling. "You were our best field agent after all."

Zane wanted that more than anything. He loved the thrill of it. Running, breaking into things, threatening people... But this time it was different. He was being forced to work for Mrs. Valentino. He would much rather go back to Max and Gemma. But that wasn't a choice he could make. Not if he didn't want to accept the resulting consequences.

He rolled his eyes. "Yeah, a field agent who stole information from

*your organization." He pointed around her office, everything orga-
nized perfectly from the waterfall in the corner, to the bookshelves
lining the walls. The lotus banner stared menacingly at him. The
symbols were scattered throughout the Evermoving's base.*

*"It is what it is." She adjusted her dress straps, a long and winded
sigh escaping her. "You're back with the Evermoving." Her eyes
narrowed. "Even if it isn't by choice. You're working for a better cause
now anyway." Mrs. Valentino shrugged.*

*"How exactly are you going to help the world anyway?" Zane tried
his best to keep the sarcasm out of his voice. "With whatever is in level
zero?"*

*Her eyelid twitched, meaning she detected the sarcasm. "Only a
select few know what we're doing here."*

Zane frowned. "Which is?"

*"We're helping government officials and world leaders run their
countries more smoothly."*

"With what?" Zane asked.

*Mrs. Valentino smiled. "You'll find out when you're older. But I
guess you could say the world's wheels only turn faster with our methods. There's so much being done that the brainwashed people of today
will never realize."*

Zane leaned back in the chair. "What's the job?"

Her smile widened. "I'm glad you asked."

He let out a quiet scream of frustration. What was the job?
His head felt like it was in a juice presser, so he tried to take off a
few of the tube attachments on his arms, but the next picture
was already displayed. This time it showed the carnival that Max
and Zane hid in. But... What he didn't remember was the tent
being covered by violent flames.

*Zane accidently inhaled smoke, sending him into a coughing fit.
He strained his eyes trying to find Max through the haze.*

*"Zaneee! Maxxxx! Please stop running. It's getting on my nerves!"
Mrs. Valentino shouted. "If you turn yourselves in, we'll let you two*

*live!" The carnival tent started to fall, the raging blaze only growing.
"You've caused enough trouble!"*

*Zane scowled at the words. He walked over an array of carnival
toys, a lot of which he assumed to be deflated balloons and stuffed
animals. He bumped into someone, and he quickly got into a fighting
stance.*

*"Zane!?" Max said, loud enough to be heard over the crackling
flames.*

*Zane set a hand on his friend's shoulder. "Let's get out of here."
Through the smoke he saw that it was too late. Blurry figures
surrounded them.*

"I—"

The memory cut off, and he took a moment to process. He
waited for more images to come, but nothing happened. And the
only sound he heard was a frustrated Dr. Valentino sighing.

"It was too much for his body to handle," Dr. Cass said,
in awe.

"Absolutely ridiculous!" Dr. Valentino shouted, slamming his
fist down on his desk.

Zane glanced at his arms, which sported so much sweat that
it had fried some of the equipment.

"He needs a break," Dr. Cass insisted. "He looks half-dead. I
guess that's what happens when you force the memories."

Zane struggled to lift his head, and when he did, he turned
towards the scientists. "What..." he whispered, his voice as dry as
desert sand. Zane cleared his throat. "Why did she do it? She
could've killed–" His voice cut off, and he coughed. It was almost
as if he was still surrounded by the smoke. "She was going to kill
us!" Zane shouted, trying to pry the remaining equipment off of
him, including the strange suction cup-like things on his chest
and pulse points.

"He's delirious. Drug him and we'll find a more efficient way.
I just wish she'd let us use the real lab," Dr. Valentino growled.

Arms lowered him back down, but he fought back, scratching and biting whatever flesh he could find. "Let me go! I need to get out of here!" Zane screamed as blood trickled down his chin. A needle was injected into him and after a few more moments of struggling, he went limp. Before he completely passed out, he heard something that sent the warning bells in his mind ringing.

"Zane remembered something he wasn't supposed to. We lost the patient's trust. Are we free to break protocol?"

Nothing was going to be the same.

CHAPTER
TWENTY-SEVEN

Zane woke up with a splitting headache. It felt like his mind had been stretched out too thin. He was lying on what was supposed to be a comfortable bed, but his body refused to relax. What was Level Zero, and most importantly, what exactly did Dr. Valetino mean by *breaking* protocol? He swung his feet over the bed and stood up, his entire body shaking. Whether he was terrified or cold, he wasn't sure. He walked to the floor-length mirror, and to his surprise, tears were slipping down his face. A strange part of him felt relief. With every memory, he started to feel a little bit more like himself. More complete. He finally had a sense of direction, almost like he knew what to do. And Zane definitely knew he couldn't stay here. Whatever Dr. Valentino was planning, he couldn't stick around for. It was too dangerous, even if he got a few more memories out of it.

Zane pressed his ear to the door of his room, listening for voices or footsteps. It was eerily silent. He had to trust that Max would find a way to break him out. Actually, that was his only option. Zane headed back to the window, and he wondered if he would be able to break it. Probably not. His room might not look like a prison, but it sure as hell was one. He laid down on his bed, his hands behind his head. It reminded him of his time in the Smith's apartment, when he stayed up late at night, desperate to remember something important. He would give anything to go back in time and do things differently. Zane squeezed his eyes shut, but this time let his tears flow freely. The bug was destroyed, so nobody could hear his loud sobbing. He was terrified. Beyond terrified. He didn't know what was going to happen to him. What *they* were planning on doing to him. He had only a few days of safety, but they were already gone. His ribs had started to peek through his skin, and the eyebags under his eyes were especially dark. Ten minutes passed, his face sticky with pointless tears. Zane just wanted to go back to the Smith's apartment. He would like to have a home there, if they would take him back. Zane stumbled down the steps and turned the water on for the bath. He quickly took off the tuxedo jacket before pulling the dress shirt over his head. Zane set his shoes aside, using the water to wash the useless tears off his face. After stripping down the rest of the way he stepped into the bath, grabbing the nearest shampoo and bar of soap they had so kindly provided him with.

Someone began to knock on the door. "Hello, Zane? Are you in there?" The door started to open.

"No! Don't open the door! I'm not dressed!"

A shriek replaced whatever Dr. Cass was going to say next, and she quickly closed it. Zane was pretty sure that she hadn't seen anything. Even so, his face flushed with embarrassment.

"Get some clothes on!" Through the door she added, "The woman you know as Mrs. Valentino would like to explain to you the memory you received the other day."

Explain what? Exactly how she had planned to kill him and Max? He'd rather have a shred of dignity still intact, so to avoid being dragged to the Evermoving's leader while naked, he got dressed and followed Dr. Cass. He chose something a bit more comfortable this time, a light blue dress shirt, and the softest pair of black dress pants he could find. Nothing that she could say would convince him to trust them. Nothing would excuse what she had done either. She set fire to a carnival just to find them, then when she did, threatened to kill him and his friend. Weird that he was getting used to things like that happening.

"Aren't we going to the interrogation room?" Zane said, confused when they headed to the door across from his room.

"No. We're going to her office."

Zane let out a sigh of frustration. "After all this time I don't even know what to call her."

They stopped in front of the door, and Dr. Cass's eyebrows knitted together. "Good luck." She opened the door.

Zane turned to her before he entered the office. "I know you're just like everyone else here, but I want you to know that if I go missing it wasn't by choice." Dr. Cass didn't say anything and instead turned around.

It was just like the office from his recovered memory. Nothing had changed. It had the same books on the shelves, the same miniature waterfall, and the same small chairs, one on each side of the desk. He stayed standing, not that Mrs. Valentino had offered for him to sit.

"Hello, Zane. I really wish you hadn't received that part of the memory. This makes things more difficult." Her blonde hair was in tight curls, a familiar red lipstick coating her lips. She was sitting in the chair behind the desk, her elbows propped on the arm chairs.

"Dr. Cass said you could explain why you threatened to kill me and Max." Zane's voice was laced with crippling doubt.

"That was after you left the Evermoving." She sighed. "You were still the enemy at the time. We weren't actually going to kill two teenagers. We just had to make you believe it."

Liar! His mind screamed.

"You burned down a carnival," Zane snapped. "Explain that."

She leaned forward, her hands clasped together. "No one was hurt." Eventually she stood up, her eyes darkening with a realization. "Nothings going to change your mind about me being a monster." It wasn't a question. "You never used to have a good intuition, but you managed to see through me this time. Congratulations, Zane." Her eyes seemed to gleam. "You're finally going to find out what Level Zero is all about."

Zane took a step backwards. He doubted Max had Level Zero in mind when he said he was going to help Zane escape.

"You remember it?" She didn't look surprised. She reached forward, her hand sliding under the desk.

"The guards will be here in a moment. I really wish we could have done things differently." The leader of the Evermoving narrowed her eyes at him. "We could have avoided so much pain and suffering. However, I'm kind of relieved. It will be so much easier to rip the memories right out of your little head."

He tore open the door and made a run for the exit. She let him. He couldn't wait for Max. Zane ran past his room, stopping in front of the two stairways. He slid down the railing of the stairs, wobbling when he landed on the floor. Zane rushed forward, and his hands managed to brush against the glass doors. Zane could see a gap in the chain link fence, and he silently pleaded for it to be big enough to squeeze through. Just as he started to open the doors, hands wrapped around his limbs. They dragged him back toward the elevator.

"NO!" Zane shouted. "LET ME GO!" He strained against them, flailing wildly. "LET ME GO!" They continued to drag him, and eventually, he tired himself out. Zane stopped struggling, the fight draining from his body.

He turned towards them and as a last resort said, "She's a murderer! How could you follow someone like that!" That was technically a lie. He'd never seen her lay a hand on anyone. Zane hesitated. He had nothing on her, besides a burned down tent. And even then he couldn't prove that happened.

The guards didn't listen, continuing to drag him to the elevator. He was shoved inside, alone, and the doors closed. Gas started to come from the bottom of the elevator until it reached the top of the elevator. He held his breath for several minutes, but eventually, his lungs gave out. He breathed in some of the gray gas, causing him to collapse on the floor.

"Help." He mumbled, fingers twitching. "Help," he whispered. The elevator suddenly dropped, and the lights began to flicker. It was almost like it was falling. But it couldn't be. Soon enough it slowed down, but not fast enough for the landing to be painless.

He woke up inside of a small glass cage, shivering. Outside of the prison, he could see Dr. Valentino hunched over a monitor. Several of them had pictures of brain scans. *His* brain scans. The room was brightly lit, and there were several more doors. Zane and Dr. Valentino were inside a place that was small, barely fitting the two of them. It clearly wasn't the only room in Level Zero. *If* this place was Level Zero. As soon as he touched the glass, the computer monitor turned red. The lead scientist glanced at him and said something he couldn't hear before turning off the silent alarm. Zane touched the glass again, but the monitor stayed the same.

"Great!" he snarled. "Just great!" Zane kicked the glass several times, and Dr. Valentino gave him an unimpressed glance.

"Is this Level Zero?!" Dr. Valentino pressed a button on his computer. "Answer me you piece of sh—"

"Yes," Dr. Valentino interrupted, his voice coming from inside the glass box.

Zane flinched at the unexpectedly loud voice. "What do you plan on doing to me?"

"The same thing as before. Retrieve as many of your memories as possible and study the effects this amnesia has on your brain. If you'll excuse me, I need to get back to work. Dr. Cass says hi."

Click.

All of the noise from outside the glass completely disappeared. Max wouldn't be able to save him. Nobody would. Level Zero was a high tech facility. He wasn't sure how he knew, but there was no chance of escape. A memory trickled into his mind, slow at first.

Max and Gemma stood in front of him, keeping their distance. They had finally managed to track him down. Zane felt a hint of pride at the fact that he had managed to avoid them for so long. They both scowled at him from the end of the dark alleyway.

"This is getting kind of old," Zane said, his eyebrows raised. "You're both acting like I'm some sort of villain."

"Why did you go back to the Evermoving? I know they have some sort of blackmail against you, but I thought you and Max agreed to never return." Gemma shifted her feet, fiddling with her fingers.

"Yeah I know. But it's... It's not as easy for me to leave them," Zane muttered. "Just..." He took a deep breath in. "Stop coming after me. Please."

"You've been acting really weird lately," Max added, studying him intently.

Zane's thoughts drifted to what he had overheard. The blue lotus banner had been ingrained in his mind. Zane knew exactly what the Evermoving was trying to accomplish, and his only bargaining chip was information about the rebel group he had belonged to. He never should have investigated. He was pretty sure the information he had was the only reason that the Evermoving's leader kept him around. If he screwed up one more time, then... He didn't want to think about it, but his friends would no longer be safe.

"You can't keep running from us, Zane." Gemma took a step forward, causing Zane to tense.

"Yes. I can." As soon as they started to move toward him, he held up a hand. *"There are members of the Evermoving a block away. If you even take one more step toward me, then everything would have been pointless. I'm already trapped. I don't want you two to be as well."*

But why would they wipe his memory if they were after the information he had? Did they finally decide it wasn't worth it? None of it made sense. Did they wipe his memory just so he wouldn't share anything about the Evermoving's little secret? And why would they let Max keep *his* memory? He turned towards the monitor which showed a dramatic change in the brain scans and heart rate. It was almost like those ten seconds or so had changed him.

"What does that mean?!" Zane demanded.

Dr. Valentino turned the monitors away from him, giving him another unimpressed glance. After some more typing, Dr. Valentino abruptly stood up, looking around frantically. He turned towards the cell, tapped a key on the keyboard, and the glass turned opaque. Through what was supposed to be a sound-proof cell, he heard a siren. Was somebody coming to rescue him? His hopes rose.

But nobody came.

No one was coming to save him.

He was alone.

Completely and utterly alone.

Hours passed, and he had walked from one side of the cell to the other at least a thousand times. The upside to the glass cell was that there were no cameras. That meant that nobody would see the stream of tears that once again ran down his face. He felt a sort of shame. In all of the memories he recovered, and even the stories he heard, it seemed like he was this tough and completely fearless guy. His past self wouldn't have been having mental breakdowns daily. But he was also pretty sure his past self hadn't been held captive for weeks on end with no hope of escaping.

Zane sat down, burying his face in his arms. The fabric of his sleeves ended up soaked. He had felt hopeless before, but now the feeling slammed into him like a truck. He rubbed his arms to try and get some warmth back into his body, but it barely made a difference. Eventually the glass walls shifted into a clear color again, but he kept his face hidden. A gloved hand touched his shoulder, and he covered his face even more with his arms, dreading what would happen next.

"We need to leave. Now," the voice snapped.

"What are you talking about?" Zane whispered, eyes drifting towards the guard. He scooched away from what was probably a trap.

"Is the doctor going to run another one of his tests?" he asked, exhaustion leaking into his voice. The guard took off his mask, revealing a familiar face framed by black hair.

Zane stood up abruptly. "Is that really you?"

"Yes, and we have to leave!" Max said angrily. Oddly enough, he seemed to hold a personal hatred for Zane in his eyes. It was nothing like the mild annoyance from before.

"Ugh, I'm hallucinating aren't I?" Zane rubbed his eyes.

"You're not." Max tapped his foot impatiently.

Zane rolled his eyes. "Yeah, sure. Nobody just breaks into Level Zero. You're just a stupid hallucination. I can't believe I thought you would be able to help me escape," he muttered.

"I'm real!" Max shouted. "And if we don't hurry, we're going to get caught!"

He was real. Zane blinked slowly. Relief flooded his face. He proceeded to tackle-hug his old friend to Max's surprise. He awkwardly patted Zane's back.

"You don't have all of your memories back." Max let out a breath of air, and with it all of his anger towards Zane.

"What are you talking about?" Zane withdrew from the hug.

Max shook his head. "I'll tell you later. Let's just focus on escaping. Follow me." He put his mask back on, and flipped his hood over his head.

Zane trailed close behind, eyes looking for any signs of Dr. Valentino. They headed past the monitor, heading out the door Max had previously opened. A long hallway led to a stairway that led to yet another door. Small flashing lights were on the ceiling, but Max paid them no mind.

"Do whatever I tell you to," Max said, climbing down the stairs two at a time.

Zane bit back a mocking remark. He took a step back when he saw what was on the other side of the door. Huge screens were displayed on the sides of the walls. And the most frightening part of it all was the footage of Gemma. It was a recording of her in a street near the bar Tim and Troy frequented. Utter horror caused Zane to freeze.

"Don't just stand there! We have to go before they figure out you're gone!" Max grabbed his arm, dragging him forward. Max's head was turned, but Zane could have sworn he saw the same fear in his eyes. He avoided looking at the creepy and stalkery images, continuing to sprint across the lab. The siren started to blare again, and red lights lit up the room. This time Max was the one who froze in place.

"Max?" Zane glanced at him nervously. "What are you doing?"

Max shook his head, as if clearing fog from his brain. They stopped at a set of doors, and Max unlocked one of them with his keycard. After stepping through, they traveled down a series of hallways, until they reached a very familiar elevator.

"If I die, run to the large green vehicle," Max said as they went inside. When he inspected it further he realized it wasn't the same elevator. They weren't out of Level Zero yet.

"I don't know how to drive," Zane warned.

"You thought I was helping you escape alone?" Max asked, a hint of a smile lurking on his face. "Who do you think caused the diversion?"

His eyes widened in surprise. "The rebels?"

Max smiled briefly. "Yeah. The rebels." He leaned forward to press the only button in the elevator.

"You didn't bring me a weapon?" Zane asked nervously, as the elevator jolted upwards.

"That was before I knew you didn't have all of your memories back."

"What difference would that have made?" Zane muttered.

Max winced. "I'll tell you later."

Zane's thoughts drifted to the confrontation in the alleyway. "Thanks for getting me out of here."

"We're not out of here yet." Max pointed out.

"But you're risking a lot." The thought of what the Evermoving's leader could do made him shudder. "They could wipe your memory if you're caught. Or worse."

Max shrugged. "I'm more concerned about what they'd do to you. Almost escaping out of their high security building twice?" He shook his head. "That has to be a record."

"You're seriously not worried about being caught?" Zane's lips twitched upwards.

"I mean... Kind of." Max frowned. "I'm kind of used to this stuff now. You don't really remember, but I can be kind of an adrenaline junkie."

"In all of my memories you seemed terrified." Zane teased. "Especially when we were stowaways on The Annabeth." He snickered. It felt strange to talk to Max outside of a memory.

Max's eyes widened. "What else do you remember?" He

seemed genuinely curious, a question from a friend instead of an interrogation.

"We went to high school together as transfer students," Zane grinned. "I don't remember everything but I do know we were assigned a really easy English assignment." His grin faltered. "Before the Evermoving found us." Zane added quietly.

Max laughed. "Yeah, well they didn't catch us that time." He leaned against the elevator hand railing. "Believe it or not, they never captured us. At least until you turned yourself in."

"That was a stupid decision." Tears pricked the corners of his eyes, and he folded his arms across his chest. "How exactly did you get out with your memory intact anyway?"

Max shrugged. "I wasn't the one with secrets."

The door opened before Zane could say anything else. Panic swirled around his chest like a tornado. Members of the Evermoving were in this part of the lab. He glanced at Max, waiting to see what the plan was. He simply walked past them, Zane following closely behind. Surprise lit up his eyes when he noticed they were asleep. One of them had his head on a notebook, drool gathering in his sandy-blonde hair.

"How long have you been planning this?" Zane glanced around at the various vials and pills, although he had no idea what everything was for.

"We work well under pressure." Max hesitated. "And we've been trying to get into Level Zero for a while."

"Isn't this place supposed to be super secure and impossible to break into?"

One of the members of the Evermoving raised their head, eyes drifting groggily to them. She was sitting on a black chair, fingers gripping a pencil. "Not anymore." Max hit her on the back of the head with the barrel of his gun. Zane couldn't help but laugh, although it was without humor. Max squinted at him, silently urging Zane to explain why he was laughing.

"Is that the only thing you know how to do? Smack people in the back of their heads?" His thoughts drifted to when Max had done the same thing to him.

He rolled his eyes. "I had to make it believable."

"The guards seemed to follow your example."

Max's face scrunched up with guilt as he tore a hand through his hair. He said nothing, and they continued to walk to the end of the second lab, until they reached a filling room. The walls were painted a light brown, and every single cabinet was labeled with things like Frontal Lobe, Legal Work, and something that really caught his attention was... Experiments.

"Uh there's nothing in here." Zane pointed out.

Max kept his face emotionless as he stepped forward and opened one of the older cabinet drawers with a torn off label. He tried to pick up one of the folders, but it was stuck. The filing cabinet suddenly started moving to the right, revealing another elevator door. Max turned around, an innocent smile on his face.

"Shut up." Zane said, eyes narrowed.

Max held up his gloved hands. "I didn't say a thing."

Zane stepped into the hidden elevator. By the end of this he was going to be sick of them. Actually, he was pretty sure he preferred stairs at this point.

"Do you have any other memories of me?" Max asked as the cabinet and elevator door started to close.

Zane adjusted the collar of his shirt. "I have a few of you, Gemma, and me but..." He blew a breath of air out. "I also remember that at one point I was the only one left on the side of the Evermoving, against my will." Zane avoided his gaze.

"Hm." Was that why Max had looked so angry before figuring out Zane didn't have all of his memories? Was it because of whatever choice he had made?

"Did I really treat her that badly?" Zane blurted. "When Gemma and I were dating I mean."

"Yeah," Max murmured. "You did. It just feels like I'm talking to a stranger right now. You look like Zane, you have the same mannerisms but..." He shuddered. "You don't really know me, and I don't really know you anymore, because you're technically not him without the memories. And it's freaking me out."

The old elevator finally started moving.

"I am Zane!" He elbowed Max in the side. "How else would I know the code words?"

"No." His forehead wrinkled. "I mean yeah, but it's not the same."

His stomach tied itself into knots. "Yeah. I guess it isn't." Zane whispered.

CHAPTER
TWENTY-EIGHT

G unshots ricocheted off of metal. Guards surrounded a military grade vehicle in a smaller version of the Level One parking garage. The garage looked similar enough to the Level One version, although the doorway to the tunnel was open. Not to mention dozens of weapons and cargo were being stored here.

"Get out of the vehicle!" one of the guards shouted, his rifle pointed towards the driver's side. He was on top of a green jeep, oblivious to the now open elevator.

"Stay here," Max told him, as he raised his gun to shoot. Zane watched as Max shot three of the guards in the head. They fell forward, blood gushing onto the concrete. He tried shooting again, but the gun remained silent. Max set the gun back in the holster, making him wonder who else had been shot. Max slid behind a blue truck when bullets started to fly towards him.

One of the guards who had been shot was still alive, the crumpled figure twitching. Zane's eyes widened and he covered his mouth with one hand to avoid vomiting. He ducked behind the elevator wall, hiding from the guards and violence. Zane closed his eyes tightly when Max started shooting again. He must have had more ammo for the gun. Zane really hoped that was Max shooting. Shouts broke out, and he heard the escape vehicle flare to life. Once everything was quiet he peeked out, anxiously scanning the area. He glanced towards the rebels, who started cheering when they saw him. A blue-haired woman opened the driver's seat, her feet planting on the concrete. She had a button nose and delicate features, the opposite of her outfit. Baggy ripped jeans covered her tiny frame and she wore a half-tucked in tank top.

"Get in the back you two! The others will be at the meetup place!" she said, already getting back inside. The man in the driver's seat saluted him, his spiked hair falling over his eyes. His nose was slightly crooked, and freckles dusted his face. Zane avoided looking at what he assumed were dead people, as he sprinted toward them. Max ran alongside him, a drop of blood running down his face. Zane genuinely felt like avoiding everything gruesome for the rest of his life. But that wasn't possible was it? They hopped into the back of the escape car, shutting the doors immediately. Zane resisted the urge to shove them open again. He didn't want to feel trapped again. But he knew the doors were unlocked. He had the option of leaving, not that he wanted to. The only thing that was missing was a tranquilizer dart. He sat down at the back of the van next to Max. They started moving, the vehicle jumping after running over some rocks. At least he hoped they were rocks.

He glanced at where he thought Max was. It was hard to see in the almost pitch black trunk. The window on the side sort of helped. "We really escaped?" Zane asked, his voice hushed.

"Not yet," Max admitted. "As soon as we get out of this tunnel, we'll be fine."

"When did you get so relaxed about breaking into the Ever-moving's facility?"

Max sucked in a breath. "Can I tell you a secret?"

Zane frowned. "Sure?"

"I'm not. It just gets easier after doing stuff like this so often." His fingers curled into a fist. "I wasn't sure whose side I was on, and now that the conflict is gone it's not as bad. Still scared though." Max held out his hand, which he noticed shaked every once in a while. Zane wanted to ask about the now dead bodies in Level Zero, but he wasn't sure if Max wanted to even think about it. He had done that to save Zane, and he wasn't sure how he would ever repay Max. Or look at him the same. The strong morals clinging to his heart loosened, in a bittersweet way.

"Hey." Max nudged him with his work boot. "Stop worrying. It's freaking me out." He wrinkled his nose, his face the only thing Zane could see since he wore dark colors.

"Is that something I don't normally do?" he asked dryly.

To his surprise, Max nodded. "You always had an ego-like confidence. Almost like you were untouchable."

Zane brought his knees to his chest, his hands gripping his hair. "I wish I had that again. I feel like a weird husk of who I used to be. A part of me didn't really want to leave, if it meant I got my memories back," he added quietly, instantly regretting it.

Max's eyebrows shot up. "Why are you telling me this?"

"Being kidnapped kind of drained me of my paranoia," he muttered.

"Paranoia? That's one thing that stayed the same." Max snorted. "It took you years to trust me."

"What are some other things you remember about me—" The vehicle came to a screeching halt, sending Max and Zane flying forward. Several curse words were uttered. Max got to his feet, turning towards Zane.

"Stay here," Zane said for him.

Max tried opening the door but the vehicle started moving again. "That was weird."

Zane knocked on the wall separating them from the driver and the other passenger.

"Everything is fine!" A muffled voice said.

"Okay!" Zane called back. He wasn't going to be experimented on anymore. He laughed, a smile creeping up on his face.

"What's up with you?" Max squinted at him. "That's the second time you've laughed like a psycho."

"Nothing." Zane took a deep breath in, and for the first time in weeks he felt good. Tired and hungry but good.

"Where are we going exactly?" he asked.

"You'll see." He paused. "One of the higher ups will fill you in on everything when we get there." Max took off his gloves, tossing them on the ground. He unwrapped the bandages on his hands, placing them where the gloves landed.

Zane sat back down. "When will I see the Smith's again?"

Max looked at him, doubt in his gaze. "I don't know."

A certain blonde-haired girl crept into his thoughts. "What about Gemma?"

"Hopefully." Max sat down beside him, placing a hand on Zane's shoulder. "I haven't seen her for a long time. How is she?" he asked.

"She's acting like she's fine, but I don't think she is. The last time I saw her she was..." He trailed off, suddenly tensing. "Inside of Dr. Sandra's office. I completely forgot!" Zane slid down the back wall, covering his face with his hands. "Ugh. I hope she's okay."

"Isn't that where you got captured?" Max asked.

"Yeah. She was actually underneath the desk when I got taken away."

"You're lucky she wasn't taken away as well," Max said, his tone even.

Zane shot up. "She wasn't, right? Things got a little fuzzy after I was hit with the tranquilizer dart." The vehicle jostled when they drove onto what felt like a highway.

"No. As far as I know she made it out without a fight."

"Why did we join the Evermoving?" Zane had a vague idea from his memories, but he still wasn't sure.

Max shrugged. "We were lost little kids with no sense of purpose. That purpose was given to us, but we got wrapped up in situations like this."

"What kind of situations?"

Max shook his head. "Doesn't matter."

"It does to me," Zane shot back. "If you won't tell me about it, at least tell me why we left the Evermoving in the first place."

"We were being stupid rebellious teenagers who thought the adults were strict. We thought it was cruel that they trained us to be agents, or spies, or whatever you want to call it. But it was long after we joined. That wasn't enough for us to question our loyalty to them. And in a way they were looking out for us. Teaching us to defend ourselves, be wary of the people around us... We never asked for a normal life. But we found files containing our progress, and they had details about private areas of our life, so naturally we ran." Max shrugged. "The files contained information about our personalities, favorite food, phycological issues, everything in between. Including things we didn't even know about ourselves. So we chose to run."

Time seemed to slow down when he found himself on the roof of the vehicle, Max halfway suspended in the air. It didn't stop there. He found himself on the wall, back on the floor again, and finally back on the roof. His breath had been snuffed out like a flame, and it took him a few more moments to process. The vehicle had been flipped over. Zane tried to sit up, but his entire body felt like it was covered in fire ants. He turned his head to look at Max, who was in a similar state, his eyes half-closed in pain. Zane muttered a curse word, forcing himself to crawl towards the doors. He fidgeted with the latch until they opened, revealing familiar city buildings. Through blurry vision, he saw muddy boots stomping towards him, and he winced.

The Evermoving had found them.

CHAPTER
TWENTY-NINE

The two pairs of boots stopped right in front of his face, one of them crouching down in front of him.

"Are you two okay?!" The two rebels asked at the same time, their words too loud for his still ringing ears.

He relaxed. "Is..." He coughed, his face scrunched up in agony. "Did the Evermoving do this? I think I broke a rib..."

"Uh. Sort of. I'm Millie. I'm pretty sure the Evermoving managed to attach something to the bottom of the car. Whatever it was caused our vehicle to flip over. They didn't follow us so don't worry." There were a few gashes on her face, but Max and Zane were worse off. His eyes shifted to the spiky haired guy.

"Sean." He nodded at Zane before creeping further inside the back of the van, helping Max to his feet. Zane's injuries were pretty bad, but Max... His eyes were droopy, and with every movement Max's face scrunched up with pain.

"Are we far from the meet up place?" Zane asked. "I'm not sure if Max will be able to make it." He glanced over at the pointing pedestrians. Several of them had their phones out. If they didn't hurry the police would get involved. He stood, using the trashed van as support. Zane took a few wobbly steps forward.

"It's close enough." Sean narrowed his eyes at an approaching pedestrian.

"Are you guys okay?!" His family watched from a nearby sidewalk, the mother holding their young children's hands. Instead of being scared, the kids looked fascinated by the crash.

"We're fine," Millie told him.

"You don't look fine. Let me drive you to the nearest hospital. My name is Dave by the way."

Zane could hear the faint sound of sirens. The police were going to arrive soon.

"Thank you, Dave, but we're fine. Our friend is going to pick us up in a few minutes." The lie slipped off of Sean's tongue effortlessly. "Besides, it's only a few scrapes and cuts."

"What about him?" Dave pointed at Max. Max's head fell forward, his eyes barely open.

Sean lifted Max's chin. "Nah. He's fine, aren't you, bud?"

Max lifted his hand and gave a thumbs up, along with a smile-grimace mix. "Yup." His words sounded like they were being put through a cheese grater. A crowd was gathering around the crashed vehicle. The police would only slow them down enough for the Evermoving to catch them.

Zane sighed. "You know what? We'll take that ride."

The four of them piled into Dave's car. Zane sat in the back next to Millie and Max. Sean took the passenger seat. Although he seemed like he wanted to get them to a hospital as soon as possible, Dave still followed traffic laws and only went a few miles above the speed limit. A cloud of awkwardness filled the mini cooper.

Dave turned on the blinker as they waited for the red light to turn green. "If you don't mind me asking, what happened to you guys?" A tiny hula dancer bobbed back and forth on the dashboard.

"We mind," Sean snapped.

"What he meant to say," Millie shot a glare at Sean, "was thank you. But we're not even sure ourselves." Max was still silent, his head resting against Millie's shoulder.

Dave pulled in front of the hospital. "Alright. I have to get back to my family. I hope you guys will be okay. I'll be praying for all of you."

Zane opened the car door, followed by Millie and Max. Sean joined them seconds later and they watched Dave drive away. His kindness had been refreshing after spending such a long time with the Evermoving.

"We're not actually going into the hospital, right?" Zane waved at the disappearing mini cooper.

"Nope. Not unless you LIKED being held captive by the Evermoving." Sean moved toward an unoccupied car. "Do you remember how to start up a car without keys, Millie?"

Zane frowned, not okay with the idea of stealing a car. But there weren't really any other options. Sean picked up a rock from the side of the road, taking a few steps back before chucking it at the passenger window. The glass shattered, gaining attention from the people around them. He opened the door from the inside, pressing a button to unlock the other doors. Max was set in the back, and Millie took the wheel. This time Zane took the passenger seat, avoiding the broken glass on the leather seat. After messing around with a few wires, Millie managed to start the car.

"Will Max be okay? He's looking a little pale." Zane twisted around in his seat, eyeing Max with worry.

Millie's eyebrows twitched upward in surprise. "You really don't remember anything do you?" She began driving past the pointing civilians. Zane was beginning to think Millie and Sean were idiots. Both the police and the Evermoving would be after them.

Zane shifted awkwardly. "No. Why?"

She shook her head. "It's nothing. Zane would just be focused on other things besides, as you would put it, collateral damage." He chose to ignore what she said.

Sean poked Max in the side. "He's breathing. He has the worst morning breath, but other than that I think he'll be alright."

Zane laughed, instantly regretting it when a bomb seemed to explode against his ribs. "Please don't make me laugh. It hurts too much." He missed Gemma in this instance. She would have made jokes that made everything a little less... Terrible. Zane's chest ached when he pictured her mischievous smile, the way her eyes always crinkled, and the way she laughed...

Millie laughed softly. "Yeah. Sure thing, Zane."

"Don't you have a way of contacting the other rebels?" Zane's stomach grew sour at the thought of seeing them.

Millie squinted at Zane as she turned right. "Rebels? What do you mean rebels?"

"I don't have a better term for whatever we are," Zane muttered.

"No way! If we were captured and they found a phone or anything else it wouldn't have ended well. The vast amount of scientists and people with all sorts of degrees could have found us using anything. Even a simple radio or burner phone," Sean explained.

Zane frowned. "I thought those were untraceable."

Millie closed her eyes. "Not to them." She quickly opened them, her eyes scanning the streets. "We'll just have to hope we get there in time."

"We should hurry then." The soft rumbling of the car did nothing to calm his nerves.

"And pray that the Evermoving didn't follow us," Sean said under his breath.

CHAPTER
THIRTY

Z ane grew confused when they pulled into a very familiar alleyway. The back entrance to the bar Tim and Troy frequented was on the other end.

"Why are we at a bar?" he asked.

"To grab a quick drink on the way!" Sean shoved open the car door. "That was sarcasm by the way." He helped Max out of the car, slamming the door shut.

"I could tell," Zane muttered, following them to the back entrance. Millie shut off the compact car, following close behind.

The color drained from his face. "Are Tim and Troy seriously a part of whatever we are?"

Millie hesitated, her hand hovering over the entry door. "Sort of. They own the bar together as friends. And they let us use the back room for whatever. It's cheap and those two wouldn't tell on us if their lives depended on it."

"And there aren't any security cameras," Sean added.

Millie pushed open the door, and obnoxious music blasted from inside. They made a beeline toward the bar, slipping into the employee room. The bartender didn't even spare them a

191

glance. Once the door behind them was locked, Zane exhaled in relief. The room was slightly dark, and almost empty except for a few chairs in the corner. Max was set down on one of them.

"I thought we were supposed to meet someone here?" When Zane saw Millie and Sean weren't going for the second chair, he took it.

The door opened, and someone walked in. "You actually managed to break him out. That's impressive." Dr. Smith looked him dead in the eye.

No.

No, no no no.

It was impossible.

But...

She was standing right in front of him.

The voice really did belong to Dr. Smith.

Zane quickly stood up, ignoring the pain that shot through his ribs. He wanted nothing more than to slam his fists into the walls. But he kept his composure. His eyes shifted to Trent who was behind her. "Why didn't you guys tell me we were meeting *these* two?" Zane's shocked expression turned into a furious scowl. Sean and Millie didn't say a word, instead avoiding eye contact.

"It only took you twenty minutes being unsupervised to get yourself kidnapped," Trent commented, but his familiar expressions were gone. Because the whole thing was an act, wasn't it? All a part of some manipulative script.

Zane took a shaky breath in. "Of course, you two weren't real doctors," he murmured, gaze hardening. "You all better start explaining everything." Zane's gaze shifted to everyone in the room. "*And* give me a reason to trust you."

Max shifted in his seat, inhaling sharply from the pain. "We just saved you from the Evermoving," Max protested, his voice still weak. He was the only one at the moment Zane could listen to without getting the urge to strangle someone. "And besides they were just looking out for you."

"By lying and manipulating me!" Zane bit back, his voice whinier then he meant for it to be. "I don't want excuses." He rubbed his temples, a headache slowly creeping up on him.

After all that they'd done and said, Trent and Dr. Smith had the decency to look guilty. They didn't apologize, however.

"What did you tell the Evermoving?" Trent asked, shame swimming in his eyes.

Millie groaned. "Trent, just relax." So he didn't lie about his name. "He just escaped from the Evermoving and he spent weeks in there, so spare the interrogation for later. He's fragile right now."

Trent opened his mouth once again, but surprisingly listened to Millie. He clearly had respect for both Millie and Sean.

"Fragile!? I'm not fragile!" he protested.

"Yes you are," Mille countered.

"No I'm no—" Zane started to say, but was cut off by Sean.

"You were poked and prodded by scientists, so shut up, Zane." Sean pointed at him, eyes narrowed. "And considering how you clearly haven't eaten in a while..."

Zane dragged a hand down his face, the skin stretching. "Yeah, whatever you say." He started pacing around the room. "I'm still really pissed off!" Zane threw his hands in the air. "Has there been a single person who hasn't lied to me?!" His anger simmered down slightly when he remembered Gemma. Zane really missed her.

"Don't you think that's a little hypocritical?" Dr. Smith took a step further into the room. Zane found himself shifting slightly toward the exit. "That used to be the only thing you did."

"No. I don't think it's hypocritical because I don't remember doing that," Zane said through his teeth. "Look. I get that you two were looking out for me or whatever..." He made his voice especially high-pitched and mocking. "But after everything that has happened, I don't want to be a part of the Evermoving or whatever you guys are. And besides..." Zane's gaze shifted between Trent and Dr. Smith. "You two did a terrible job." They both opened their mouths as if they were about to say something. His gaze darkened, as he edged closer to the door. "Want me to give you a few examples? There was a member of the Evermoving in the same cafeteria as the three of us. I have no doubt that you saw him, but you didn't do anything to stop him from stealing the surveillance footage. Another thing. You brought me directly to Dr. Sandra's office without investigating anything! You know, the place I was literally kidnapped at! Yeah you two really did a great job of protecting me." Zane's fingers twitched toward the exit. Every part of him wanted to run and not look back.

Trent frowned. "We'll make up for our past mistakes," he said carefully. "Trust me when I say we'll try our best to ensure nothing like the kidnapping incident happens ever again. And right now we'll explain everything. Starting from the beginning."

Zane folded his arms over his chest. "Okay."

"You're aware that you ran from the Evermoving, correct?" Trent asked. Zane nodded. "Part of the Evermoving's system is leaving behind no evidence. You and Max were loose ends. It wouldn't have mattered because the Evermoving could have destroyed any trace of your existence. However..."

"I had information they didn't want anyone else to know. I'm aware. Why do they want me to gain my memories back if that's true?" Zane focused his eyes on the ground.

Dr. Smith spoke this time. "We believe that some members of the Evermoving were trying to get you to remember certain things. Things that would make you want to go back to their side. You did a lot of great things for them. No one wants to give up someone like that if they have to. But not everyone agrees on subjects regarding you, Zane. And that became apparent when you went back to their side. Not everyone agreed with that decision. So some people decided to wipe your memory. And they did."

Millie turned toward Zane. "The Evermoving is careful, and always a few steps ahead of us. They likely erased any proof of whatever memories are in your head. And that's one of the reasons you should trust us. Whatever hidden memories are in your head... They're useless to us."

CHAPTER
THIRTY-ONE

The twitching in his fingers stopped, and he relaxed slightly. "But if I'm useless why am I here and not rotting in Level Zero?"

Trent pressed his lips together. "About that. Wherever you were being held wasn't Level Zero."

"Max said—" Zane started to say.

"Yes, we've been trying to break into Level Zero," Max interrupted. "But I never said I actually broke into the place."

"The Evermoving's leader told me directly I was being taken to Level Zero," Zane muttered. "That still doesn't explain why you helped me escape. It was a great subject change though."

Sean leaned against one of the beaten-up walls, his nose crinkling. "Well, even if we can't use you, at least the Evermoving can't. That and it was sort of convenient. Max was working as a double agent long before you were kidnapped. He already got all the information he could."

Zane sighed. "So you guys helped me because... It was convenient."

"And sentimentality played a role," Dr. Smith admitted.

"Despite your past of questionable choices, there are people that still care about your well-being."

"I'm not being held captive, correct?" Zane took another step toward the exit.

"Correct..." Millie's blue eyebrows furrowed together.

"If you guys can't use me, and the Evermoving no longer has me captive, I'd like to leave all of this behind me. I don't care how my past self lived for the whole escaping and explosions kind of thing. It's over. I'm going somewhere far far away." Zane took a deep breath in and turned his back on them, reaching for the doorknob.

"Zane..." He stiffened, turning toward Dr. Smith. She looked at him with a mix of sorrow and concern. "It's not over." Zane looked toward Max for confirmation.

"Remember the footage of Gemma we saw? They might go after her next." Max's words sent Zane on a dizzying roller coaster. Despite the jagged turns his mind was taking, Zane was deathly still. He had almost forgotten about that.

Zane stepped back into the room. "Okay. But after we get Gemma away from danger, I'm done. Understand?"

Trent winced. "It's not that easy. The Evermoving is watching her every movement. We have to wait for the right moment.

Sean scoffed. "If you ask me, we need to get her out of harm's way as soon as possible."

Zane sighed. "Okay. So what can we do now?"

"First, we're going to go somewhere we'll all be safe," Dr. Smith explained. "Preferably soon, because Max needs medical attention."

Millie helped Max to his feet, supporting half of his weight. For the first time he noticed the flower tattoo on her shoulder. "Congratulations, Zane. You're about to discover where all six of us at one point used to work. For the second time."

Zane frowned. "You guys better explain more on the way."

"We will." Sean brushed past him, opening the door. "Don't get all huffy about it. We already wasted enough time." He clapped his hands together. "Vamanos!" Sean's accent sounded like he practiced frequently. The obscene music, without being muffled by the door, was loud. Zane followed closely behind Sean, Millie and Max being the last ones out. They were glared at on their way to the back entrance, which was expected. Their group was kind of odd, between Millie and Sean with their odd hairstyles and tattoos, Trent and Dr. Smith who were dressed like they attended church on a regular basis, and... Max who looked completely wasted at first glance. Trent was the one to push open the door, and Zane gladly breathed in the fresh air. Instead of asking questions he followed the others to a large blue truck. Zane ended up squished in the back with Millie, Sean, and Max.

Trent started the truck, before turning the wheel. "Zane before we reach this place you should probably know more about what exactly we are. And who the Evermoving is." Trent didn't wait for a response. "The easiest way to explain it is that the Evermoving is kind of like a form of CIA or FBI that got corrupted from the inside. And that leads me to what exactly Beatrice, Sean, Millie, and I are. We're exactly what the Evermoving is. We're part of a nameless group founded to prevent the Evermoving from behavior that is illegal or morally unjust."

"Like what?" Zane demanded, gripping the car seat when Trent made another turn.

"Like whatever they're doing in Level Zero."

Zane exhaled slowly. "Which is why you're trying to break in there. I can't imagine what they're doing, especially after what happened." His voice wavered without his permission. "Max knows. They triggered some of my memories in a really weird way. As in painful and excruciating." He left out the part where he let them do it. "It worked sort of but I think the machine was killing me." The only noise was the rumbling of the truck. "It just kept getting worse, especially after Dr. Sandra left." One side of his face lifted in contempt. "Just from what I've seen, I can't imagine what's in Level Zero."

Millie tilted her head at him, studying him in what seemed to be a different light. "And you managed to get through it without any previous knowledge of withstanding torture of that degree."

Zane shifted uncomfortably. Using the word torture made it so much worse. But that was true. He had been tortured.

Manipulated

Starved.

Hit.

Abused.

Zane looked out the window as they headed further into the city. A thought dug into him like a kitten's needle sharp claws. His first memory of torture was still very clear in his head. "Dani and Tom. Will they be at this place as well?"

He could see Trent frown in the rearview mirror. "The new recruits? Probably. How did you hear about them?"

"They kidnapped me." Even after all that happened, everyone in the car managed to achieve a flabbergasted expression.

It was Dr. Smith who broke the shocked silence. "WHAT?!" Trent swerved slightly when he heard the shout. Nearby cars honked at the truck. "Sorry," she quickly added, twisting around in her seat so she could look at Zane. "Please accept my apology on their behalf. I want you to know it won't go unpunished. What happened?"

"Oh, you know." Zane laughed nervously. "They used chloroform out in the park by the apartment you guys used. I ended up tied to a tree. Then after that they asked all sorts of questions.

Actually they kind of..." He hesitated, unsure if he should continue. "Used a form of torture."

Dr. Smith's eyes narrowed. "I don't think you'll be seeing them for a while. They did that against orders." She twisted back around, facing the window. "Dani and Tom haven't even passed basic training," Dr. Smith added under her breath. "I don't think you understand the severity of the situation Zane. What they did should not be taken lightly. It is disobedience of the highest order. It's not like they joined our cause easily. They had to agree to certain terms and conditions. They even signed something. I don't think you understand what this means for them and I hope you know that those two will have nothing to do with us from now on. And if anyone at all gives you any trouble besides a few snarky comments just let us know. They all have certain rules they have to go by. We told them that they can only talk to you and there will be no abuse or negative talk of any kind. Although we can not stop anyone from giving you weird looks, Zane."

"I don't expect anyone to treat me kindly. Obviously my past self did a lot of messed up stuff that they probably wouldn't forgive me for even if I apologized. Profusely." Zane glanced out the window as the car made another turn. He wondered what the workplace actually looked like. Or if it was just some dump. He wasn't even sure if the rebels had any sort of funding.

"Do Troy and Tim know about this place?" Zane asked.

"Nope," Trent said. "They've asked a few questions about what we really do but they mostly leave the issue alone. Unless you told one of them."

"I wish I knew if I did or not," Zane admitted. "But who knows. Amnesia kinda sucks." He exhaled slowly, his fingers rubbing his temple. "How far away is this rebel base place?"

Millie spoke this time. "Far. We can't exactly have a place right next to the Evermoving. They've been looking for us for a long time." Millie still had Max leaning against her shoulder and Zane really hoped that she was exaggerating for his sake.

"They could be following us," Zane pointed out. "Shouldn't we be more careful?"

Trent snorted. "I doubt it. I'm pretty sure we lost them a long time ago."

A memory suddenly struck him, and he found the car disappearing around him. Slowly colors came into his vision and he was surrounded by familiar walls.

Zane looked around the interrogation room, his gaze landing on Mrs. Valentino. She looked worse for wear, and her normally blonde hair was turning brown at the roots. "Zane, we're giving you one last chance. And then that's it. No second chances. No third chances."

He focused his gaze on the interrogation table, his mind turning like rusty wheels. "Okay." The word seemed weightless despite the colossal consequences it would bring.

Mrs. Valentino's lips curled into a smirk. "That means no more contact with the rebel base. No contact with Max or Gemma. You know that right?"

Zane nodded. "I know. I accept that." He didn't really. He just needed to make her believe that. Zane wanted to make up for his mistakes. And he was going to do that.

The memory was ripped from his mind, and the real world flooded back to him. He blinked rapidly to adjust to the new surroundings.

"Was that a memory?" Dr. Smith's words were strangely echoey, slowly becoming louder. "Or are you struggling not to fall asleep?" Her last words took on a teasing tone.

Zane shrugged. "A memory I guess. They never make any sense without context. It's like being given a board game but without the rules to play." However, it was of some comfort that in the end he truly was on Max and Gemma's side. It eased some of the crushing guilt he felt on a daily basis.

"Hey are you guys hungry?" Dr. Smith opened the dashboard, revealing various snacks. She grabbed a bag of trail mix and reached around the seat. Zane snatched it, and the thought of food made him increasingly aware of his stomach trying to eat itself. The stress of escaping the Evermoving had almost made him forget about how they had starved him. He tore open the bag and grabbed a handful to shove into his mouth. It tasted like the best thing he'd ever eaten.

Dr. Smith handed back a few more bags. "We still have an hour before we're there."

Zane sighed. "The Evermoving isn't following us, right? Can't we stop to get medical supplies."

Sean nodded. "Actually that's a good idea. Max is looking a bit pale. Paler than normal I mean."

Trent tapped his fingers on the steering wheel thoughtfully. "Alright. I'll find a gas station." A few turns later and they arrived at a run down but still functioning pit stop. Trent headed inside the gas station while the truck was being filled. He could still hear the sound of traffic from the city, honking cars and pedestrians chattering. Trent arrived a few moments later with a handful of different supplies. He began to drive again until they reached a dark parking garage. They spilled out of the car and Sean lifted Max into the back of the truck.

"Alright buddy boy. Where does it hurt the most?" Sean asked beside him.

"My leg is killing me," Max admitted.

"Okay. Forgive me for ruining your modesty but the pants have to go."

Max sighed. While Sean bandaged and applied different treatments to Max's injuries, Zane continued to eat the snacks in the truck. It wasn't that he didn't care about Max. He was just really hungry. Zane could hear muffled screeches from Max, but he trusted that Sean knew what he was doing. He wouldn't be a part of the so called rebel group if he didn't. After eating almost seven bags of the trail mix, Zane sprawled out across the back seats. After the muffled screeching subsided they were back on the road again.

The rest of the trip was driven in silence. Zane thought about telling Dr. Smith to turn on the radio, but the mood was too gloomy for that. Then the car began to slow down. A large office-like building with three stories started to come into view. They pulled into a garage leading underground and the hairs on his skin prickled. It reminded him too much of the Evermoving's parking garage.

"Nice place." He tried opening the vehicle door, but it was locked.

Trent snorted and took the key out of the ignition, before unlocking the vehicle. "Yup, welcome back Zane. I think it's been a year since you were last here." He pressed the same button and the garage door began closing. He glowered as he stepped outside.

"Where is everyone?" Zane asked, scanning the parking garage. No one was inside.

Millie exited the vehicle as well, brushing her blue hair behind an ear. Her silver earrings glinted underneath the fluorescent lights. "You'll see." She helped Max out as well, supporting his weight.

The six of them headed towards a stairway leading up to a door and on the other side... Was chaos. Dozens of people of different sizes, colors, and vastly different outfits walked up and down stairways. Some of them wore disguises, so he couldn't tell what was real or not. Some held coffee mugs, and most carried guns they didn't bother concealing. The large room was similar to a lobby, with a large roof that made the space open. It was designed to function, and everything inside had a purpose. Not to mention this particular room had dozens of medals displayed on the walls. Not medals. Memorials for those who had been lost. He felt nothing. The names were exactly that. Just names. Zane knew he should probably feel sad but he was indifferent. Doors were slammed every few seconds, dozens of voices blurring together. But suddenly it stopped. They all turned towards Zane, making him shrink in on himself. They started whispering amongst themselves.

"He's back."

"He doesn't deserve to be here."

"When's he going to betray us again?"

"I can't believe they spent their time saving him."

"He could be useful."

"They should have dragged him in like a prisoner."

"They made the wrong decision."

"He's kind of sickly looking isn't he?"

"He's scrawnier than I remember."

"I hope I don't have to work with him."

"The youngest spy who's actually good at what he does. Too good. He's dangerous."

Sean coughed loudly. "Carry on. And don't let your superiors catch you gawking." Sean's voice shook them out of their trance, but every once in a while someone would stare at him.

Zane looked at Millie. "You were right. This is a lot worse than I expected," he whispered.

She nodded, giving him a half smile.

"Sorry there aren't any balloons," Sean said under his breath, although his tone implied that he wasn't. "You're safe now." Sean placed a hand on his shoulder. "So don't worry about it."

Zane hesitated. "Are you sure about that? The Evermoving probably has ways to get to me. There were witnesses, remember?"

Sean frowned. "What part of don't worry about it do you not understand?"

Zane took a deep breath in. "Let's just get Max somewhere he can recover."

Trent shook his head. "Not you. We were supposed to bring you straight to one of the higher ups, and not make any detours." Millie, who seemed annoyed with the discussion, whispered something to Dr. Smith. They took Max away, and Zane lost sight of him when he disappeared into the crowd.

Trent tried to reach for Zane and he moved out of the way. "Don't touch me." His body turned rigid.

Trent held his hands up. "Got it. Lead the way Sean."

Each step he took brought him further into the familiar workplace. And farther away from being normal. A spark of anger lit in his chest. He deserved normal. But what kind of teenager has amnesia, is a part of an organization aiming to take down secret villains, and gets kidnapped frequently?

Idiot. You put yourself in this situation. He thought, trailing after Sean.

"It's over, Zane. You can relax," Trent told him.

Zane nodded, snippets of calm building up until he could breathe normally again. Everything was going to be fine. He was fine. Max was fine.

Gemma might not be okay, Zane thought, his sense of calm shattered. His fingers curled into fists. He winced when a jolt of pain went through his hands, and he quickly uncurled them, a slight ache still remaining.

"What does this person want from me?" Zane's eye twitched as they went up the stairway.

"All he wants is to help you," Trent stated.

"And to make sure you're not dangerous," Sean added, despite the glare Trent gave him. "Plus I'm sure you have a few more questions, especially about who you used to be." After reaching the top of the stairs they headed down a long hallway.

The door was made from a rich hazelnut. A large silver

knocker was on the front, a small letter slot below it. Everything about it was strange, but he pushed his nerves away and raised his hand to knock. Zane knocked once, his face scrunching up in pain. He cursed, silently praying for his hand to stop hurting. Now that the adrenaline had worn off, he realized his ribs weren't in the best shape either.

Sean stepped forward. "Let me." He stepped forward, knocking three times with a two second space in between.

"Come in. Not you Sean. Just Zane."

He stiffened. He knew that voice. Zane threw open the door, and it slammed into the wall. He had to be hallucinating.

"Hey, Zane. Surprised to see me?"

THIRTY-TWO

"What?" The floor seemed to disappear beneath his feet. "No that's not—" Zane shook his head rapidly. "That's not possible." The office was small, with five tv screens on the wall, and a white chair in the middle of everything. The only thing in the room besides that was a green couch in the corner.

"Isn't it?" His dark hands were placed on his hips, his coffee-brown eyes staring right at Zane. The dirt smudged apron he normally wore was missing, replaced by a white shirt and black slacks. However the first two buttons on the shirt were undone, giving off a hint of his normal messy style. It really was Danny.

"You're a part of this place. I used to work for you. But why..." He trailed off, words failing him.

"Sit down. You probably need the breather. I heard you had a rough time with Evermoving." He gestured to a green couch in the corner, and Zane approached it, his mind numb. Smith sat next to him, a faint smell of plants and dirt wafting towards Zane.

"I have a lot of questions," he whispered.

"And I'll answer all of them." Danny chuckled. "You're tough you know that? After everything you went through you're still standing. You always have been, even when you first started working for me."

"I had Gemma," Zane said. "First question. What did you really mean when you warned me about Trent? It was something about making him angry."

"I'm surprised you still remember that. I did mean it. It hadn't just been part of the show." Danny put his hands behind his head, a serious look in his eyes. "Trent has a history of angry outbursts. He's never really liked you before."

"Do you actually work at that nursery?"

"Pretty much. I had to improvise when you got there, but luckily for us you didn't remember me."

"I still don't." Zane reached up to tear a hand through his hair but stopped. His injured hands wouldn't have been happy with him. "Tell me everything. And tell me about when I first started working for you."

Danny nodded. "I think I know a good place to start at. I doubt that the others told you about this yet. The Evermoving wasn't always bad. It started as a good cause. I was a part of the Evermoving too you know." Zane almost choked on his spit. "We wanted to help our country and she went too far. You know her as Mrs. Valentino." Danny's eyes darkened with a deep sadness. "The first thing I caught her doing was experiments that made people like you." Zane almost flinched at the words. "She experimented with the human brain, without my knowledge. You should have seen the people she was using. After the first few experiments, they were completely and utterly broken. Some braindead, the others with no personality left. No life experiences. At the end of the day, I was the only one left in the dark. Our original purpose was gone, replaced with... Something else.

She turned the organization into something sinister. You remember Level Zero right?"

Zane winced, the memory of the glass box still fresh in his mind. That had been bad enough. He couldn't imagine how much worse Level Zero was. "I know it exists."

"It was created after I left, which is why no one knows where it's located." Zane bounced his foot up and down, chewing on his inner lip. "Where you were being held was one of their other labs, and if you had been inside Level Zero, you wouldn't be sitting next to me right now." Smith stood up, took a remote from his vest pocket, and turned on the screens. A 3D model of the Ever-moving's base showed up. It was labeled EM. All of the rooms on the surface level, including the parking garage were extremely detailed. Except for the floors below the parking garage. Vague sketches filled the space underneath the parking garage, several question marks next to certain spaces. Large lettering at the bottom of the model read, 'Level Zero?' "Level Zero, we're assuming, is a secure holding facility for wanted men and women all over the world. Dangerous individuals that were hunted down by the FBI, government, you name it. But what these people don't know, is she uses them to experiment on. And the thing is you were the only one who knew exactly where it was."

He shook his head. "Not anymore."

"We have our theories but—" Danny sighed. "It could be anywhere. Once she removed me from the equation, things got much worse. She's clearly gaining a significant amount of money from this."

The ability to completely wipe out specific memories was insane. But what else was she doing with it?

"Soon after I found out, I left with some of the staff. I tried to talk to her but..." He pressed a button on the remote. It showed footage of the different rooms in the building they were currently in. Different people were putting on disguises, others taking them off, and it also showed a weapons room. "Here I am." He gestured around the room. "I created an organization with the world's best spies and agents to take her down. With help of course." Zane wrapped his arms around himself, the information making his head swim. "Decision Office Central. They decide what to do for all of the important stuff. I'm a part of that. Some people call us the Docs. Please don't, it's a very stupid abbreviation."

Zane fidgeted with his pant leg. "Who are the other Decision Office people?"

Danny blinked slowly, and several minutes passed before he said anything. "You'll find out soon enough, although it doesn't really matter."

Anger seemed to press against his head. "I thought you said you'd answer all of my questions?"

"Not that one." The corner of Danny's mouth lifted. "Do you have any others?"

Zane scoffed. "Yeah. When are we going to save Gemma?"

"Eventually. But right now we have to be cautious. She's being watched constantly according to Millie." It was exactly what Max had said.

"You already risked that with me!" he protested.

"Because you're the one the Evermoving wants. Not Gemma." Danny straightened. "You're also one of their lab rats that escaped. And they want you back. We're keeping you safe. Not to mention the information you store in your brain about their organization is something the Evermoving are scared of—"

Zane cringed, not wanting to hear the rest. "Yeah. Speaking of scared, why do people look at me like I'm some sort of monster? Is it really because I was a part of the Evermoving? Or is there something else?"

Smith set his hands in his pant's pockets. "That's a conversation for another day."

He tugged on his hair in frustration, barely feeling the pain. "You said you'd answer all of my questions."

"If you're sure that you're ready." Zane stood up, nodding his head eagerly, ready for anything Smith would say. "The reason they hate you so much, on top of betraying them is..." Smith looked away for a moment, a nervous, small smile on his face. "I'll just say it. It was before you worked for me. You've killed people, Zane."

He hadn't been ready for that.

THIRTY-THREE

D anny took a step towards him, the sharp smell of herbal plants not helping with his scattered brain. A tsunami of emotions crashed into him, and his head seemed to split open. Slowly fuzzy images knitted themselves together, but it all seemed to spin in circles. Sometimes the people flickered in and out of view, and other times they were perfectly clear. The memory almost felt incomplete. There were a few different figures but he couldn't make out their features or who they were.

"We were always on the same side. But I guess you turned out even more messed up than me." The voice came out distorted and like an echo.

Everything went blank, and he couldn't see anything. "Go ahead. Kill him." A deep, gravelly voice said.

"Nothing is wrong with me." His vision returned, and he looked at a mirror, only to see blood splattered on his face. Muffled voices filled the empty space, almost as if it had been ripped from his mind, like unwanted weeds. A horrible scream threatened to shatter his mind. He wanted the memory to end, but at the same time he wanted to see what happened. But the rest was fuzzy. Sometimes he saw

hints of color, but then it ended. Why couldn't he remember? The memory almost felt fake, composed of pure emotions. Smith waved a hand in front of his face, stopping when Zane blinked.

"I can't remember it." But he did feel guilt attached to what he couldn't fully remember. He really had killed people hadn't he? The worst part was, Zane was thankful the Evermoving had removed those specific memories.

Danny crossed his arms, his jaw tightening. "What?"

"Trying to kill people. I caught a few glimpses but it's almost like parts of the memory were..."

"Completely gone," Danny finished, letting out a frustrated sigh. "I might as well tell you. You already know pretty much everything anyway." He paused by the door, fingers hovering over the knob. "Max doesn't remember these things that well either. You're not the only one with a few missing spots in their brain. I don't think the Evermoving wants you to remember everything that happened either. Or whose lives you ended. Why else would they go far enough to make sure you don't remember at all?"

Max was missing some of his memory too? Why didn't he say anything? Zane's eyes shot to Smith. "But you're not certain?"

"Just a theory."

"I have one more question. I woke up covered in blood, with no memories. I need to know how it happened. I sort of got answers to this but I want the specifics." It had been the one question he had been craving to figure out. The question that had gotten him in so much trouble too. He couldn't believe he had almost forgotten to ask.

"I don't know," Danny said carefully. "We think that whatever procedure happened occurred in Level Zero. They're too careful to let anything slip."

Zane groaned. "Great. More stuff that no one knows. What exactly should I be doing here anyway? Secret agent spy stuff or...?"

He opened the door. "Ask Millie. She'll help you find something. Can you find your way to the medical room?" Zane suddenly grew self-conscious of what were probably scars and bruises on his face.

He was able to find Millie and Sean and they brought him to the medical room. Zane was told that Max was inside of the miniature hospital. There were dozens of beds pressed against the walls. Oddly enough there were no curtains separating the cots, giving the room an open look. The tile floor had several blood stains that had been scrubbed over and over again but hadn't come out. The result was a light red stain, half covered by a rubber mat. A man and a woman were getting disguises taken off, bits of stretchy material being pulled off of their skin. One of the men in charge of the medical practices took fake tattoos off of an older, olive-skinned woman. She looked twenty years younger when her double chin was removed.

But these people weren't why they were here. His eyes scanned the room for Max, widening when he finally found him. His eyes were closed, but he was breathing. An IV machine was attached to him, and one of the medical staff sat by him, scribbling notes down on a clipboard. Zane blew out a sigh of relief.

"Millie and I already got our injuries treated," Sean told him. Zane nodded, flexing his fingers, painful tremors running through them. Everything was going to be fine. His injuries didn't feel that awful. If only the stupid Evermoving hadn't blown up their getaway vehicle. His fingers curled into fists. He winced when a jolt of pain went through his hands, and he quickly uncurled them, a slight ache still remaining.

"Let's go." Sean adjusted his black jacket, kicking open the hospital door with his foot. "You'll finally get some time off. Isn't that exciting?" he asked, his voice monotone. He made jazz hands, a smirk on his face.

Zane side-eyed him as he exited the room, giving Sean an unimpressed look. It really was exciting. Almost scary. No. Terrifying. It was terrifying.

After taking X-rays of his skeleton, the doctors found out that some of his fingers, and the wrist on his right hand suffered from fractures, so his dominant hand was put in a cast, and the affected fingers in miniature versions of the chunky white material. Luckily everything else was just bruises, scrapes, and sore limbs. Zane sat on one of the hospital beds while the finger and wrist casts were carefully put on. He had been lucky compared to Max, who, according to the doctor, had a few broken ribs, a large amount of blood loss, and plenty of sprains. Millie and Sean visited soon after his casts were put on, although they didn't seem too happy about it. The man who helped him moved on to another patient, his demeanor switching from a sort of resentment to friendly.

"What are you two doing here?" Zane asked, not bothering to hide his exhaustion.

"We have to continue being your babysitters," Sean grumbled, eyes widening with annoyance.

"Both of you?" he asked skeptically.

Millie winced. "I guess."

"We have to guide you around since you remember literally nothing about this place. We were considered the best choices since we already spent so much time with you," Sean explained, pausing to yawn. "I don't know about you guys, but I want to sleep before I do anything else. I guess you'll get your old room back."

"Nobody took it?" Zane hopped off the hospital bed.

Sean shrugged. "Nobody wanted the room of a traitor. Plus it smells funny. Like sweat and guilt."

"Sean is lying. The guy you just talked to, Danny, was saving it for you in case you ever changed your mind. He always saw the best in you," Millie admitted, glaring at Sean. His spiked hair was slicked back, and his skin was still dewy from a recent shower. Zane stood, trying to figure out how to open a medical cabinet with the limited use of his hands. He opened it with his pinky and the finger next to it, before snatching a pair of scissors with his good hand. Millie and Sean watched him carefully.

"Where is my old room?" He remembered it vaguely from a recovered memory, but his past self hadn't been focusing much on where it was.

After dozens of twists and turns, and climbing more stairs than Zane thought was possible, they reached a plain wooden door. He twisted it open, revealing... An extremely plain room. There was no dust, and the bed was made. An old white shirt and black jeans were placed on top of it, along with socks, and briefs. Beat up shoes were sitting beside the bed. The open closet had nothing in it, except for a small walkie-talkie. The pair of scissors in his pants pocket felt heavier.

"Who cleaned it?" Zane took everything in, from the white paint that was slightly peeling, to the small window on the wall. On the other side of the glass was a view into a small alleyway created by two buildings being smushed together. And was there a rope hiding above the window? Somehow it was disappointing. He wasn't *that* boring was he? Where were the decorations that gave glimpses into his dare-devil personality? Where were the guns, knives, and secret files?

"Danny," Millie said, peering into the room. She seemed just as curious as Zane was. Sean stood outside the room, kicking the door frame out of boredom.

He froze. "Seriously? Why does he care so much?"

Sean snorted. "You were one of the top agents. But yeah, I wonder why." He rolled his eyes, kicking the door frame with added aggression. Sean took a step back, stretching his arms. "Alright, well there's food downstairs if you need it. There's an entire floor dedicated to it. You can't miss it. The showers are on the same floor." Zane nodded, still processing the plain bedroom. He expected something that would give him hints about his past. But no. Literally nothing.

"Goodluck," Millie said.

Once they left, Zane closed the door. There had to be something useful. He grabbed the Walkie-Talkie, but there was nothing but radio silence. He thought about saying something into it, but it seemed extremely short range. And he had no idea who the other radio belonged to. He decided to close the closet-door, the inside too depressing to look at. Zane opened the window, fingers grazing rope.

Zane threw the backpack out of the window, and it landed with a thump. It was a good thing he hadn't put any breakables inside. Max would arrive soon, and they had a limited time slot. He grabbed the rope coiled on his bed, twisting it around the metal loop above his window. He scaled down it, lifting the bag back over his shoulder. Zane was making the right choice. He knew it.

"Good luck," Max whispered. Zane's eyes shot towards Max, who threw him car keys, the faint light reflecting off of a nervous smile

He jolted forwards, his head hitting the window sill. The memory had presented itself in a new way. It was almost like he had been there, experiencing it. Zane hesitated. He could go get a shower and stuff himself with food. He already had so many answers to questions he had been asking since the beginning. But something about the walkie-talkie wouldn't leave his mind. Zane reopened the closet door, snatching the tiny device. He flipped it over, searching for something familiar. The only thing out of place was the small dent on the bottom right corner.

Zane blinked rapidly, pushing his bedroom door open. He hesitated, rushing back in to grab the change of clothes.

Somehow the memories he had recovered made zero sense. Were they before or after the carnival? Hopefully Max would be able to clear everything up. Plain doors like his lined the hall, but he walked past them, and towards the white staircase. He opened the door at the bottom, revealing a cafeteria-like room. Everything about it was different from the Evermovings. For one there was excited, loud chatter. Large white tables were in the center of the room, everyone's plates piled high with sugar-filled foods. No one gave him any odd looks despite his ripped clothes and bandage covered limbs. He noticed that he wasn't the only one. Dozens of the agents still had healing wounds, deep bags under their eyes. He let himself smile briefly. Part of him wondered whether they would act the same if they knew who he was. If they knew he was a traitor.

His thoughts drifted to when he first arrived, and to all the odd looks he got. A red haired woman made eye contact with him, first recognition sparking in her eyes. Then anger. He adjusted the clothes under his arms before discreetly jogging to the showers. The entrance was behind a wall, giving a small amount of privacy. He went inside the men's version, steam pressing against his face. It reminded him of a locker room, which included the wooden benches. Several of the showers were already running, each one covered by a curtain. He grabbed the garbage can by the entrance, before dragging it towards the mirrors. He set his clothes down on a bench, taking the scissors from his pocket. Zane looked at his hair in the mirror. It was greasy, unkempt, and he was looking forward to chopping it off. He learned over the can, bringing the scissors to his hair. There was something bittersweet about it. His hair was the only thing he had kept all his time. He did have his old clothes, but there were no memories attached to them. Zane took a deep breath in and made the first cut.

THIRTY-FOUR

"Catch!" A shirt was thrown at the back of his head. Zane turned towards the bedroom door, grinning. He grabbed the shirt off of his head, Millie reluctantly smiling back. She wore a gray tank top, and for the first time he could fully see the butterfly tattoo on her shoulder.

"Found em." She slung a black garbage bag onto his twin sized bed. "The rest of the clothes are in there. Good thing we didn't get rid of them."

The first night had gone smoothly, and he felt good. It helped that he had been getting regular meals again. His right hand had a cast, but he couldn't complain.

Millie sighed. "Zane, could you join me for lunch?"

"Why? And don't you have stuff to do?" Zane opened the garbage bag, taking a peak at some of his old, but new clothes. "Like maybe getting information from the Evermoving, or whoever they work with?"

"Breaking into a secure facility gets you some vacation time." Millie leaned against the doorway, arms crossed casually. "I also wanted to talk to you more about Dani and Tom." Zane's mouth fell into a silent 'o'. He hadn't run into them yet, and he considered himself lucky. "And about what you can do while you're recovering, if you're bored."

He nodded. He could recall in detail his kidnapping. "Step outside please."

After putting on a white dress shirt and a pair of black pants, the two of them headed down the white staircase and into the cafeteria. Zane adjusted his shirt, which was too baggy for him. Had he really lost that much weight as the Evermoving's prisoner? They chose a table in the corner, away from everyone else. A group of younger adults tried to sit close by, but after glancing at the two of them left to find another table.

Millie spread her hands out, her silver rings clicking on the cheap plastic table. "I need an official report from you. Right now they're being transferred across the state, and once you write it out on paper, they'll be fired for good."

"Okay?" Zane's lips pressed into a thin line. "Do you have something I can write on? And don't they know too much? I thought you didn't want the Evermoving to discover this place."

She chewed on her lip, bringing her arms back to her sides. "About that. We aren't going to fire them yet. Currently, they're being re-evaluated."

His head hit the table, making a small thud noise. "Of course," Zane mumbled. "It takes a lot to get kicked out of this place. I would know."

She slid a piece of paper over to him, along with a pen. "Just write the report. I'll let you know if they're terminated."

His eyes widened. *Just like Dr. Sandra?* Zane thought.

"Not killed," Millie emphasized, and the slight panic he had disappeared.

"So you said that I could do something in my free time?"

She grinned. "Yup."

Zane regretted asking. She led him to the basement elevator, and they stepped inside. She inserted a keycard into the elevator panel. His stomach dropped as it slowly descended. The dim lights weren't any help either. Eventually it stopped, and the doors opened, revealing a large cataloging room with a dozen filing cabinets. Which didn't seem like it was enough.

He squinted at a large bin off to the side, overflowing with different papers inside folders. "What the heck is this place?"

"Even secret organizations need to keep track of things," Millie mumbled. "There are so many secrets in this place, and almost no one is allowed inside." She glanced at him. "You already know everything which is why you're even standing here in the first place."

"Uh, I have amnesia, remember?"

Millie chuckled. "You're going to remember these secrets eventually. But this place needs serious help with organization so... Unless you want to back out you can work on organizing these important documents. I'll show you how." She headed toward the bin with the overflowing envelopes.

"It's better than doing nothing," Zane said under his breath, but he was dreading the tedious work.

She picked up one of the envelopes, eyes scanning the front before showing it to him. "When you organize these you have to focus on the keywords." Her finger tapped the word traitor. They both headed toward the file cabinets, and she stopped in front of the first one. "This one is for ongoing investigations." Millie stepped to the right. "And this contains the identities of some members of the Evermoving." She pressed her thumb on the lowest drawer's handle, and it made a small beeping noise before opening. There were very few files. Then Millie opened the four drawers above it, and those were completely empty. "Yeah.

Not a lot, I know. Most of them came from you and Max. Also they're organized by level of importance." She flipped the folder she was holding over. "This has a number of two and..." She brought him to the seventh file cabinet. "It goes here." She opened the second to last drawer and set the folder inside. Unlike the second file cabinet, this one was almost completely full. There were a lot of traitors. Millie explained what the other file cabinets were for before she left him to it. He got to work, and fell into a rhythm. The task felt familiar, and a few hours later, he decided to take a break. Zane headed toward the elevator but hesitated. There wasn't much else that he could do except eat. He might as well keep working. Zane headed back toward the slightly smaller pile, eyes scanning it. His eyes shot toward a small letter with Gemma's name on it. It probably just contained information about the Evermoving watching her, something that he already knew. Zane grabbed a different envelope, flipping it over. A 'one' was on the back. He smacked the envelope against his other hand repeatedly, chewing his inner lip. Zane spun around, lounging for the letter with Gemma's name on it. He tossed the other envelope to the side. Zane opened it, taking out a piece of paper. It was folded, and on the front had 'To Zane' written on it. His hands shook as he unfolded the piece of paper, but he was too numb to react in any other way. This wasn't just information that had been written down.

Hey, Scaredy-cat. I don't know where you are but the Smith's haven't been to the apartment in ages. I know you were kidnapped, but I heard rumors that you're back on the streets again. I'm really hoping that's true. If you're reading this, can you please meet me at the Coneflower Theater? I'll be behind the door at the end of the hallway. I'll be waiting there every Friday at noon.

Love, Gemma.

Why didn't anyone tell him this paper was found? His thumb lightly trailed Gemma's handwriting. And what would have happened if the Evermoving had been the ones to discover the letter? The better question was what if they planted it? But they didn't know she called him Scaredy-cat. It had to be real. And there was no way Danny or anyone else was going to let him go. Except maybe he could try convincing someone. Sean seemed like the best bet. Out of everyone else, he was the most likely to say yes. And besides, it's not like he would be able to sneak out again. Zane was going to need help from someone on the inside. A small smile curled his lips. He was going to see Gemma again. And soon.

Zane decided to wait in the cafeteria for Sean. Sean was a little more elusive than Millie, but he had to eat at some point. That's the thing that brought him back to the cafeteria. Also, he was hungry. Zane munched on a few french fries, until he finally spotted Sean. Zane almost missed him, and he would have if a small crowd hadn't moved out of the way. Sean walked past the group, taking an apple from the self-serve area. Zane stood, taking his lunch tray and putting it in the used pile on his way to Sean.

Sean saw Zane out of the corner of his eye, turning around with a huff. "What do you want? I thought you were supposed to be organizing files."

"I was. I need you to take me somewhere. It's important." The fresh smell of hashbrowns wafted toward them.

Sean raised his eyebrows. "What's this about?"

Zane glanced at the floor and back up again, before gesturing for Sean to come closer. Sean took a step closer, waiting for him to explain. "It's about Gemma. I found a note she wrote in the cataloging room. She wants to meet me at the Coneflower Theater."

Sean scoffed, taking a step away from Zane. "Just go there yourself, weirdo. You don't need a babysitter."

"I can't!" Zane whisper-hissed, following Sean as he headed

toward a table. "I don't think anyone here is going to let me leave with a car to go after Gemma, especially with the Evermoving watching her. I need your help to pull this off."

Sean sat down, lips pressed together in a thin line. "Tell me more about this note."

Zane's eyes brightened and he sat down across from Sean. "I guess she originally put it in the apartment that I lived in for a while with Trent and Dr. Smith. I found it while I was organizing files, and when I saw her name I couldn't resist opening it."

"I can take you there, but if anything happens you're taking full responsibility." He took another bite out of the apple. "Also we're not taking her back with us." Zane nodded in agreement. Sean narrowed his eyes. "I'm serious Zane. The Evermoving can't know you visited her."

"I'm serious too, Sean. I would never do anything to endanger Gemma." Zane hesitated. "Anymore."

Sean nodded. "Okay. And what time do we have to meet her?"

"What's today?"

He frowned, before standing up. "Friday."

"Now."

Sean sat back down. "No. We can't go today."

Zane groaned. "Okay. Next Friday works too. We have to be there at noon."

Sean grinned. "Alright. Next Friday it is."

Once next Friday arrived, he immediately sought out Sean. He rounded the corner to the cafeteria, checking the clock on the wall. Eventually, the time was 11:00, and he was getting worried. Where was Sean? Did he rat Zane out? Sean might not have been in the cafeteria, but Millie was.

He approached her, setting his elbows on the table. "What room does Sean stay in?"

She looked up in confusion. "Uhhh. I don't remember but he's over there." Millie pointed behind him. Zane turned away before letting his face flood with relief. He headed toward Sean. He was standing in the entryway to the cafeteria.

"Meet me in the parking garage in ten minutes." Sean told him. Zane nodded, guilty for having doubted him.

In ten minutes, they were on their way to the Coneflower Theater. The van jostled, sending him flying across the floor. His shoulder hit the wall of the van, and a fiery pain shot up his arm. Sean was driving, and apparently this was his way of shaking off any potential tails. Zane took a deep breath in, steadying himself by putting his hands against the metal wall. There were no seats in the back, and Sean hadn't been kind enough to let him sit in the front. Zane couldn't risk being seen and blah blah blah. The car eventually came to a stop, and he felt like vomiting. Not only because of the bumpy ride, but he had bad memories of places like this. He always found himself in the back of a car, either recently drugged, or escaping from the Evermoving.

The back door was flung open, and Sean grinned. "Hope the ride wasn't too bad for you."

Zane winced, standing up and stumbling towards the door. He hopped down, glaring at Sean. "Was that really necessary?"

Sean's grin evaporated. "Yeah. It was. We can't risk anything with this meeting of yours."

Zane glanced at the nearby movie theater. They had parked a few blocks away, and he felt sick, a bit excited but mostly nervous. He hadn't seen Gemma in so long, and there she was. Waiting inside.

"Don't come in with me. I don't want to scare her," Zane said.

Tom nodded, already getting back in the driver's seat. Zane regained his balance and crossed the street to the movie theater. It stood tall, movies displayed on the front. He pushed open the doors, looking around wildly. The smell of butter and salt was overwhelming. There was a long line, and he easily slipped past, toward the movies. The employee was too busy to notice. He headed down the dim hallway, and per Gemma's directions, opened the door at the end.

She was sitting on a chair, a bored expression on her face. It instantly changed when she saw him. "Hey Scaredy-cat!" she greeted, the corners of her eyes creasing.

"Hey," Zane whispered, smiling in return. "It's good to see you again." Joy exploded inside him like fireworks from seeing her familiar face. She wore baggy clothing like usual, but there was something different about her. Something off.

"You have to go to the rebel base with me."

"You have to come with me to the Evermoving."

They said at the same time.

Zane widened his eyes in alarm. "You're joking."

"No I'm not!" Gemma whisper-hissed, sneaking behind him and closing the door. "You need to come back. I don't know what you're doing with the rebels but whatever it is, it isn't good."

"No way! You can't be with the Evermoving now. They practically tortured me if I forgot to mention that!" he snapped.

"Yeah, well so did Dani and Tom," she pointed out.

"This is different! They messed with my brain!" He glared at her. "Seriously, Gemma, how did you get involved with them? Are you an idiot?"

"I'm not! I recovered some memories and they're the good guys!" she whispered.

"Shut up!" he snarled. "They are not the good guys. Just please reconsider this! I agreed to meet you because I thought... I thought you were on my side."

Gemma's eyes darkened. "Not anymore, Zane. I just didn't think you'd be so stubborn about this."

"What are you talking about?" he demanded.

"You don't really get a choice in this."

"Hell if I don't." Zane turned around and started to open the door.

She grabbed his wrist. "I wouldn't do that if I were you. Just come with me. Back to the Evermoving. This can all be sorted through. Please Scaredy-cat," she added softly.

Zane twisted around and threw her back, swinging the door open and making a run for it. She tackled him from behind, and his chin connected with the scratchy carpet.

"What are you doing! Get off of me!" Zane kicked her in the stomach and she let go. "You're making the wrong choice. The Evermoving aren't—" He didn't give her a chance to finish her sentence.

He kept running but he was intercepted by, surprisingly enough, the police. "Stop what you're doing!" He recognized the man in the back. It was Anything. Zane remembered the way he stood, and his height. But it was strange to see his facial expressions. He wasn't wearing his usual mask and disguise, which had been replaced by a police costume. He had short, dark hair, and warm colored skin. This definitely wasn't law enforcement. He ducked into one of the movie rooms, the Evermoving following closely behind. Loud music blared in his ears, and his feet crushed popcorn. He slid into the front of the room, the projector blinding him.

"This is a dangerous man! Stay away from him!" The members of the Evermoving said, eyes locking onto his. He wasn't dangerous. Why were the civilians looking at him like that? The betrayal finally sunk in, and the weight of devastation felt like a slap to the face. He made a break for it, jumping over the red theater chairs. The people started to shout, and one attempted to grab his ankle, but they were too slow. The Evermoving followed closely behind and several shots fired. He kept running and almost made it out. He was inches away from the exit doors. But hands began to drag him back, and a needle was inserted into his side. Talk about deja vu.

"You really thought you got away," one of them whispered. Zane cried out, desperately trying to escape their grasp. He lost sense of where he was, and they kept dragging him away. Somewhere. Where was he again? His limbs relaxed against his will, and he became dead weight. His only knowledge was that he was somewhere dark. Zane coughed and coughed, each hacking breath adding to his misery. But she was there. Gemma was there. She stood on the sidelines and watched him with a triumphant gleam in her eyes.

"I hate you," Zane wheezed out, his eyes locking onto Gemma's, the words barely escaping his lips. "I hate you," he said a little louder. "I HATE YOU!" Zane shouted. "I HATE YOU—"

"That's enough."

His gaze swiveled around to meet Mrs. Valentino's. She crouched down beside him, placing a hand on his shoulder. "Maybe it wasn't such a bad thing that you were rescued. You always come running back to us." She smiled innocently. A stupid innocent smile. Zane wanted to punch it off of her face.

"I'm not tell..." His words fell off his tongue, his mind slowly getting more drowsy by the second. The hands holding him released Zane, and he jolted forward, his face meeting the hard ground. "I'm not... Won't tell..."

Gemma winced, looking away quickly. "You should have just come with me..." she whispered. tears gathering in the corners of her eyes. "This is for the best. You're my friend..." The words fueled his hatred and followed him as his mind drifted to the deepest darkest angriest corner of his mind. He plotted. He planned. Because no matter how much the betrayal had hurt, he couldn't afford to be set back any further. He knew who he was. And he was NOT going to waste time proving that he was a good person. He was going to tear the Evermoving apart brick by brick until all that was left were memories.

Then the lights came. He didn't know what they were but they were almost blinding. Several more gunshots rang in his ears, and he covered his ears. His last bit of conscience fled, and he vaguely remembered seeing Sean's face.

CHAPTER
THIRTY-FIVE

Z ane practically fell out of the hospital cot, arms restraining him. "NO!" he shouted. "Get off of—" He trailed off when he noticed Max. "I'm not..." He looked around at the familiar hospital room. The same blood stain on the tile floor, the same medical staff... He was back in the rebel base. "The Evermoving was there," he finally said, his throat parched. He leaned back against the pillow, his eyebrows knitting together. "They were there."

"We know," Max said, his voice low. He was standing now, but it still looked like he was in pain.

"How did you know to... I was almost... They almost got me," Zane said, his gaze swiveling to Sean. "I thought you said you were going to wait in the car."

He snorted. "Then you're dumber than you look right now. We put a listening device on you," Sean said, and Max shot him a scowl.

"You did what?" Zane asked, shock lacing his voice. That was a total betrayal of his trust. His heart hardened. "Not cool. At all. And you didn't even tell me," he muttered. "You thought I would betray you?"

Max shook his head. "No. Sean worded that wrong. We were just making sure... Gemma wasn't with the Evermoving. Unfortunately she was."

"You told him about this?" Zane asked.

"Danny knows as well," Sean pointed out. "I let him know on the ride there."

Zane shook his head rapidly. "But Gemma wouldn't join the Evermoving. She knows what they're like. There has to be some sort of misunderstanding." He started to get up, but he was pushed back down. He glared at them. "She wouldn't do that."

"Well she did!" Sean shouted. "Do you get it now? Do you understand through that thick skull of yours? She betrayed you! SHE. BETRAYED. YOU. And the only reason you're here right now is because of that listening device. You've been acting stupid lately, but honestly I don't think there's been a time where you've ever acted rationally. Every decision you make is important, Zane. If the Evermoving got a hold of you, well... We don't even know what would happen."

Zane covered his mouth with his hand. "I... There's no way. It's just... They have to be manipulating her. They had to have done something with her brain."

"Did she seem manipulated to you?" Max asked, giving him the same look of pity that Sean was giving him.

Zane groaned, sinking further into the pillows supporting him. "I don't know." He finally said, glancing at the hospital exit. There was nowhere he could go to get away from his thoughts. He flexed his fingers, familiar pangs going through them. He'd finally gotten the cast off, but they still hurt from time to time. "She could be. It's always a possibility. We need to get her away from them."

Danny entered the room, a grave expression ruining his normally joyful grin. "No. She's too far gone."

"I was too far gone!" Zane shouted. "BUT I'm STILL here. She's a good person. She can still be saved." He blinked away the tears gathering in his eyes. Somehow he knew on the inside she couldn't be. But he still wanted to deny it. The truth was so much harder to face.

Danny stood close to him, humming under his breath. "Maybe." he said, but Zane could see the lie in his eyes. "But maybe she doesn't want to be saved. She joined of her own free will."

"Did you get her?"

"Get who, Zane?" Danny asked.

"The leader of the Evermoving was in the building!" Zane hissed. "You could have grabbed her.

"We barely got you out of there," Sean said. "We didn't plan for so many of them to be there."

"Of course you didn't! And don't think I'll forget about the tracking device," He added bitterly.

"Oh I'm sure you won't," Max said under his breath.

"Did we at least get something useful out of that!" Zane said. He was frustrated to his very core. The three of them shook their heads. "Go," he said. "Just leave me alone." He crossed his arms over his chest, and one by one they left. His eyebrows furrowed together, lips pressed into a thin line, his body tense and his mind whirling. Zane's eyes were rebellious and filled with tears. He swallowed the lump in his throat, blinking rapidly until the tears in his eyes disappeared. Zane felt completely and utterly betrayed. Ironic wasn't it? In his past he was a completely untrustworthy person, and now he was being betrayed by those close to him. No. Zane wasn't going to continue wallowing in self-pity. He wanted his old job back. And if they weren't going to give it to him, he would have to take measures into his own hands.

THIRTY-SIX

A distraction. That's what he needed. He was currently standing in front of the intricate door leading to Danny's office. The chance of him saying yes to what he was about to ask was low. But Zane wasn't asking for permission. He knocked on the doors.

"Who is it?" A voice called from inside.

"Zane," he said.

He heard several papers shift around. "Please come in!"

Zane opened the door, which made a creaking noise as it swung open. Danny was sitting on the green couch, a notebook beside him. His hands rested on his knees.

"Is this about Gemma?"

Zane stiffened. "No. It's about my old job. Millie has been having me organize files downstairs but... I'd like to do something different." He paused, digging his nails into his palms. "Danny, I want to go on the missions I used to." He avoided using the word dangerous.

Danny looked up at him, his expression frozen with worry. "That would create a lot of work for me to do. You'd need a new

identity to go by and a less recognizable face. The answer is no."
His words were said carefully.

"I get that it's dangerous." A burning sensation built up in the back of his throat. "But I need this, Danny. After what happened with Gemma I could really use a distraction."

Danny sighed. "I'm not going to put you in danger just for you to use that as a coping mechanism. We have a few people here who are licensed therapists—"

Zane shook his head. "No therapists. Not after Dr. Sandra."

Danny stood. "I've done a lot for you already, Zane. But I am not your friend. You need to listen when I tell you that there's no way I'm putting you in any more danger."

"Fine," Zane snapped. "I guess I'll continue organizing files."

"You can't do that anymore either," Danny said. "You've made it very clear that you're not to be trusted. Millie has other things for you to do."

"But—"

"Get out of my office," Danny said calmly, eyes narrowing. "Now." His eyes softened. "Take a break, Zane. None of this is your problem anymore."

Zane avoided eye contact, his mind drifting to a quiet place. For a moment his thoughts floated on an ocean cold enough to numb him. He left, and the door closed behind him. There was no way he was going to do what Millie or Danny wanted him too. There were people in the building that didn't know he wasn't supposed to go anywhere near the Evermoving. Maybe he could use that to his advantage.

Zane walked back to the cafeteria before taking a seat at the table in the corner. He wasn't hungry, but he knew that a lot of conversations happened in the cafeteria. So he was watching. If he didn't have his memories he was going to figure out how things worked. Technically, he was supposed to still be recovering, but he never really listened to authority, did he? He was already hearing rumors of a huge project coming up, and Zane wanted to join this so-called secret.

"He's finally stepping up..." A whisper from across the cafeteria. "Brute force is necessary in this hidden war. We need to take this action..."

"We're leaving soon..." Another whisper. "Don't bother bringing a disguise."

Interesting. Very interesting.

"We're taking them down from the inside." The last whisper was drowned out by the sounds of the cafeteria. That changed things, and he was going to find out exactly what was happening.

Zane abruptly stood up, joining Millie and Sean at their table. "What the heck is this secret mission? And who's stepping up?" He demanded.

Millie glared at him. "It's none of your business that's what. You lost your right to information after the stunt you pulled with Sean."

Zane rolled his eyes. "Yeah okay. But this is different. It's serious. Ground breaking even. It's not something you can push under the rug! Everyone has been talking about it. I'm pretty sure I'm the only one who doesn't know at this point."

"Dani and Tom don't know. They still aren't allowed back by the way." Sean poked at his food, and he noticed the two were sitting farther away from each other than normal. Millie was still angry at him for bringing Zane to visit Gemma.

"Good." Zane bit the inside of his lip. "But I wasn't the one to kidnap as well as torture someone. What they did was worse than meeting up with an old friend."

Max sat down next to them. "Is Zane asking about the thing?" He looked at Zane in an unimpressed way.

Millie nodded. "Which is still none of his business. But

everything that's about to happen is because of what occurred at that movie theater."

Zane sighed. "Right."

"And settle down. This thing that's happening will take months of planning," Max added.

"Would this have happened if I hadn't tried reaching out to Gemma?"

"Actually yes. We've been wanting to do this since the beginning. You just put the plan in motion faster," Max said.

"Are we taking down the Evermoving for good?! Is that what's happening?" Zane blurted, slamming his hands down on the cafeteria table.

Sean glared at him. "Congratulations. You know all of the secrets in this place once again."

"I want to go," Zane demanded.

Millie took a deep breath in. "Don't you think you've done enough damage?" Her voice shook. "Everyone here has had to go out of their way for you including us! First it was when you were captured by the Evermoving and we had to rescue you. Now this thing with Gemma, not to mention everything you did while on the Evermoving's side. I used to think you were this mysterious guy with a knack for sneaking around and gaining intel. But maybe you're just an entitled kid." The words seemed to come out of nowhere, and Zane watched her storm away from the table.

Max's eyes focused on the ground. "Maybe for once, you should leave things alone and not try helping. I know you're going through a lot right now, but you can't stop the Evermoving and save Gemma all by yourself."

Zane glanced at Sean. "Max, can I talk to you? Alone?"

Sean snorted, throwing his hands up. "If he asks you to take him somewhere, say no."

Max grinned. "Noted."

Once Sean left, Zane spoke. "Danny said you also have spots missing from your memory. Is that true?"

Max shifted his weight, the table creaking beneath him. "Yeah. Mrs. Valentino wipes the memories from anyone who finds out something they're not supposed to. I don't think a single member of the Evermoving doesn't have a few spots missing from their memory. Including Mrs. Valentino."

Zane's foot taped against the tile floor repeatedly. "Really? Do you think that's why no one knows her real name? Because she doesn't even remember herself?"

Max laughed, his chest heaving from the effort. "Oh that would be the cherry on top. A leader of an organization but she doesn't have any memories from her past. That would be something else."

Zane folded his arms over his chest. "How are you feeling?"

Max shrugged. "Could be better. Could be worse. I'm just thankful that I get a long break."

Zane inhaled slowly. "They won't hurt her, right?"

Max stayed silent. He didn't need to say a word. The Evermoving had already hurt all three of them.

CHAPTER
THIRTY-SEVEN

Z ane was inside of a room he had never been in before. Okay, that wasn't true. He had probably been inside of it all the time in his past. It was one of the upstair's rooms, and it contained all sorts of weapons. But his eyes were focused on the guy speaking and the whiteboard behind him.

"So." The man used a whiteboard marker to draw something as he spoke. "One of the higher ups wants a group of us to investigate a nearby mall. Apparently a member of the Evermoving was there according to Dr. Smith. The thing is there's reason to believe they forgot to scrub the camera footage, and we're going to use it to track this guy down." He turned around revealing a head of messy black hair. The guy wasn't even that bad looking, he just needed a haircut. Not that Zane could judge, considering the hair he'd had in the hospital.

There were six other people in the room. He managed to overhear that a few people were going to meet up in the room, and that they needed an extra person. So far nobody had said anything about him being there.

"If we do this successfully, we might even gain more intel on the Evermoving." A heavy weight filled the room. Zane knew personally that no one from the Evermoving gave up any information without a fight.

"But what are you doing here?"All the heads in the room turned toward Zane.

He swallowed, gathering his thoughts. "This guy that was at the mall... Uh... I have had several encounters with him already and Danny thought it would be beneficial if I tagged along. I witnessed him taking footage from a computer, and I saw him at the mall the same day Dr. Smith saw him."

The guy narrowed his eyes at Zane. "I thought you weren't supposed to go on any more missions?"

Zane shrugged. "You can delay this whole thing by checking in with Danny if you really want to. But I'm right here, ready to go on this mission no matter the risks."

"Alright, kid." He shrugged. "And you can address me as Mr. Rolland. Just know that I'm not happy about this in any shape or form." He moved away from the board, revealing what was on it. It was a small map of the mall. He tapped one of the rooms. "This is where the security office is. A group of you will trade off with some of the mall cops and gather intel. But they're not the real issue. Another group of you is going to go through the mall and make sure none of the Evermoving are located inside." He paused to take a deep breath in. "Dave, Ken, and Tam will go inside the security office. The rest of you, while communicating with us on coms, will scout out the mall for any dangerous individuals. Is that clear?" Mr. Rolland looked directly at Zane, almost daring him to ask a stupid question. "No? Let's go, crew." He gave a brief smile before they all exited the room.

Zane followed Mr. Rolland to the parking garage, where they all piled into two different cars. The ride there was excruciatingly silent, but he knew better than to break it. These people weren't like Trent, Dr. Smith, or even Max. They didn't know him, and didn't care to. In their eyes he was just a danger to everyone. He did learn the names of the others in his group. Briana was a brown haired woman with an imp-like face, Ben was a guy with a jawline sharp enough to cut through a rock, and then there was Ian. So far Ian hadn't said a single word except yes and his name, so Zane was assuming he was just shy.

Eventually, a com was handed to Zane, and he put it in his ear.

"Hey kid?" Mr. Rolland said from behind the wheel. Zane looked up. "Take one of these." A gun was tossed to him, and he quickly caught it, his palms turning clammy. His heartbeat quickened, the realization of what he'd just done catching up to him. Zane went directly against Danny's orders, and he wasn't sure what would happen if he was caught. All missions were logged, and surely Danny would be told all about what happened. If anything important happened that is. The most likely scenario would be that nothing happened and no footage was found. And yet... The thought of narrowly avoiding being discovered was thrilling. He tucked the gun into an inner coat pocket, making sure the weapon had the safety lock on.

The suv pulled into the mall parking lot. Mr. Rolland twisted around to look at all of them. "Last chance to ask questions. It should be easy enough. Don't forget to communicate on the coms." Everyone around him got out of the car, and he stumbled after them, as unsure as a newborn deer. They all seemed as if they knew exactly what to do and where to go.

"Are you going to focus or do I need to drive you back?" Mr. Rolland asked, not bothering to turn around.

Zane sighed. "Nope. I'll focus."

The group split up, heading in different directions. Zane stepped through one of the entrances, eyes scanning the crowds inside. So far it was just a bunch of teenagers and families roaming the mall mindlessly. He passed a brightly colored store with stuffed animals lining the walls, eyes snapping back toward the crowd. Zane was starting to hate malls. It reminded him of Trent and Dr. Smith, which didn't make it any better. He accidentally bumped into a brown haired girl and she glared at him.

Zane held his hands up. "Sorry about that."

She rolled her eyes. "Whatever."

He heard static in his ear before it turned into words. "So far so good. We're in the security room."

"No sign of the Evermoving," Briana said. Two other voices joined in confirming the same thing. It took him a moment to realize he needed to say something too.

"All clear on my end," Zane added, as he made a turn around a corner. The coms went silent once again, and he made another turn. Oh no. His eyes met with the last person he wanted to see right now.

It was Robin, and she was looking right at him. She was wearing a pink crew neck with a heart necklace, and a soft blush covered her cheeks. Her mouth fell open, her neutral expression turning into fury. She took a step toward him. He panicked and ran the other way. Yes, he'd promised her an explanation. But unfortunately he couldn't give her one right now. And if there really was a member of the Evermoving in the building, then they couldn't know that he cared about Robin. His legs picked up momentum when he heard her footsteps behind him. Zane's eyes snapped to the men's bathroom sign. Surely she wouldn't follow him in? He came to a screeching halt in front of the bathroom, before charging inside. He finally stopped in front of one of the sinks, turning around to face the door. A minute passed. And then another.

The door burst open, and Robin stomped inside, finger pointed directly at him. "What the heck, Zane!? Why did you run from me? ALSO you promised me an explanation WEEKS AGO!"

Zane grinned, scratching the back of his neck. "Uh... Right.

An explanation." He pressed his lips together in a thin line. "That's not really possible right now."

Tears began to well in her eyes and he instantly regretted saying that.

"Uh but maybe I can make time!" Zane spluttered, eyes widening. "Because I did say you deserve one which you do..." His eyes shot to the ground and back up again. "I'm just on a bit of a time limit."

Robin set a hand on her hip, pouting her lips. "Then make it quick!" She was trying to be fierce but it wasn't very effective considering she was one of the sweetest girls that existed.

He glanced at the bathroom stalls and urinals. "Uh... Do you wanna find somewhere a little more private?"

CHAPTER
THIRTY-EIGHT

Zane locked the door to the family bathroom, before turning toward Robin.

"Who was the guy you were running from?" Robin demanded.

"Okay uh…" He probably shouldn't reveal government-level secrets to a teenage girl. But knowing that didn't stop his next words from spilling out. "I should probably start from the beginning. A few months ago I woke up in a hospital with amnesia. Somebody visited me there, someone who I thought was a nurse. The strange part was she told me my name. And I found someone else with amnesia too. You've met her. The blonde girl at the library? Anyway, Mrs. Valentino visited her too. We were trying to investigate, and I found out that my guardians had something to do with it." He decided to leave out the first kidnapping. "That led to my capture. I guess I was this important guy before my memories were erased and—"

Robin started laughing. It turned hysterical. Then it turned into crying. "You're insane. Zane, you have a serious lying problem." Her voice cracked, and she used the palm of her hand to wipe tears from her face.

Zane squeezed his eyes shut. "I—"

The static in his ear was back. "A member of the Evermoving was spotted near Hot Topic and Hollister. Report there immediately and get the footage somewhere safe," Mr. Rolland instructed.

"Have to go," he finished. "I'm sorry Robin." He threw open the bathroom door, and sprinted toward the two stores. Once he got there, he spotted several of the others, and... A familiar face with high cheekbones, and brown eyes. The same guy that wiped the footage of Mrs. Valentino. So far he hadn't spotted any of the rebels, but it wouldn't be long.

"What's the plan?" Zane whispered into the com.

"Get him into an area with fewer people and capture him. Do not fire unless necessary," Mr. Rolland explained.

Zane pretended to tie his shoe, his face turned away when the member of the Evermoving started to come his way. He wasn't sure why but somehow he knew it was the best thing to do. Sometimes the best way to hide was in plain sight.

"He's heading toward the exit. He knows we're here," Ian said.

"Don't let him get away," Mr. Rolland ordered.

Zane began to follow him, alongside a few of the others in the group. The Evermoving member began to walk faster, and the four of them matched his pace. The walk turned into a sprint.

"He's making a run for it! What should we do?" Zane spoke into the coms, while avoiding crowds of people.

"Well don't stand around! Go get him!" Mr. Rolland snapped.

"He's going out the south exit! Pull one of the cars around!" Briana said.

Zane quickened his steps, and just as the guy stepped through the exit Ian caught up with him. The member of the

Evermoving was tackled to the ground, face smushed into the sidewalk beneath him. A few civilians were looking through the glass door. A van sped toward the apprehended man. Ian knocked him out using the handle of his gun, and he was set into the back of the van. The door to the back was shut, and luckily the window was tinted. Ben approached the witnesses showing them a fake police badge, although technically their organization outranked the police department. They were more on level with the FBI instead of the police department. The rest of them piled into the seats, Ben joining them moments later. Zane peered over the top of his own seat, just to make sure the guy was still knocked out. He looked innocent without the permanent scowl mangling his features.

"Someone is bound to call the police. Ken, make sure nobody follows us, and have someone check for more members of the Evermoving." Zane was able to hear Mr. Rolland in the coms, and from the driver's seat in front of him.

"Got it. I should be back in an hour or two," Ken responded through the coms.

This time Mr. Rolland spoke to them. "Make sure he doesn't have any bugs, or ways of contacting the Evermoving."

"I got it." Ian hopped over the seats, landing beside the unconscious body. "Gross. He's wearing their symbol," he whispered.

"You're a little rusty, kid, but you did fine today," Mr. Rolland said as he took a particularly speedy turn.

"Cut that out!" Ian complained.

Zane nodded. "Thank you, Mr. Rolland."

He saw Mr. Rolland raise an eyebrow in the rearview mirror. "I didn't say you did good. All I said was that you did fine."

"Oh. Right," Zane muttered.

"I found a tracker sewn in his clothes!" Ian called out.

"Hand it to me," Briana told him. "I'll toss it out the

window." After they disposed of the bug, and got confirmation from Ken that their license plate number wasn't given to the police, they continued driving back to the rebel base. Once inside the car garage, he slipped away and headed back up to his room. Zane collapsed on his bed, tensing when he felt the gun press into his side. He set it beneath his bed, before closing his eyes. It had been a success, and he just had to hope Danny didn't hear about it. And... It felt good. It felt really good to chase the guy down. The adrenaline was still coursing through his veins, a constant source of energy. After a few deep breaths, his heart slowed down and he was able to relax. But his only thoughts were about the next mission.

CHAPTER
THIRTY-NINE

Zane opened the door to the weapon's room, and familiar faces looked back at him. Mr. Rolland and his team were all inside.

Zane coughed. "I heard you guys were planning something else."

Mr. Rolland rolled his eyes. "Get in here and close the door."

Zane's eyebrows shot upward. That was easy. He closed the door behind them, setting the gun from yesterday with the other weapons before joining the miniature circle that had formed. Briana gave him a slight nod.

"I don't know if today will be interesting enough for you, Zane. I have plans to interrogate the new captive." Mr. Rolland adjusted the sleeve of his white button up. "He's currently sitting in the interrogation room and I want you all to observe. After we get information from him he's off to a secure prison."

Zane resisted the urge to raise his hand. "Don't we need actual evidence to send someone to prison?"

Mr. Rolland laughed, and a few of the others joined in as well. "He was wearing the symbol of the Evermoving. We don't need any more evidence than that." Zane felt his face heat up, but he kept silent.

"We're going to let him sit for a while before the interrogation so go get something to eat or relax. Just be sure to meet back here in half an hour," Mr. Rolland instructed.

Zane was the first to leave. He found himself drawn to the hospital room. He had just gotten his friend back and he wasn't about to take that for granted. Zane started to open the door, stopping when he heard his name being spoken.

"I don't know, Sean. Have you seen the look in Zane's eyes lately? There's almost this wild look in them. There's not much else we can do considering he refused to see a therapist. And this new coping mechanism of his isn't healthy." That was Max speaking.

He heard Millie sigh. "I know. But Danny already told Mr. Rolland to keep the missions light. He's not in any real danger."

And that stung. Really bad. He turned away from the door, keeping his expression calm and collected. Voices echoed in his head until it became tangible.

Cooper Wild. That was the name of the guy speaking to him. He looked deceivingly young, despite being twenty four years old. "She wants to remove a few more memories of yours. Mrs. Valentino believes you won't be as dedicated to us as you could be, especially since she believes the reason you rejoined us was to protect your friends."

That meant another trip to Level Zero. Zane hesitated. "I will be. Just don't remove them." After another moment of hesitation, he added, "please."

The memory was plucked and stashed somewhere in the regained memory section of his brain. He knew the identity of the guy they just captured. Maybe Mr. Rolland would finally take him seriously.

CHAPTER
FORTY

H e walked into the weapon's room, eyes narrowing slightly at Mr. Rolland.

"I guess we're all here then. Come with me." Mr. Rolland and the rest of the group made their way downstairs, passing the cafeteria and heading toward a less occupied series of hallways. The door they reached was black, and needed a key to open it with. There was a door next to it that was just as secure. Mr. Rolland opened the door on the left, revealing a room with one-way glass. Cooper Wild was on the other side. Everyone except Zane and Mr. Rolland entered through the door.

Mr. Rolland sighed. "What are you doing kid?"

"You might need me in the interrogation room."

"And why's that?" Mr. Rolland looked at him in an unimpressed way.

"Because I know his identity. And I used to know him when I was..."

A part of the Evermoving. Zane shook his head, dismissing the thought. "His name is Cooper Wild. And he's been inside Level Zero."

Mr. Rolland's eyes widened. "I'm still going to do the interrogating. If I need you I'll bring you in."

Zane nodded, joining the others in the left room. Once the door was closed, Mr. Rolland entered the room with the apprehended man. Cooper was sitting on a chair attached to the table in the middle of the room. He was facing the one way glass. It reminded Zane of the Evermoving's interrogation room.

Mr. Rolland sat down across from Cooper. "Hello. I am Marcus Rolland. When did you join the Evermoving?"

He kept silent, a permanent scowl disfiguring his face. "Who's behind the glass?"

Mr. Rolland rolled his shoulders back. "Please state your name."

Cooper rolled his eyes, focusing on the glass behind Mr. Rolland. "Is the kid behind there? I thought I spotted him in the mall. He was a part of the Evermoving once so I'm surprised you're even bothering to interrogate me. I'm sure Zane has told you all about our ability to keep secrets. Unless he was disposed of." Cooper smiled at the one-way glass, and Zane took a step back. Briana glanced at him, her eyes revealing concern.

"We're getting off topic." Mr. Rolland shifted in his seat. "Answer the original question."

Cooper Wild seemed perfectly content to sit there, and a small smile continued to play on his lips.

"You know things," Mr. Rolland began. "But the thing is, we know things too."

Cooper's grin widened. "Oh yeah? Like what?"

"Your name for one."

Cooper's smile began to fade. "Excuse me?"

"Cooper Wild, your uncooperative behavior will be taken into consideration when you're sent to a secure prison." Mr. Rolland stood. "I'll see you tomorrow." He left the room, locking the door behind him.

"Mr. Rolland knows who he is?" Ian shifted his feet, his tan face scrunching up in confusion.

"Nope," Zane said. "I do though." He turned toward the door, which began opening.

"Nice work, Zane. We made him uneasy." Mr. Rolland's praise filled him with pride.

The next day they were all in the usual meeting place.

"I gave the name to one of the techy people upstairs, and they were able to dig up some information," Mr. Rolland began, holding up a folder for all of them to see. "This contains information about his family, where he used to live, and exactly when he dropped off the grid. That means he likely started working for the Evermoving five or so years ago." After they were briefed they went back to the interrogation room.

Zane watched Mr. Rolland interrogate Cooper Wild from behind the one-way glass.

"Please state your name," Mr. Rolland requested.

He slumped in his seat, glaring daggers at Mr. Rolland. "Cooper Wild."

"And how long have you been with the Evermoving, Mr. Wild?"

Cooper sighed. "Don't you have that information already?"

"Yes. But I'd like to hear that from you, Mr. Wild."

Cooper gritted his teeth. "Six years."

"And that would make you how old?"

"Twenty five since yesterday. Sort of rotten luck to be captured on my birthday." Cooper snorted, but his eyes revealed a hidden frustration.

Zane's eyes widened. "Wow. I almost feel bad for him."

"I know right?" Briana murmured from beside him.

"Happy belated birthday, Mr. Wild. What do you do for the Evermoving, besides hang out in malls?" Mr. Rolland asked.

"These questions aren't getting us anywhere," Zane complained.

Ian turned toward Zane. "He's working up to the big questions. Rolland is just testing the waters first."

"I'm an errand boy," Cooper said cautiously, eyes focused on the table. They shot back up toward Mr. Rolland. "I still don't understand how you figured out who I was."

Mr. Rolland tapped the table a few times before responding. "Are you feeling alright, Mr. Wild? For a member of the Evermoving you aren't very quick."

Cooper's eyes widened slightly. "Zane told you?"

"Yes?" Mr. Rolland said, confused.

"Zane wasn't supposed to remember that." His face scrunched up as he thought. "The Evermoving promised me that. But I guess that's what happens when you rush the procedure."

What was that supposed to mean? How many memories would Zane never remember?

"They really messed up with him. It's a good thing they didn't do the same with Gemma..." Cooper Wild trailed off, regret filling his face at the information he'd let slip.

Mr. Rolland set his hands on the table, face up. "Care to expand on that?"

"Nope. I'm done talking." No matter what Mr. Rolland said, Cooper Wild didn't respond.

FORTY-ONE

Zane woke up to the sound of excessive knocking. "Come in?" His voice was slurred by drowsiness.

Danny pushed the door open, fixing Zane with a glare. "I told you not to go on any missions."

"But you already knew I was doing this!" Zane countered, swinging his legs to the ground.

"That was because I thought they weren't going to be serious. You weren't supposed to be the one uncovering information, or regaining memories from your past. You were supposed to relax and take a break. Zane, you went against my direct order." Danny stepped further into the room.

Zane hesitated, studying Danny's face. "You already knew I wouldn't listen, because you warned Mr. Rolland. And isn't what I'm doing a good thing? Nobody else would have known Cooper's real name." Zane sighed. "Look. A while ago I was totally fine with being uncooperative. But if I can help with the information I have, why shouldn't I do that?"

"I said no—" Danny began but Zane cut him off.

"I've been to Level Zero before too. And you need me for the interrogations with Cooper Wild. I might remember more things." His words weren't entirely true. But he was so desperate to stay away from his thoughts and save Gemma at the same time. If that was even possible. The Evermoving might have messed up with him, but Gemma? She had complete unwavering loyalty toward the Evermoving. Whatever they had tried to accomplish had worked.

Danny squeezed his eyes shut, before opening them again. "If you remember anything about it go ahead and tell us. I've told people to keep an eye out for you so don't even think about sneaking away again."

Zane exhaled slowly. "Why do you want me to stay away from these missions?"

"Because if the Evermoving gets their hands on you, we lose. They might have messed up with you the last time, but as soon as they figure it out guess what happens? Everything we've been working for will completely disappear. They'll prepare for what we've been planning, and suddenly they have someone on their side that knows all of our secrets and knows us personally. Once they make you more cooperative and loyal, there isn't going to be a thing you hold back from them."

So what would have happened if they had been successful the first time? The thought filled him with soul crushing dread.

"Zane, I want you to start seeing one of our therapists. I atleast want you to talk to someone you already know, like Max or Millie. Can you do that?"

Zane rubbed the sleep from his eyes. "Yeah. I can do that."

Danny left the room, and Zane thought about who he could talk to. He heard Millie, Sean, and Max talk about him behind his back. He wasn't sure if he could even talk to those three. Who did that leave? He barely knew the team he went on missions with, and it seemed weird to talk to Danny. Dr. Smith and Trent weren't an option either. Gemma wasn't available, and wouldn't be as long as she was with the Evervmoving. And Robin? She wouldn't talk to him if her life depended on it. He had never felt so alone. Maybe a therapist was his last option.

Zane peeked out of his room, relieved when he saw Danny still heading down the hallway. "Hey Danny!"

Danny turned around. "What is it, Zane?"

He hesitated for a moment before speaking. "Where do I find one of those therapists you mentioned?"

Danny smiled. "I'll show you where to go." Danny waited for Zane to catch up to him, and they headed to the downstairs lobby. Zane descended the stairs, shrinking under the mixed looks he received. He saw anger, disappointment, disdain, and worst of all pity.

"Keep your chin held high," Danny told him. "You can't change how they think of you but you can change your reaction. Act like you belong here, and maybe one day they'll believe it."

Zane rolled his shoulders back, instilling an obviously fake confidence into his movements. But eventually there was some level of truth to it, because he began to believe his own lie.

Danny brought him to a plain door. "Ms. Johnson should be in there. And please take this seriously."

Zane nodded, and Danny left him there. He raised his fist, and knocked on the door. It opened in seconds.

Ms. Johnson had a head of red, curly hair, which contrasted her white button up. "Hello, Zane." Her green eyes narrowed for a moment before she stepped back, letting him inside. "Welcome back."

The room was small, but cozy. There was a filing cabinet on one side, and a couch on either side. One of the cabinets was still open.

Ms. Johnson crossed the room, pushing the cabinet closed. "Pick whatever couch. Or remain standing if that's what you prefer."

"I don't want this to be documented," Zane blurted.

Ms. Johnson froze. "Okay." She took a seat on the couch to the right of Zane. "What brings you in here? Trauma from a mission, seeing a loved one die, perhaps a betrayal?" The last suggestion was a little too accurate. Zane sat down on the couch across from her.

"I don't want advice." He folded his arms over his chest.

"Okay. Just talk then." Ms. Johnson set her head on her hands, tilting her head. "I'm here to listen."

Zane inhaled sharply. "I have no one I can trust, and the one person that I could trust was brainwashed. I don't know if I'll ever get her back. She looked me dead in the eyes when the Evermoving was trying to capture me." He paused. "My past self made a lot of mistakes, and most of them I can't even remember. Actually, I'm pretty sure I won't remember a lot of things. The one thing I don't regret was trying to keep Max and Gemma safe. But even then I screwed up!" His tone gradually grew louder. "Gemma's mind is completely screwed up, and Max has missing spots in his brain too! And if the EVERMOVING captured Gemma then they're definitely coming after MAX too—"

Ms. Johnson held up a hand, cutting him off. "Max is safe, Zane. He's still lying on his cot recovering. Look at me." Zane did as she asked. "He. Is. Safe. Say it with me."

"He is safe," Zane muttered.

"You are safe," Ms. Johnson added.

He nodded. "I am safe."

"There are people here that you can trust, Zane. I won't keep any files on you."

"Right," Zane mumbled. "I think we're done for today."

Ms. Johnson's eyes widened in surprise. "Does that mean you're coming back?"

Zane shrugged. "Maybe."

CHAPTER
FORTY-TWO

Okay, so maybe he overreacted a tiny bit. It was true; he had been acting a little wild since Gemma betrayed him, and after getting kidnapped. Twice. His footsteps took him to the hospital room, and he entered, approaching Max's cot.

"How are you doing Bluejay?" Zane smirked.

Max snorted. "Fine." A long sleeve shirt covered what he assumed were bandages and bruises. "But this place gets kind of boring. People are always using the lounge room, and I'm getting kind of tired of watching crime documentaries. It's always first come first serve, and somehow people always get there before me."

Zane frowned. "There's a lounge room?"

Max raised his eyebrows. "Yeah? Have you gone this long without going in there? You must have been bored out of your mind. Actually, let's go there now. We could both use a distraction."

"Right now?" Zane blinked slowly.

"Am I clear to leave?" Max called to one of the medical professionals. A woman waved him away distractedly.

The lounge room was surprisingly close to the bedrooms. It was eight doors away from his room. There was a pool table on the inside, and a group of people playing.

"Oh, nice! No one has claimed the tv yet." There was a glass wall with a door separating two sides of the room. Max and Zane went inside the other half of the room, which had the tv and a few different seating options including beanbags and a couch. They both took a seat on the couch. The place was surprisingly cozy, especially with the scented candles and paintings on the wall. It was the last thing he expected, but it was nice.

Max grabbed the remote from the ottoman in front of them. "You probably don't remember Indian Jones do you?" A slight smirk curled Max's lips.

"No? Why?"

"It was one of the few movies we watched growing up. The Evermoving wasn't a big fan of television. But we found an old copy on a mission and sometimes we'd sneak away to watch it." His eyes darkened. "Mrs. Valentino caught us once, but she didn't try to stop us. She just asked where we got it. This was a long time before we tried leaving the Evermoving. Anyway." He turned on the tv, pressing different buttons until he found the Indiana Jones movie. It started playing. Zane's eyes remained glued to the screen. But every once in a while he glanced at Max sitting beside him. There was a conflicted expression on his face. Maybe they weren't here just to relax. It ended, and Max paused it.

"What are we really doing here?" Zane asked.

Max blinked slowly. "What do you mean?"

"Too much is happening for us to have a random hangout."

"You're right." Max set the remote aside, but didn't turn off the tv. "Zane." He sighed. "This plan that's being set into motion is going to be dangerous, and I'm worried that Gemma will be caught in the crossfires. I've talked to Danny about it and he agrees."

Zane dragged his hand down his face. "Yeah I figured."

Max lowered his voice to a whisper. "I still have faith in her. I think some part of her hasn't been screwed up by the Evermoving yet. You might be the only one to change her mind. I knew she screwed you over, and you don't have to try to help her."

"No! I do. I want to try. But how exactly does Danny want me to do this? I can't exactly waltz into the Evermoving headquarters." Zane snorted.

Max laughed nervously. "About that. We gained more intel from Cooper Wild." Zane almost choked on his spit. "I guess the Evermoving promised him that you wouldn't ever remember who he was. He's a bit angry at them, which is why he let us know how to get to Level Zero."

CHAPTER
FORTY-THREE

Z ane felt like shouting for joy. He had actually done something good for once.

"It's underneath some warehouse by the ocean. Both the place you were taken to, and Level Zero is going to be infiltrated tomorrow. Danny wants you to go to the building you were held prisoner in five minutes before we storm the place. We think Gemma is there too. You can use my old costume and mask. We don't have a lot of key cards to spare, but you'll be given one. Don't even think about losing it." Max paused. "I know that originally we weren't going to involve you. But she used to be a part of this place, and if we can save her from spending her life in some prison, then we'll take that chance."

Zane narrowed his eyes. "There's something else isn't there?"

"She's also one of the few people we know for sure the Evermoving experimented on. In order to know what they did, it would definitely be nice if she was willing to uh... Be studied."

Zane had to restrain himself from smacking Max.

Max clearly saw the angry building in Zane, because he held up his hands. "I wasn't the one that said that. It was Danny."

Zane crossed his arms over his chest. "Right. So tomorrow?"

Max nodded. "I know it's not a long time to prepare. Will you be okay going back there again? I know that... It wasn't the best experience for you last time."

"Yeah. I'll be fine."

"So what'd you think of the movie?"

Zane laughed. "Uh... It was good. Kind of cheesy, but good."

"Danny asked to meet us in his office in..." Max glanced at the clock on the wall. "A few minutes."

Zane exhaled slowly. "Oh jeez. If I'm discovered and killed, you're invited to my funeral."

Max shook his head. "Thanks. And if I get killed tomorrow, you're invited to mine."

Zane grinned. "Alright." He stood. "If we want to get to Danny's office on time we should probably head there now."

When they got there, Millie was standing there waiting for them.

"Good job, Zane." She nodded. "I'm pretty sure everyone here is going to be able to forgive you after this."

"Including you?" Zane asked.

Millie smiled. "I already have. I'm just here to wish you good luck. I really do hope that you can convince Gemma. I know the three of you were close." She was wearing her usual tank top, which revealed her butterfly tattoo. Her fingers twitched once in a while, and there was a slight smell of coffee in the air. Mille stepped aside.

Zane was the one to knock.

The door instantly opened, with Danny standing there. "Hey. So you're up for it then?" He raised an eyebrow at Zane.

Zane nodded.

"Good," Danny said. "Come on in." Once the two of them stepped inside, Danny closed the office door. He handed him the outfit and boots that had been set by the couch, including a gun.

"Once you get to the entrance of the parking garage, someone is going to ask you a question. Respond with 'for a greater purpose' no matter what they say." Danny explained. "Now all you have to do is wait for tomorrow."

"Right. Thank you for letting me do this," Zane muttered.

Danny's smile was strained. "Of course. Now go get some rest for tomorrow. It's going to be a long day."

CHAPTER
FORTY-FOUR

A wire fence surrounded the outside of the Evermoving's facility. His driving wasn't the best, but it was clear at some point he had learned the skill. Zane passed the front entrance. He needed to get to the tunnel entrance, but most importantly Zane had to find Gemma before the others got inside. It took a few minutes to find it and just like Max promised a voice came through his com.

"Why are you here?" The voice was deep and impossible to identify.

"For a greater purpose," Zane said.

The entrance to the tunnel opened slowly, and he swallowed the lump in his throat. Zane couldn't believe he was going back inside. It was easy to drive into the parking garage, and even easier with the costume he had borrowed from Max. He got out of the car, fast-walking to the elevator. The rebels had very few key cards, but thankfully he was given one. Zane was pretty sure she wouldn't be in any of the parking garages, or one of the prison cells. His only guess was that she was in one of the rooms he had stayed in. After swiping the keycard, he got in the elevator and pressed the button to go up. The doors opened to reveal the lobby. He had minutes before the rebels stormed the building. A member of the Evermoving looked directly at Zane.

Stay cool. You belong here. Zane thought. He looked away from the other masked individual, heading toward the stairs. The lobby was still the same, with the fancy carpet and fountain. He tried not to walk too fast, but Zane felt like everyone was looking at him. Zane hoped that it was just in his head. After reaching the top of the stairs, he made a beeline to his old room. Just as he got there, he stopped. The Evermoving wouldn't have given her that room if they thought he was coming back, right? Zane knocked anyway. He heard footsteps hitting the stone floor.

"Who is it?" They really did give her his old room. It was definitely Gemma's voice. The door started to open. Zane used the opportunity to slip inside, quickly shutting the door behind him.

"Hey! What are you doing!" Gemma glared at him. Her normally wild hair had been pushed back into a ponytail.

Zane held up his hands, using one of them to take off his mask. "It's me. Please don't say anything," he whispered.

Her mouth fell open. "I knew you were a Scaredy-cat, but I didn't think you were an idiot. What the hell are you doing here?" If Zane looked hard enough, he could see a tiny bit of happiness in her eyes from seeing him again.

"I'm not here to hurt you, and I'm definitely not here to join the Evermoving." Zane took his hood off. They stood in awkward silence, which coated the room like sticky honey. "I didn't forget about what you did."

Gemma fidgeted with her hoodie. "Yeah, I figured. But I can't come with you—"

"You need to get out of here, Gemma. We can leave together. This place is going to be stormed in a matter of minutes, if they haven't already."

She froze. "What?"

"Gemma," Zane pleaded. "Just come with me." He reached toward her.

She tore her arm out of his grasp. "No way! If something is happening I need to help!"

"You're just saying that because they messed with your mind. Just come with me and I'll try to convince them to help you! I can't stand the thought of you getting killed by one of them instead." Zane was only getting one chance to convince her. That's what Danny said.

Gemma's gaze softened and she took a step toward him. "Zane. I know you're trying to do the right thing. The little group you're a part of clearly made me and everyone here out to be the bad guy." She took another step forward and wrapped him in a tight hug.

Zane arms felt glued to his side, and he slowly brought them up.

"It's okay," she whispered. "I understand what you're going through."

He hugged her, eyes squeezed shut. Danny was right. There was nothing he could do. So why in the world did it hurt so much knowing that? For just a few more moments he stayed in the embrace. Zane opened his eyes. She had a com in her ear. They were hearing everything if the static was anything to go off of. He had to act fast before more members of the Evermoving came.

Zane pushed her away. "I'm sorry that things couldn't work out." Zane set the mask back on his face, flipping the hood over his head. He tried leaving the room but Gemma followed him out.

"It's not too late! You could stay and help! Me and you, like it was back in the hospital!" Gemma pleaded. "Team Gemma-Zane right?" She added something else in a heart breaking hushed whisper. "Zane's team?"

He got to the railing overlooking the lobby. Some of the rebels were flooding into the building.

"Stop right there! Code nightshade!" One of the Evermoving members yelled. Gunshots fired, and he turned away from the deaths. After the Evermoving saw their own go down, the ones still standing surrendered.

Zane quickly took off his mask. He didn't want to be mistaken for one of the bad guys. Once the Evermoving members were taken care of, they began to scale the stairways.

Millie was in the lead. "Is the situation under control?" She glanced at Gemma, before handing Zane a com. He put it in his ear, handing her back his other com.

Zane nodded, anger rising in his chest. "Yup. I'll take care of her."

He couldn't help but notice Millie's finger was still on her gun's trigger.

He turned back toward Gemma. "Stand down. Please." She didn't really have any other option.

Gemma sighed. "Yeah sure." Her eyes drifted to the gun Millie was holding. If the moment presented itself she was going to make a run for it, wasn't she?

"You can keep going. I'll be fine," Zane told her. Millie nodded, joining a few of the others in the elevator downstairs.

After a second of guilt, Zane rushed forward, twisting her arm behind her back.

"What the heck are you doing! I already surrendered." Gemma struggled, but he held her there. Zane hesitated for a second, his expression blank. He wasn't going to let her cause any more trouble.

"Because I know you, Gemma. As soon as I turn around you're either going to attack me or run away." Zane knocked her out, and once she went limp he set her back inside her room.

Zane rushed back toward the lobby, hands gripping the railing. He leaned over it, but he saw nobody. That was alive at least. gunshots and footsteps echoed throughout the building. That and screaming.

Zane pressed the device in his ear. "Has anyone found Mrs. Valentino yet?" He paused. "The leader of the Evermoving?" Zane clarified. The response was radio silence. He straightened when he spotted her familiar fake blonde head. She turned toward him, and if looks could kill, he would have been dead a long time ago. He felt a sense of satisfaction watching Mrs. Valentino be taken away in handcuffs. She deserved to rot in prison for the rest of her life.

Words came through the com in his ear. "Check the remaining rooms. I think that we got everyone." Level Zero was finally being infiltrated. Zane watched as the rebels spilled into the different rooms. He saw the elevator descend. His heart swelled, but instantly shriveled up when he thought of Gemma. What was going to happen to her? Zane headed back to his old room, to say one last goodbye to Gemma. His eyes drifted to her unconscious body, but he had no more tears left for her. She had made her decision.

Zane squatted down next to her. "I really wish we could have done this together. I'm sorry we couldn't." She didn't respond but he wasn't expecting her to say anything. She was going to stay knocked out for a while. "I guess you'll be put in juvie. I'm sure you'll be able to escape but... I'll miss you, Gemma." He turned away from her. Zane knew if he turned back around he wouldn't be able to leave her there. He still stayed by the door, just in case she managed to escape. Besides, the others didn't really need his help. Eventually the sounds of gunshots died out, and there were no more enemies left. They had all been captured or killed.

After a while he finally heard something. The static in his ear suddenly turned into four important words. "Level Zero is ours." The words gave him a sense of peace he was sure he had never felt before. The hidden war was over.

CHAPTER

FORTY-FIVE

Gemma was in prison, along with Mrs. Valentino, and most of the Evermoving was being held in secure facilities. But there was one thing he wasn't sure of.

Zane knocked on Danny's office door. "Come in!"

He opened the door, and Danny turned around to face him. "Hey Zane." The TVs in the room were on, showing different footage of the Evermoving members being taken to very secure and hard to escape prisons. Zane wondered if one of them was the guy he had nicknamed Anything.

"What did you end up finding in Level Zero?" Zane asked.

Danny's forehead creased in concern, and he ignored Zane's question. "It was a bust, wasn't it? You weren't able to convince her?"

Zane shook his head. "She was as stubborn as always."

Danny inhaled slowly. "To answer your question, let's just say that Level Zero is something else. I'll show you what we found. If anyone deserves to know, it's you." Danny grabbed the coat laying on the couch. He paused, setting a hand on Zane's shoulder. "Now that everything is over, I'm sure you'll want to move somewhere far away. We'll figure something out for you."

Zane nodded his thanks. "I appreciate everything you've done, Danny."

There was no longer a need to be discrete, so they took a small truck straight there with no detours. A few hours passed, and they pulled up to a barely standing warehouse. A feeling of gloom seemed to strangle the warehouse. Dozens of other cars surrounded the place, and the rebels, or good guys, or whatever you wanted to call them were walking back and forth talking into coms or carrying cameras. Zane opened the passenger door, the sound of gravel crunching underneath feet greeting him. The anticipation built in his chest. They headed inside, light shining through the holes in the roof. Strangely enough, there was a large rock in the middle of the warehouse. Danny approached it, lifting it up with ease. The boulder wasn't real. There were hinges on the side, and once Danny lifted it all the way up it revealed a small hatch.

"This is only one of the entrances," Danny explained. "Cooper Wild kept the other entrances secret from us, not that it matters at this point."

The two of them climbed down to an echoey steel hallway. The metal felt cold to the touch. Danny opened the door at the end of it, and on the other side was a laboratory. It was massive, and the amount of papers and data on the computers would take years to study. On the far right were dozens of cells.

"Did you figure out who was on the other side of those?"

Danny frowned. "Yeah. People who knew things they weren't supposed to. That or people that the Evermoving were being paid to hold captive. I don't think they knew what the Evermoving was doing with them."

Zane could have been trapped inside one of those cells for the rest of his life. He glanced at the medical tables, which had restraints attached to the side. Scalpels were on the table beside it. It was a horrible thought, but Zane wondered if they performed surgeries on people's brains directly on those tables. And he wondered if he had been on that table before. But his past was behind him now. Zane didn't want to be the person he used to be. And he didn't want the memories that came with it. He did awful things in his past. Zane almost wished he could forget those things again. Zane was someone else now, and he was going to live out his life by his own rules.

ACKNOWLEDGMENTS

THE END.

Thank you for reading. I hope you enjoyed it! Forget Again is my very first book! I am fifteen years old and I started plotting out this book at thirteen. I plan on writing more books after this, but this is the end of Zane's story.

I want to thank the people who cheered me on, including my parents. They were very supportive of my goals.

My creative writing teacher Mrs. Hoopes who has taught me alot about the writing process, helped me improve my writing, and helped me publish this book.

Mrs. Heffner, who was my eighth grade English teacher, the person who inspired me to start writing. If she hadn't, Forget Again might never have existed.

Mrs. Egryabroat, my ninth grade English teacher, the person who was always interested in my writing. She cheered me on throughout the process, and she is one of the sweetest people I know.

And lastly my friends, who were always there for me. They were almost as excited as me about publishing, and I'll always be thankful for that.

Once again, thank you for reading my story! I would love to hear your thoughts on my book, and you can reach out to me by email.

likechocochoco@gmail.com

ABOUT THE AUTHOR

Cielo Devlin is a young adult fiction writer. Though this is her first book, she has plans to write more books in the future.

Made in the USA
Middletown, DE
17 May 2023

30717812R00165